𝒯.

D0240596

THE
WILD
BEYOND

PRAISE FOR *THE LAST WILD* TRILOGY

'I haven't read a book this good since *The Hunger Games*'
Guardian Children's Books

'As thrilling as *James and the Giant Peach*'
The Times

'An amazing story . . . deserves to win prizes'
Guardian

'Action-packed'
Daily Mail

'A wonderfully strange and strangely wonderful book'
Financial Times

'Written in a vivid, urgent style, *The Last Wild*
may be as critical to the new generation as
Tarka the Otter'
The Times

'Inventive, with laughs, tears and cliffhangers'
Sunday Times

'Brings to mind the smarts and silliness of Roald Dahl'
New York Post

'Deserves full marks – I hope other children will enjoy it as much as I did!'
First News

'A page-turner that makes you think; *The Last Wild* won't be the last we hear of Piers Torday'
Inis Magazine

'Do not miss this magical and astounding debut: a truly inspirational book for kids'
LoveReading4Kids.co.uk

'A hugely inventive adventure'
Eoin Colfer

'Splendid stuff'
Eva Ibbotson

'Gripping, original and memorable'
Francesca Simon

'Wildly inventive, moving and gripping'
Frank Cottrell Boyce

'Full of suspense without ever sacrificing warmth'
Katherine Rundell

'An excellent, punchy adventure tale with vivid characters . . . [it] tells us that we're all interconnected, humans and animals, and that the least of us can make a difference, even a mouse'
Financial Times

'An enchanted adventure with a message of empowerment and hope'
Booklist

'A magnetic adventure . . . find yourself glued like tar to this satisfying, spine-tingling book'
Samuel H. (aged 10)

THE WILD BEYOND

PIERS TORDAY

Quercus

First published in Great Britain in 2015 by

Quercus Publishing Ltd
Carmelite House
50 Victoria Embankment
London EC4Y 0DZ

An Hachette UK company

A CIP catalogue record for this book is available
from the British Library

HB 978 1 84866 8 485
EBOOK 978 1 84866 8 263

10 9 8 7 6 5 4 3 2 1

Typeset by Nigel Hazle

Printed and bound in Great Britain by Clays Ltd, St Ives plc

'O, wonder!
How many goodly creatures are there here!'

    The Tempest, William Shakespeare (1611)

NOW,
A
DREAM

By the light of a silvery moon I lean out of the window to stare at the last great city on earth so I will never forget it.

How it looked: paper-blue squares, shadows. How it sounded: the silence of the grave. How it smelt: acid, water, smoke.

I try to drink everything in, remember every detail. Faded adverts on the top of apartment blocks, fire escapes hung with drying clothes, twinkling lights on skyscrapers in the distance.

I wonder what will go first. These things, us, or the city itself. All the places I've ever known. The glass towers, the deserted houses of the Culdee Sack, the stinking slums of Waste Town, maybe even the chimneys of Facto.

Right now, in the moonlight, the river running through the city looks still and solid, misted like a mirror when you breathe on it. The Ams, now as broad as a sea. Far on the horizon, I can see the white glow of the Amsguard. Nine concrete columns supporting giant steel gates, still keeping the world's sea at bay. Only a week ago a crazed dog and his dark wild would have opened the gates to wash this city away, if we hadn't stopped them.

But even with Dagger no longer around – gone who knows where – the water has risen up over us once already. There's nothing to say that it won't happen again. Next time it might not even matter whether the Amsguard is open or shut.

Who am I kidding?

Everything is fine. We won. We are safe. I should be happy. But instead, I am as flat as the River Ams itself.

If I didn't know better, I'd think the city had been abandoned. It's the dead of night, and it's so quiet you could hear a mouse shiver. If only there was a mouse shivering by my side.

Until we find her, no matter how many skyscrapers and factories we build, we won't bring our world back. Because she has the Iris. The DNA of all the animals and plants we lost to the red-eye, collected and secretly stored by Polly's parents in a page of her notebook, as microdots. A page the mouse was hiding in her cheek pouches. She ran off when Skuldiss confronted us outside this flat. And now . . .

I don't want to think where she might be.

Besides, I should be asleep. Dad says I still need

4

time to recover after Dagger's attack on the Amsguard. Is it any surprise that I'm wide awake, with a million unanswerable questions spinning around in my brain like a mini-cosmos? I wonder if looking at the real stars in the real sky instead will help. I gaze over the rooftops, towards the haze of bright spots that start swimming before me, and my eyes begin to close.

As they shut, I hear a noise.

A drone in my ear, the buzzing of a fly. An ordinary fly, so small it could fit on my fingernail.

Come with me, it says.

So I climb out of the bedroom window and sit on the ledge, my legs dangling in the air.

The fly takes off into the night and I'm no longer hanging over the windowsill, but flying out above the city. At first I worry my feet will strike aerials and chimneys, but when I glance downward I can see not rooftops but things I remember from the countryside. Animal bones gleaming white through tangled branches. A foaming waterfall. The smokeless chimney pots of a big house. Searchlights criss-crossing a cliff.

A lake hidden within a ring of trees.

We keep on flying right up high, till even that water is just another glinting mirror on the surface of the earth. We soar to where the air is thin and hard to breathe, burning my throat. I start to hear cracks and explosions. I don't want to look below, but my feet are growing hot. The world of forests and seas beneath me has become a cracked black ball, oozing with molten fire.

The planet, what's happening to it? I say, but the fly doesn't reply and keeps on buzzing ahead. Next we're among the stars, floating and tumbling. They are so bright and beautiful that for a moment I forget the explosions.

The buzzing stops and the fly disappears, leaving me in the middle of space, every star looking so far away. Everything else is empty blackness. I am small. I am all by myself. Which is when I start to fall.

Crashing through space so fast –

Burning through earth's atmosphere –

No cloud can break my descent –

The sea, the Island, rising up to meet me at such a rate, spikes and ridges and hard edges zooming into view. I brace myself for impact –

Which is when I open my eyes again, gasping for breath, sucking in more air than there can be in the sky.

For a moment I have no idea where I am.

The world is just shadows, which harden into lines. Faded curtains frame the windowsill I'm slumped over. Behind me are low ceilings, a dusty ultrascreen and a doorway. I fall back on to the sagging mattress.

My heart hurling itself against the thin wall of my chest like a rubber ball, I gulp in more air, calming myself. I'm not out in the city, or falling from space. I'm in our new home, Aida's flat in the deserted Maydoor Estate.

Or at least our new home for the time being.

And I'm not alone any more either. I must have screamed, because now other shadows are coming into the room, stretching towards me.

The tallest of them can scarcely squeeze his horns under the door, but he manages somehow, his warm breath on my neck.

You cried out in your sleep, Wildness, he says.

I reach and touch his flank. *I think . . . I maybe had my first animal dream. Or you might call it an animal nightmare. Do you get those as well?*

Impossible! says the oversized cockroach, marching across the tatty rug I have instead of a duvet. *Humans can't experience our dreams. They are visible to us and us alone.*

Nevertheless . . . muses the stag.

My new friend the rat doesn't say a word for a change. He curls up on my pillow, beginning to doze. The wolf gives me a funny stare, cocking his head, the expression in his eyes unreadable.

Before I can tell my wild more about the dream, human shadows are filling the room too. They are laying hands over my arms, touching my brow and checking the sling fixed tight across my torn shoulder (a sling that once was my favourite scarf).

'Are you OK, Kidnapper?' says Polly, using the name she has been calling me since I first broke into her house. 'You screamed loud enough to wake the whole city.' The toad at her feet bellows indignantly, as if he is particularly cross at being woken.

'Yes,' I say. The second word of my new human speaking. It makes things easier. One word easier, to be precise. I still can't add 'I think' or 'I hope so', so I rub my injured arm instead. I wonder if I will ever be able to say more words.

'Hmm,' grumbles Aida as she chucks herself on to the end of my bed. 'Attention seeker, if you ask me. What you making that row for, waking us up, if you not being murdered? Tell me that.'

'Is it still the fever from your injuries?' says Polly, patting my brow again.

'No.' I begin to shake . . . and shake and shake. I'm not feeling cold. In fact, I'm burning up – but I'm also shuddering, my teeth chattering, unable to stop moving.

'Now, Kidnapper,' she says. 'I can't guess what was in your dream or why it was so frightening, but remember, it was only a dream.'

'Yes,' I say, trying to smile. She's right of course. I know that outside this window hundreds of animals who answer to me are keeping guard over our enemies in the Four Towers. The surrounding city is damaged but not destroyed. The mouse is safe somewhere, I am sure, looking after the one thing that could help us rebuild this planet.

I am also in a flat surrounded by my wild, my best friends and some of our parents sleeping next door. Home, just how I want it to stay for ever and ever. But none of that can dislodge this sharp pain deep inside – as if my dream has left me with a stone blade shoved between my ribs.

I can't explain it more than that. I have never felt this way. Not even when Mum died, not when I thought Dad had abandoned me in Spectrum Hall. Not when we lost Sidney, or when I found myself trapped in the Underearth and feared I might never see daylight again.

This feeling is different. It keeps on hurting, even as Aida leans forward to take my injured hand, a curl of loose hair falling over her ear. 'It OK,' she says. 'We here, you know.'

But I hardly hear her words through the fog now freezing around my heart. A smoky mist of thoughts and fears that are as cold and black as deepest space. They all amount to the same thing though.

The feeling of being completely and utterly alone.

PART 1: SOMETHING IN THE WATER

Today is the day I am meant to rebuild the world.

I didn't expect it to begin with a rat sticking his tail in my face.

Good morning, dearest friend! Time to rise and shine!

Do you have to shove that right up my nose? I splutter, pushing him on to the floor with my working arm.

But it's an ancient rat greeting, he says, scrabbling back on to his feet. *Many rats would take that as a great honour.*

I'm sure they would. But many thirteen-year-old boys, including this one, would take it as a super-gross start to their day.

*If I didn't know how much you loved me, I could

almost think you were mocking me, dear friend,* says the rat, his eyes narrowing. *But you would never do a thing like that, would you? Not to a rodent who saved your life.*

For a moment I feel ashamed, remembering everything he did, the scar on his hind leg still sore and bare. Then I remember he also did just jump on my face for no good reason. *Of course not. Now beat it before I change my mind.*

With a shake of his whiskers the rat scurries away to the main room next door. I rub the sleep from my eyes. Images from last night's dream flash before me, but I try to block them as I stumble after him.

Dad is sitting up groggily on the sofa bed. At first I wonder if he's woken with a badger from the new wild on his head. Then I realize that's his hair.

Polly's parents, Mr and Mrs Goodacre, are in the kitchenette, boiling up tea from weeds she found in the communal garden downstairs. That and a few stale cartons of Formul-A we found stored in one of the other empty flats are all we've been living on. I can't remember when I last wasn't hungry.

Wolf and my stag are both awake and blinking in the light, curled up on a mat by the built-in fire-effect heater (which doesn't work). The toad puffs up in his box of soil and water next to them, swollen with rage at being disturbed before midday.

Polly marches out of the tiny box room she is sharing with Aida.

'Phew! It's so stuffy in here,' she says.

'I'm afraid these flats weren't designed for six people and a stag, a wolf, a rat and a toad to share,' says Mr Goodacre, stroking his long nose.

'Not to mention the General,' says Polly, pointing to the orange cockroach scouring the kitchen counter for stray crumbs.

'Yes, how could I forget the joy of sharing a flat with one of those?' he mutters.

'You being rude about our friends and my home, mister?' says Aida, the last to emerge.

'Not at all . . .' he begins, going quiet as Polly glowers at him, in the way she does at anyone who lies to her face.

'Anyhow, let's get some fresh air in,' she declares, and ties her borrowed dressing gown extra-tight around her waist, stomping forward to open the door.

But Aida lays a hand on her shoulder. 'Wait,' she says. 'We meant to be in hiding. Anyone could be out there. What if it not safe?'

Everyone looks at their feet. Because we know they're all still there. Just through that thin wooden door, down some steps and across the road lie the Four Towers. The headquarters of Facto, who spread the red-eye disease, who got rich off Formul-A in return and who tried to kill us for exposing them. Every single one of them waiting for their moment to seek revenge.

Selwyn Stone in his museum of stuffed beasts. Captain Skuldiss on his magic crutches. The young-old

Littleman, Aida's former gang leader turned traitor, the cullers with their weapons.

Since the day we stopped the floods, and created the new wild, we haven't seen or heard any sign of them. Now even the ultrascreens are silent, gathering dust like the one in this flat. The windows of the Four Towers are dark, the lights running down the sides of the chimneys dead, the doors and gates locked from the inside.

And covering every inch of the building and yard are hundreds of animals from the countryside and the city: my new wild, united until the Iris is found and activated.

The entrances and exits are guarded by my wolf's mother, the undisputed leader of the pack. No longer serving the dark wild, she has returned to her rightful place as a guardian of the last creatures left alive on earth.

Facto's helicopters sit lifeless, their screens and windows pecked to smithereens by the starling and her flock.

Even the tops of their chimneys are blocked with nests made by seagulls from the Ring of Trees.

Shrikes, yellowhammers and redpolls circle the whole site, monitoring any skylight or hatch that could be used as an escape route. (Which would be hard, as the black spiders covered every single possible exit with their gummy webs.)

Not a soul to be seen, alive or dead. We're all safe, say my grey pigeons from the windowsill outside, delivering their daily news report from the Towers.

Not a soul to be seen, says the white pigeon, tumbling in to land just behind them. *We're all dead.*

So we should feel safer than ever before, and yet . . .

'Come on! It's broad daylight on a sunny morning,' says Polly. 'Nothing bad ever happens in broad daylight on a sunny morning.'

Polly was always good at not being scared of things, but since her capture by and escape from Facto, she doesn't seem frightened by anything. I think I like the new Polly, but I'm freaked out at the same time.

Even in broad daylight on a sunny morning.

'Apart from sneezing fever,' says Mrs Goodacre, bustling around with mugs of hot weed tea for everybody. 'That's never nice to get on a sunny morning.'

'You can't get sneezing fever in a city with hardly any flowers or trees left,' replies her daughter with a roll of her eyes.

'At least something good has come out of all this end-of-the-world business then,' says her mum, beaming as she hands me a cup of steaming brown water.

I clasp the mug tight, not caring that it's too hot to hold. I'm enjoying being distracted by the burning sensation.

I just turned thirteen years old. All the people and creatures I love most are in this flat. Even if it is smelly and too small for us. But we have been shut up in here for over a week now. Beyond the door lies a flooded city that needs rebuilding. Beyond that, a whole planet without animals that we could help reboot . . . if only we could find the mouse with the answers.

There is so much to do . . . it feels impossible to even know where to begin.

Dad is sitting up on the sofa bed beneath the silent ultrascreen, with at least two of the buttons on his shirt fastened. (Which, even if they are in the wrong holes, is not bad for him.)

When do you think we can go out? I ask him in the animal voice, looking at my tea.

He runs a hand through his thick hair. *I'm not sure, Kes. Your arm isn't fully healed yet. Besides . . . I've already, you know, lost you twice . . . So forgive me for not wanting to let you out of my sight just yet.*

I love my dad but suddenly I miss my mum more than ever before. It's a physical ache, like a chunk taken out of my side. She would have known the right thing to say.

Then my heart jolts as I hear a knock.

Followed by several more knocks.

A solid, hard rapping.

Nobody moves in the crowded flat.

The knocking continues, growing stronger and louder. It sounds like it could bust the front door off its hinges as it bends and buckles with each thump, the chain rattling.

It sounds like the outside has waited for us long enough.

It sounds like the outside is about to come in.

18

'I think there's someone at the door,' says Mr Goodacre, stroking his long nose again.

Polly gives him another of her special looks.

'At least they haven't broken the door in,' says Dad, blowing on his tea. 'People who knock first go down well in my, er, book.'

He's right. Selwyn Stone didn't knock when he came and took me to Spectrum Hall. Aida's bike-riding Waste Mountain Gang didn't knock when they came looking for the Iris. Now there are words coming over the hammering. 'Open up! I know you're in there.'

'Wait a minute,' says Aida. 'I know that voice.' Before any of us can stop her, she strolls over to the door, unhooks the chain and pulls back the bolts.

It's a boy. A boy with a grimy numbered sweatshirt

and a purple Mohican.

'123!' snaps Aida. 'I told you to manage our crew at the mountain. What you doing here?'

'Sorry, boss.' The boy named after the numbers on his top wipes his nose on his sleeve. The second-in-command of Aida's gang still looks rat-faced but . . . let's just say I'm more keen on rat faces than I was. 'I know you told me to stay there, only . . .'

'Only what?' demands Aida. 'An order is an order.'

123 shrugs and points behind him. We peer round the edge of the door at the empty concrete balcony, a few pigeons pecking around in the corners.

'I don't get it,' says Polly.

The boy stretches out his thin arm even further – to the world beyond. At first all we can see are the tall columns of the Four Towers opposite, layered in the multicoloured scales of birds and butterflies guarding them.

'I told you about them,' says Aida, but 123 shakes his head.

'Yer not looking,' he says.

'Oh,' says Polly. 'I see.'

And then I do too.

He's pointing not across but down, at the crowd of people gathered in the street below. Not the rest of the Waste Mountain Gang. Not cullers in armoured suits or angry Outsiders from the Quarantine Zone, but ordinary people.

The men and women we hurried past in the centre of

Premium. Old, young, fat, thin, every sort. They fall silent as we gather on the balcony to take a look. Their shoulders are hunched, their faces downcast, as they shuffle around, like they're waiting for something or someone.

What a lot of new friends, says the rat gleefully as he peeks round the door frame.

They are not friends, you idiot rodent, snaps the General. *They are enemy intruders. Prepare to be repelled, invaders!*

I rub my arm. It's fighting talk but there's only a handful of us. And hundreds of people filling the street, the crowd stretching around the corner and beyond for who knows how far.

It can't be, but it's almost like the whole city is outside our flat.

Aida snorts. It's not the kind of thing that impresses her. 'What?' she says. 'What they want?'

123 cracks his rat-face into a big smile, with dry lips and a crooked gap between his front teeth. 'They made me come. They wouldn't take no for an answer. Because they want you,' he says. 'Every last one of you.'

Before I can use my good shoulder to shove the door shut on 123 again, he jabs me hard in the stomach.

'Nah, not like that, dummy! They want to say thanks and stuff, don't they? For saving their city.'

Aida scowls. 'You going to stand there all day letting the cold in? Or come in and tell us what going on?'

123 closes the door behind him and goes straight to

the kettle, making himself a cup of tea as if he's been staying here as long as us.

'Help yourself, why don't you?' says Mrs Goodacre with no trace of a smile, folding her arms.

Our guest leans against the kitchen counter with his drink, trying to ignore the rat nibbling his laces. *Another new friend in this tiny nest of yours!* says my rodent. *Do you think he will stay forever?*

I hope not, I say, but even that just makes him more excitable.

Then 123 explains. 'You don't get it, do yer? They saw you all on the ultrascreens, when we told 'em how you stopped them animals, the flooding and all that.'

123 was able to hack into Facto's network after I trapped Stone and his cronies in the control tower, and the Waste Mountain Gang broadcast the truth over the ultrascreens.

'So?' says Aida.

'Well, it stands to reason, don't it?'

'Spit it out!'

His face colours and he gives another gap-toothed smile, cowering from Aida even though she didn't raise a finger. 'You've gotta understand, boss. People lost everything . . . homes, food . . . everything.'

'Last I checked, that's the way it's been for a long time,' she says, picking at the mismatched fingerless gloves dangling on string from her wrists. 'What's your point?'

22

'My point is, now them lot have gone dark for the moment –' he gestures with his thumb to the factory opposite the flats – 'everyone else has seen what you can do via the ultrascreens, learnt how Facto were lying to 'em over the virus, formula – the whole lot. They reckon you're in charge now.'

'If only we were, young man, if only we were,' says Mr Goodacre with a sigh and another stroke of his nose.

123 steps back in disbelief. 'I'm not joking! What about the bridge? It's nearly swept away, it's not safe. There's the damage them animals did before the floods. Plus a power station needs repairing, the streets are full of washed-up motors . . .'

'Hey,' says Aida. 'We saved them from the storm and the animals. We didn't destroy no bridges.'

'That as maybe, but who's gonna fix it? It's all well your animals keeping Stone and his crew locked up in them Towers, but who's taken their place? That lot outside want some answers. Who's the leader now?'

The room goes extra quiet. I can sense everyone's heads turning towards me, including the stag, who gives me one of his most penetrating stares. The kind you can't hide from.

Our visitor stabs the air with his finger. He doesn't shush because everyone else has gone quiet. In fact, he gets louder. 'You don't get it, do yer? You saved us and exposed Facto's lies. You brought the animals back and stopped the floods.'

23

He pauses and turns to the others, as if challenging someone to come forward and disagree with him. But no one does. And he is definitely pointing at me.

'It's you they really want, mate. The one who can talk to animals. They want you to help them. They think you're the boss-man.'

There's a long silence, during which the only sound is the odd cry from the birds across the road. Aida jabs me in the belly, hissing, 'Well, say something then. Or do something.'

But before I can, Dad bounces up from the sofa in an explosion of beard and undone cuffs. He barges round the room, scooping up our mugs as if it was a competitive sport.

'Right!' he barks. 'The tea party's finished. Thanks for coming, young whatever your name is . . . time to go home now!'

123 holds his ground. 'I'm sorry to be out of turn, yeah . . .' he begins.

Dad slams his hand on the sideboard, and one of the empty mugs topples to the floor with a smash.

'Well, you are out of turn,' he says. 'You are children. Yes, even you, young lady,' he says to Aida, who is giving him a stare that normally puts people straight into intensive care. 'You are – all of you – incredibly brave, and wonderful young people. But you are still only that. Only young. I will not have you getting drawn into . . . the politics, rows over money, power struggles . . . strictly grown-up stuff – out of the question! So you jolly well . . . go back out to those people right this second, and . . . and tell them that, you know, these are our children they are talking about.' He turns to me, his badger hair quivering, his cheeks hot with colour. Even Aida flinches. He is like a shuddering engine that could overheat and explode at any moment. 'Kes, I have failed you enough times in the past. Never again. I don't care how many broken bridges there are. All I want – in fact, all I have ever wanted . . . is to keep you safe!'

'Well said,' murmurs Mr Goodacre behind him, and his wife nods in agreement.

Rat leaps up into my sling, shivering. He doesn't like it when we argue. The boy with the Mohican sucks his teeth and looks away.

'Fine,' he sneers. 'See if I care. I was only trying to help.'

And with that he has disappeared as fast as he arrived, Aida's calls for him to stay drowned out by the slamming of the door.

'Now, everyone, all of you, into Kester's room, while the grown-ups decide what to do next,' says Dad, glowering, his fists still clenched.

For once, no one disagrees with him.

My room is cramped and stuffy. For what feels like hours I sit on the end of the bed, staring out of the window, while my friends pace up and down either side of me. They are fuming mad.

'Why do you always do what your dad says, Kester?' It's never a good sign when Polly uses my first name. 'I thought you were a Kidnapper, but it turns out you're just a goody-goody.'

I want to snap back that I have never done what Dad tells me to. Leaning forward, I breathe on the window to create a mist for writing – and then stop.

Perhaps she's right. I have always done what Dad said, or at least what he wanted. I helped him find a cure for the virus. I rescued him – twice. What about what I want?

'Never knew my dad, and my mum went a long time ago. So I don't listen to anyone but me.'

Aida's mum was a journalist who disappeared when she discovered what Selwyn Stone was really up to inside the Four Towers. But she vanished before she could tell Aida or anyone her secret.

'Yes, that's very clear, thank you,' snaps Polly.

'So? I don't see you out there taking on your Mr Dad and Mrs Mum, do I?'

'And you are doing what exactly in here?'

'I'm not messing with the Prof, not in that mood,' mutters Aida, looking at her shoes.

I thump the bed in frustration. Like the rat, I hate it when we row.

Except this time, I get their point. Why didn't I stand up to Dad? We have to leave this flat, find the mouse and finish what we started. The world can't rebuild itself. I'm not sure anything out there could be more frightening than Dagger or Captain Skuldiss.

I spy the ghost of my reflection in the window.

My pale, hungry face. I've lost more weight than I realized. My arm in a sling. Who am I kidding? I may be thirteen years old but that still makes me just a kid. Maybe we should leave things to the grown-ups for now.

The worst bit is that I still can't tell anyone how I feel, apart from Dad. And right now he's the last person who wants to hear.

I lean forward and breathe on the glass again, this time making a nice fog, in which I write

DONT KNO WHAT 2 DO

The girls stop pacing at the squeak of my finger on the windowpane. They stare over my shoulder at the letters, and the fragments of city we can make out through them.

'You still don't get it, do you, Kidnapper?' Polly says. 'Well, Aida and I had a chat last night.'

'A real long chat.'

I wonder if I'm dreaming again. A week ago these two hadn't even laid eyes on each other, but now they're inseparable? I should never have left them to organize the escape from the Four Towers themselves. It's gone to their heads.

They sit on the bed, either side of me, and I'm worrying what might follow. To my surprise, Polly reaches across to take Aida's hand and clasps it tight. Next she takes my injured hand. I can't help blushing, which I hate myself for, making me blush all the more.

'Listen to us because you're listening to yourself too much. You did lots of amazing things: saving the city from floods, rescuing us, making the two wilds friends again.'

'And even though you lost your mouse, and the Iris,' says Aida, picking at the fraying edge of the rug with her other hand, 'you will find them again. You good at all that finding stuff.'

'You're not going to have to be a hero by yourself any more,' Polly says. 'Aida and I don't agree on everything. In fact, we only agree on one thing. Which is . . .'

'We ain't going anywhere,' says Aida, gripping my good hand, as tight as a bird's claw.

'Exactly,' says Polly. 'We're all three of us best friends. We're never going to leave you again, and you must promise the same. Whatever we need to do to find the mouse and rebuild our world – from now on we're all three of us doing it together. And that, Kidnapper, is an order. So let's shake on it.'

I look into her dark eyes, and we do, but Polly doesn't release my hand.

'It needs to be binding,' she says. 'You need to swear an oath on a sacred object.'

Last time in the garden, when Polly first told me the truth behind the Iris, it was my dad's life she made me swear on to keep her secret. I can't think of any sacred objects lying around Aida's flat.

She grips my hand and wrist tighter. I wince.

'No,' she says. 'We need something real this time. That we can use to always remind ourselves of our promise, even if we get separated.' She scratches her nose. 'Because that might happen once or twice. Although never for long!'

Aida grunts in agreement and we scan the room for

anything worth swearing an oath on, but neither peeling wallpaper, dusty curtains nor the lifeless ultrascreen in the corner would be right.

Polly grabs something from the floor by my bed. 'How about this?'

She opens her palm. Inside is a battered pile of green plastic. A pile that used to be my digital watch, that Dad sent messages on when I was rescuing the last wild, that made the light that saved me from Dagger.

The watch-camera-torch that was Mum's final gift to me.

I imagine her again as she hands it over, smiling despite the illness, being strong for me, being a mum – and I push the picture out of my mind. She's gone, and she's not coming back. I have to keep reminding myself.

Dad repaired the watch after my first journey, but he hasn't been able to rescue it since its bashing on the Amsguard, not out here away from his lab and his tools. A waterlogged battery, a cracked screen and a fraying strap where the dog tore at it, trying to bite my hand.

This pile of plastic will never tell the time, or take a photo, or shine a light again. But that still doesn't stop me gasping with shock when Polly, with a few quick tears, rips it into three bits.

Two straps and a face.

'A part each,' she says. 'Don't look so upset, Kidnapper. As long as we stay together, so does your precious watch.'

Grim-faced, I swear on the parts never to leave them

again. As do my friends. Aida unravels a few loose threads from the fraying rug we're sat on, and feeds them through the remains of my favourite-ever present.

One buckled green tongue of a strap around her neck. Another around Polly's, a skinny plastic dragon tooth. And a cracked digital face around mine. We stare at each other for a moment. Polly's right. My gift from Mum may not be technically sacred, but the effect is the same.

Our pledge is real. And I know exactly what we need to do.

It's later that evening, and we have been summoned back into the main room. Dad calls it a 'conference', but in fact it's a lecture on how we need to rest, stay indoors and keep out of trouble until 'the picture becomes clearer'.

'You mean you don't know what to do yet?' Polly says.

'It's not that simple, my dear girl,' groans Mr Goodacre. 'There is a power vacuum, as your friend explained, which means the streets outside could be extremely dangerous. Who knows who might be roaming them? They could be even worse than Facto. Besides, how could any of us actually help?'

Aida spins on her heel, frowning. 'I dunno,' she says. 'Someone needs to clean this mess up, that for sure. There might be all sorts of loot in them abandoned houses and cars—'

'This is an emergency, not an opportunity, my good young lady thief,' says Dad.

31

I've had enough of this. I glance at Polly and touch the watch face round my neck. That is her signal, and she steps forward. This time, she is being brave for all of us – just as we agreed in my room.

'I can't believe you're having this conversation,' she says to the grown-ups. 'You should be ashamed of yourselves. For even thinking this is only about bridges or power stations. But most of all, for telling us we couldn't do it because we're children. That's the worst reason ever!'

'Now mind your tongue, Polly,' says Mrs Goodacre. 'That's a professor you're talking to. It's unlike you to be so bold.'

'If he's a professor, he should know better. As should you, Mum. I don't want to make you cross. But did you forget so fast? The real reason why we shouldn't be helping them?'

She bends down to pet her toad in his plastic box of soil and water. He stares at us like only a toad can while she strokes his head.

For the first time, I understand that my wild regard Polly in a different light. Because they cannot speak to her, they have accepted her as a friend of mine. But I don't reckon they've ever looked at her the way they are now.

The stag, standing as tall as he can in the cramped flat, gazing at her with his deep brown eyes. Wolf licking her hand with his tongue. The rat leaping on the wolf's back. (Much to the annoyance of the General, who was happily fast asleep there.) The pigeons in a row on the window ledge, tilting their heads at her.

She crouches down to stroke the wolf and the rat. 'You didn't forget her, did you?' And she glares back at her parents.

'Before anyone repairs a single bridge we need to find the mouse.' I've never seen three adults act so shifty at once. 'Never mind keeping out of trouble. Trouble can look after itself. What about the planet you want to rebuild?'

She picks her toad up out of his box and holds him so tight to her chest it looks like his eyes might bulge clean out of his head.

'What about the Iris?'

The next morning, we are up on the flat roof of the Maydoor Estate, perched on dead air-conditioning units in the sun to plan our search. Ventilation pipes curve out of the concrete like gaping worms, watching us in open-mouthed silence as we work.

Dad sketches a rough map on the back of a paper tablecloth we found under the sink in Aida's kitchen. 'If we're going to do this,' he sighs, 'then we should at least . . . you know, do it properly for once.'

We argued long into the night, and it wasn't until we were all yelling at each other, and the wolf begged us to stop because his ears were almost bleeding with the pain of so many high-pitched voices at once, that the grown ups gave in and agreed to let us look for the mouse.

Under certain conditions.

(Well, one condition, in fact. That we follow Dad's plan. So I suppose Polly was right after all. Again.)

First, he divides the city into quarters.

This estate is where we last saw the mouse alive. While Aida and I distracted Captain Skuldiss, she leaped out of Polly's rucksack. With the General, they managed to evade the cullers' stamping boots and the Captain's robotic crutch, disappearing into the night. The General headed to the Waste Mountain to summon the stag and the wolf. The mouse ran off elsewhere . . . with the vital information we need to rebuild the world balled up in her cheek pouches.

If you'd told me to ask where, I would have, snaps the cockroach when I try to find out where she went. *I had my orders, she had hers. I am a military insect. I don't question orders, I either give them or follow them.*

If only we'd made a specific escape plan, I say to myself, for the millionth time since she disappeared. I just told her to go somewhere safe. Yet she is still a stranger in this huge capital. Where could she be?

This isn't the first time we've tried to look for her of course. As soon as I could walk again after my fight on the Amsguard, I paced the walkway outside, calling for her.

I started calling the moment the sun came up, and kept on calling until it had sunk deep behind the glass towers far across the river. I yelled into cracks in the floor and hollered into drains. I tapped my good fist against every brick, every vent, until the skin was ripped from my knuckles. Not one squeak did I hear. Not one tail shake did I see. If she is doing the Dance of Disappearing Forever, then it is the quietest and most invisible jig she has done yet.

While Dad draws, I shade my eyes against the dazzling sun and stand up to look at the view. I get a panoramic vista of a city which is washed out and washed up – but not washed away.

The River Ams, which once flowed steady and straight between the north and south banks of Premium, has spilt over those borders completely. It has spread out through the surrounding streets in spindly tentacles of water the same colour as Mrs Goodacre's tea. From up here it looks as if the mighty river itself is combing through the neighbourhood, searching – like us – for something it can't find.

It is pretty too, the rippling strands bouncing flashes of white light up into your eyes, a series of coded signals we can't decipher. But can I hear an animal calling me? Is that a cry, floating through the hot air . . . ?

'So, Kes, if you're listening . . .' Dad coughs extra loud and pats the map with his hand. I squeeze back in between the others, huddled over the tablecloth. Dad explains that as he can talk to animals too, he's going to lead the grown-up search party. Mr and Mrs Goodacre will use their knowledge of plants to look in the park, as they know which bushes, hedges or trees might make the best hiding place for a small furry rodent.

Then he says they're going to search the roads around our old home and the Culdee Sack. I think it's unlikely the mouse would choose to go back there. Although it was where I discovered her last time, so she might have thought it was a safe bet. Equally though, we don't know what's left of our house after the floods. Dad wants to find that out too, I suggest.

Absolutely not, he insists, in the animal voice, his eyebrows springing up. *Finding that mouse of yours is my . . . what do you call it? . . . top priority.*

We agree – remembering our earlier visitor – that if the search takes us to flooded areas in need of repair, we will help where we can.

'And everyone, remember, don't just listen out for the mouse – there might still be people trapped in their homes who need rescuing,' says Polly.

'But be careful, like we agreed! Promise you won't go anywhere you won't be able to get out of again,' tuts her mother.

Dad is insistent that the girls and I only search close to our new home. As it happens, I'm still convinced that the mouse won't have gone far from the Maydoor Estate if she could help it. She knew how important the pieces of paper from Polly's notebook crunched up in her cheeks were. So we are going to comb every inch of this estate,

37

the surrounding streets and the riverbank until we find her.

'I can imagine her squeezing into a hole and getting stuck,' says Polly on her knees, shining a torchlight across the fluff and dust trapped in the air-con grilles.

'I reckon she waiting on the other side this road till she think it safe,' says Aida, standing right on the edge of the roof. She focuses her homemade binoculars, looking towards the abandoned perimeter fence of the Four Towers.

'Perhaps you don't need to be so near the edge, dear,' says Mrs Goodacre behind us.

We're interrupted by something crawling over my feet.

Two somethings crawling over my feet, to be precise.

I have made a great new friend, announces the rat, pulling his lips over his yellowing fangs. *This cockroach and I are best pals forever.*

They must have followed us up the fire escape.

It's more of a professional relationship, if you don't mind, says the General, marching over the rat's back. 'Cockroaches don't tend to make friends with rats, as a rule.*

A friend is a friend, says the rat, only a flicker of desperation in his eyes.

I'm not sure how long this new alliance will last, but it's given me an idea. *Well, friends—*

Colleagues, interrupts the cockroach. *Comrades

serving your Wildness together.*

Buddies and best love chums for life, Rat says with a curl of his tail.

And I begin to form a notion of how our search party could be completed. It's tricky with one arm in a sling, but I kneel so I'm at their level.

Well, comrades and, er, friends – I think you could use your new . . . partnership . . . to help us find the mouse.

A mouse? sniffs the rat. *Why do you want to find a mouse? Isn't a rat good enough for you, dear friend for life?*

More than good enough. But this mouse just happens to be carrying the information we need to bring back every single animal we lost to the berry-eye plague. Imagine how many new friends you might have then?

The rat is silent for a moment, rubbing his snout with his front paws as he thinks. *New friends?* he says eventually. *Best new friends?*

Better than best, I reckon. Now, here's what you need to do . . .

Premium may have looked glittery from the roof of the Maydoor Estate, but once we are down in the streets the city feels dirty and brown.

We discover that some roads are OK if you don't mind getting your feet wet. Some you can only cross on the back of a stag. And some are like brand-new rivers, dotted with car roofs, traffic lights and ultrascreens poking out from the water like they have been dumped there by mistake.

I say rivers, but actually they are more like ponds – they're not running. They're just sitting and stinking. The only creature who actually seems happy is Polly's toad, who bounces on ahead, dripping with excitement.

What is that smell, Wildness? says the stag, as we splash our way down a muddy avenue, stepping around an obstacle course of the most random rubbish, from fallen

40

trees to strings of sodden clothes, twisted around lifeless Facto surveillance cameras. *It is not one I recognize.*

I shudder. It's nothing good. Everywhere smells of damp and decay. I had banked on the mouse being able to stay hidden and safe from the cullers. I hadn't thought about whether she'd be able to stay dry too.

'Look,' says Polly, pointing to a long, patchy black line that someone seems to have painted across the front of all the houses. 'A flood mark. That's how high the water came.'

The line runs above every front door and ground-floor window. Then I see that it isn't paint at all, but a paste of compressed soil and twigs smeared across the buildings by the force of the water.

The last time we walked past these houses it was pouring with rain, the lawns filled with packs of dogs from the dark wild keeping their owners cowering inside. The wolf by our side stops to taste the air, as if he can still smell them.

Now the people who survived the floods are out in the sun, armed with mops and brooms, pushing water into drains and untangling power lines from where they have wrapped themselves around branches.

Where we can, we help. Polly and Aida heave a smashed outdoor ultrascreen (my arm is still not strong enough for that) off someone's dented car, blown there by the force of a storm. We help pick up about a thousand scattered scraps of paper from a front garden. Piece by piece, we lug soggy furniture out from a flooded basement on to dryer ground. One couch is so waterlogged and heavy, the others can't even begin to lift it. Luckily, bobbing around in the waist-high water, I find a drawer stuffed with belts and braces, which I turn into a makeshift harness for the stag. The watching crowd cheers as he drags the sofa out into the daylight.

Polly returns tight-lipped smiles. Aida gives sweeter ones, while I just hope no one notices her also scooping up anything that sparkles – watches, necklaces, loose change – and stuffing them into a wheelie case that she found by the side of the road.

The only things Polly picks up are plastic bags. 'They get everywhere, and besides, you never know when you might need one.'

I'm not really paying attention though. My movements are mechanical (and restricted), my facial expressions distracted as if I'm not really choosing to make them. It feels like every cell in my brain is focusing on only two tasks.

Calling and listening for my mouse at every step we take. My head turns at the tiniest movement – a flag flapping in a gutter – and I twitch at any sound – the squeaking castors of a bleached office desk, being pushed along the pavement like a cart, piled high with bundles of clothes and bags.

Me riding the stag, the wolf by our side, the pigeons swooping in the air – occasionally grabbing bags and toys stranded in high branches and dropping them down – we cover as many streets as we can, calling out down every one.

But no reply comes. Every now and then I think I hear something . . . but it's gone before I can even work out where it's coming from. *Did you hear that, Stag?* I ask him.

Hear what?

I shake my head. I'm not sure myself.

Polly keeps glancing at her scribbled copy of Dad's map and directing us – 'Aida, you take this empty shop, I think just the ground floor will do. Kester, you go with the stag down the alley, the water's too high for us. Can you ask the wolf to come with me to these houses? I'll knock on the front door and ask if they've seen a mouse and he can call for her at the same time. Remember to keep the pigeons focused on the roofs.'

The day wears on, and as the sun begins to drop behind the glass towers – which now seem as if they're on the coast of another country across a sea, not just the other side of a river – I hear the sound again.

I have to strain to catch it, the damp creaking of a flooded city washing over the top, but there is something there.

Something calling to me.

The sound comes from down a dark alley between two huge square buildings. I direct the stag to take

43

us, but Aida strokes his flank, staying us. 'What you want to go down here for? Just old docks. Been shut for years.'

Exactly the kind of place a mouse might head for.

The sound comes again.

I brush her hand away, and ride into the shadows.

The buildings look deserted. There are no cameras or ultrascreens out here. Coils of rope slung over gantries swing in the breeze, and rusting shutters squeak as we pick our way over slippery cobbles. But that wasn't the sound I heard. The wolf scrambles over a pile of pallets, sniffing every inch, but there is no mouse hiding underneath. You don't need to be a wolf to pick up all the smells in this place – faint traces of things that were last here a long time ago.

Coffee. Fruit. Fish.

The buildings have sheer stone walls and rotting wooden floors. They feel old to the touch, like they are from a different time to the rest of the city. They are big enough to be temples – each one stretching on for miles. They are also completely empty. My pigeons fly through their big open doors and eventually out the other side. *Nothing in there,* they call out, then with a little echoing flutter they fly into the next one.

Nothing in here either, says the white pigeon, perching on my head. I brush him away, suddenly in no mood for his silliness.

Polly traces words engraved into the side of the deserted vaults, every letter as tall as she is, each word a building's name:

FLOUNDERS
ROACH
TENCH
PIKE

'They the owners?' asks Aida, also rubbing a hand over the worn-down letters.

'No,' says Polly, looking inside the empty halls. 'They're the names of fish. They must have caught them in the river and stored them here.'

We all peer into the gloomy hangar-like space. It still smells of fish, all right, but there aren't any here now. Just a few slimy-looking pieces of broken barrel in the corner.

And I hear the sound again, a bit louder this time. *How about just now? Did you hear that, Stag?* I say.

I think perhaps I did, he replies.

I heard it too, says the wolf. *And a wolf's hearing is much better than a deer's, so I also heard it much better.*

The stag twitches. *But did it sound like a mouse to you?*

Wolf shakes his head. *I've never heard anything that sounded less like a mouse. It is an animal call, only . . . one I've never heard before.*

45

I try to listen, but everyone's chatting to one another and I can't focus. I put my finger to my lips. They all freeze, even the white pigeon. (Although he freezes in mid-air, which is never a good idea, and plummets head first into an overflowing water butt.)

And then I hear it again.

A single animal sound, floating above the city. One watery sound, that leaks deep into my bones and makes me shiver; so slow and so old, I feel I am clutching an ancient parchment that disintegrates into thousands of fragments in the breeze. A call so loud I can think of little else.

It's definitely not the mouse.

We all stand silent in the dusk, which seems to be creeping up on us from the depths of the buildings, curling along the river like a dark mist. All of us frozen still, straining to hear.

Then – there it is again. That deafening call in my head, rippling and crying, urging me on . . .

Signalling to the others to wait, I slide off the stag and head round the corner, tiptoeing as if the cobbles were heated stones. The wolf crouches low alongside me, padding so softly you wouldn't know he was there if it wasn't for his upright tail brushing my leg.

At first it looks like there's nothing to see. Just a cobbled courtyard and a wharf, with steep steps running down to the water.

Drifting in the river beyond are dozens of boats – washed clean off their moorings by the floods, jostling in the twilight. Capsized hulls bobbing about like hollow shells, snapped masts dragging behind them. A speedboat has been rammed right up on to the shore, plastered with a web of seaweed and rigging. Jutting through, its prow looks as white as bone.

Who knows where they all came from? There are upside-down boats with hand-painted names, too hard to read in the dark. Out in the deeper water there are cargo ships with flags and logos I don't recognize stamped all over them. There is even what was once a river ferry, black holes smashed through its tinted windows. A little rubber dinghy rocks about in between these larger wrecks, a lost baby looking for its mother.

Every boat is silent, swaying and abandoned. There's nothing here.

Come on, Wolf, I say, and we turn back towards the warehouse. Which is when his ears prick, and he stops.

We both slowly turn around, and then, there it is – rising clean out of the river ahead, as if a shadow took shape in the dusk, only dripping with beads of wet . . . a flick of a giant tail.

A tail belonging to something huge and unseen, something that called me here with its echoing cry.

Something in the water.

Under a triangle of light from the old lamp, the wolf and I creep to the edge of the harbour and peer down into the watery gloom. There's nothing there. Whatever we saw emerge from the depths has vanished. I wonder if it was my imagination, my hungry brain playing tricks on me. Except my wolf saw it too.

But now all we can see is the black river, eddying between the wrecked boats against the side of the pier. Wolf shivers. *I don't like looking at that drowned wolf in the fish-road.*

That's not a drowned wolf. That's you.

He wrinkles his snout. *I'm not that big, or that old.*

I grab the ruff of his neck, pull him forward so that he can see for himself. *You are, trust me.*

The wolf gives a start and steps back from the

edge, before nosing over it again, then jerking away every time he sees his face. He is only recently full grown.

He is looking over the side again. *So, Wildness,* he says, *The more I stare at that drowned wolf, the more I see the most handsome creature ever to have walked this earth, so I accept he must be me. But whose is that giant eye?*

I rush back to the harbour edge, gripping it with one hand as I lean over. And there, beneath the rippling reflections of the wolf and me, looking up between us both, is a huge disc of an eye.

An eye the size of my head, surrounded by barnacled and blistered skin, the oldest-looking I have ever seen. An eye that, though hard to make out through the ripples and clouds of dirt, is definitely bright, burning red.

It blinks.

We both jump, and I only just stop myself from falling in the water. The eye vanishes from view.

But we don't have to wait long before further out there's the roll of a glossy hump, bigger than any boat here. The hump gives a sudden spurt high into the sky.

Make that an explosion. A cloud of foam, shot out by a fountain that spouts up as tall as a glass tower. Puffs of white droplets hang in the air, sparkling in the harbour light, before showering us with a salty, fishy spray. The wolf shakes his nose and tries to rub away the scent with his paws.

49

Shouts ring out behind us as the others rush forward from their hiding place, the stag's hoofs clopping along the cobbles.

'What that – a bomb in the water?' says Aida.

I motion at them to be quiet, and we huddle along the edge, the stag also frowning at his reflection.

Then, before I can explain, a circle of ripples begins to form among the glistening pools of oil gathered on the surface. Little eddies of bubbles that grow into silvery crests and then into waves. Emerging from their centre, dripping like a sunken wreck raised from the deep, is the smooth back of the biggest beast in the world.

I grew up in a world without animals, but even I know the name of this one. It's the kind they used to call a whale.

Up close, a more beautiful creature than I ever dared imagine they were. And bigger, so much bigger than the ones I've seen in films or photos. Water pouring off its sides, as if the river had given birth to it.

The wolf nips my hand, terrified. We are all scared, staring at this giant who is raised near full out of the water. Then it sinks below the surface again, merely a few bubbles floating along to suggest that it was ever there.

What do I do? Why is it here? I ask the stag, the questions streaming out of my brain faster than I can process them.

I think you should try and find out, he suggests. *But be careful. We do not fully understand the ways of the walkers under the wet.*

What do you mean?

The inhabitants of the fish-road are . . . different to us. They have strange customs.

A talking stag tells me a singing whale is strange. It must be *really* strange.

You remember the water snakes at the whiterforce? he asks.

How could I forget? I glance at Polly, her face screwed up as she scans the river for another sign of the whale. She could also be remembering what happened at the whiterforce. The snakes there spoke in mysterious hums and chants.

They still couldn't save Sidney.

I borrow Polly's torch and seek out the rusted hoops of a ladder further along the wall, hanging straight down into the water.

'Do you think that's a good idea, Kidnapper?' asks Polly. 'On your own? Remember our pledge.'

Her fingers brush the green watch strap dangling round her neck, and instinctively I touch the clock face tied around mine. How could I forget it? But I'm the only one who can find out why this creature is here. I know that nothing this beautiful and gentle could ever wish us any harm.

Taking her hand, I fold the torch back into it. 'Yes,'

I say, pointing to the river. She nods, understanding – I hope.

The water is much colder than I'm expecting, and my free fist clenches tight around the rungs as I take a sharp breath. My legs are under the surface now, my sodden trousers clinging to them, my feet lost from view as they dangle in the deep.

I can't see it any more! I tell the stag.

Have patience. How do humans ever see anything, when they never look longer than the beat of a fly's wing?

So I wait. How can something so big disappear?

My toes begin to turn into icebergs.

And then . . . a rubbery and smooth thing grazes past them and keeps on grazing. On and on and on it goes. This whale must be as long as the river itself.

I take a deep breath and sink into the water, feeling no bigger or more significant than the tiny specks of flotsam drifting on the surface beside us. Swallowing as much air as my lungs can take, I duck my head under, and Polly shines her light in, making the murky water less frightening. 'Remember, she's probably more scared of you than you are of her!' she shouts.

Maybe in Polly's universe.

Here in the river, it takes every ounce of concentration in my body not to let my jaw hang open and all the air right out again.

This monster is old and withered, riven with scars and wrinkles, its underside scored with barnacles and weed.

But mostly, in the light of Polly's torch, it is blue. I have never seen anything so blue. Bluer than the bluest sky or the water at the Ring of Trees. This is blueness that goes on forever, that feels like it has been here an eternity, that you disappear into.

The lonely blue of my dream.

I know that I am looking at the deep shades of the ocean, of places I have never seen. I could stare at it until the end of time. But I can't because the whale powers off in another direction, sending me spinning, just missing a flick of the huge tail.

I rush up to the surface, gasping for air, the others crying out – 'What is it, Kester?' 'What does it want?' 'Is it friendly?'

From the water beneath me there comes that cry again, the cry which called us here. The rippling call becomes a moan, that forms into a song. But it is unlike any music I have ever heard before. This is a sharp cry of pain, as if every sound is forced out, echoing up through the waves and into my head.

While singing, it swims further and further out, deeper into the middle of the flooded Ams. It is too big to look at in one go. I only catch slippery glimpses of something great passing by in the dark.

I strike out, doing my best one-armed crawl, and follow the cries.

They are not hard to track.

The call of pain echoes around us so loudly that I

know the stag and the wolf and the pigeons can hear it too. The birds begin to circle above us in the air – whether out of sadness or fear, I can't tell.

The whale's deafening song fills my mind, transporting me from the filth of our city river to the depths of an ocean far away, where the light cannot reach. Which is when, her cries echoing on the tide, the whale in the Ams begins to speak.

The underside of the whale's jaw is covered in barnacles, stuck with withered fronds of seaweed. They have lost their colour in the water, going grey as a beard. Her red eye glitters as the ancient whale fixes me with her gaze.

Her voice is as old and cracked as her skin, and I am powerless to resist her words. I tread water, ducking my head for as long as I can, before coming up for air at the last possible moment. As the stag warned, she speaks in an underwater animal tongue of her own, similar to the chanting water snakes. Only this sounds like a language from very long ago; half sung, half spoken, a strange poem.

Listen, littleness. You must hear my heart-song. For it reveals the truth of this world – which I have journeyed far to tell you, suffering many hardships, carrying in my bone-breast the fate that awaits us.

I notice ripples on the surface, the vibrations of her words strong enough to make the water tremble. Her voice is so loud, so powerful, that every animal in the city must be able to hear.

Tossed in the great-wet, I was near death-dashed on stone-cliffs by sea-surges. Under frost-wastes, ice-chains wrapped themselves around me till I thought my life-blood would drain away. I lone-swam for many moons with no company but the waves washing. But all the while I never forgot this tale, which was our beginning – and will be the end, if you do not heed it.

I dare to interrupt. *Is this the animals' dream?*

A story they tell one another, that foretold me finding a cure for the virus and bringing the dark wild into the light.

The whale gives a barking laugh, her belly pulsing. Its sheer force pushes me back, the boats behind rising and falling on the wake.

'Are you OK out there, Kidnapper?' calls Polly from the shore. Treading water hard, I raise my hand so the others can see me.

Littleness, there were great-fish in the world's wet long before your furred ones walked on the dry. Have they sung the beginning of the dream?

Yes, they told me about when the men of the First Fold started keeping animals for food, and stopped sharing the animal voice. They said one day a boy would come who spoke their tongue—

*That is only the beginning of *their* dream. Ours begins much earlier. Once, before time itself, there was a great-fish who wandered-wide in the wet. Now this great-fish was good, but she also lone-swam. So she started to sing a song. It was a deep-music, deep enough to call all that is into being. She sang everything into life: from the belly-feeders who lived on her body to the giant-sharks who tried to feed on her head. But she was too clever and tough for them. She sang the creatures of the great-wet, all the fishes that ever were and the bug-eyed crawlers who slithered in the shadows. She sang the float-jellies, the sea-weeds and the krill shoals she grazed on. And she sang the air-flies who buzzed overhead, the white-feathers screaming high in the sky. Her music went beyond the wet, singing the dry-weeds that greened the earth, the land-giants curling their trunks, the hover-wings humming over pretty petals. For as many days as there are bright-dots in the night sky, the creatures in the wet and on the dry lived together in peace. Apart from one. A beast who grew to live alone, who did not want to share the world . . .*

The whale pauses for breath. Her whole body is trembling with the fever, and I can sense the heat from here. I have never before seen such a big animal with the red-eye. It is like a fire consumes her from the inside, the flames licking at the windows of her eyes.

All because of a virus that we could have stopped.

I hang my head in shame. *I think I know the name of this beast.*

You do, for his name was Man, and he was your ancestor. One day, a boy-man living on a rock in the middle of the ocean-blue dived right in. He swam straight to the belly of the great-fish, slicing her open with a stick-stone, tearing out her whale-heart. The ancient fish, who had sung the whole world alive, sank down to the sea-floor. The boy returned to the men waiting on the sand-shore. He brought them the giant heart, which they set hot-stones under until it burned and glistened hotter than the sun itself. Out of that fire came slicks of melt-fat and cloud-black, and with them a new age. An age of man, of tall-homes, of their smoke-holes and iron-paths which covered the dry.

Animals call trees tall-homes because so many creatures can live in them. They think our towers must be the same.

*Man filled the wet with his sail-shells, trailing knotted traps and pumping out slick. As he spread over the earth, so the creatures the first great-fish had sung vanished until there were nearly none left. By the time my mother calved me, there were just six of us swimming in those same waters where the great-fish once swam. When we broke-breeched to blow, we glimpsed swaying fronds on crystal-sand, smelling of the most golden honey-makers there ever were. There was not one trace of man. They had deserted this island-rock long ago in search of more land to build tall-homes on and fresh creatures to devour.

But in their rush to consume the world, they forgot the whale-heart. Stolen and buried under stone. And in the heart still lay the secret of the song that began the world. We named this whale-heart island Faraway, because it was now far away from the beast that killed the song: man. We swore to protect it as long as we lived. But one by one, old and grey, five of the great-fishes sank to the bottom forever. Until it was only me, lone-swimming in the great-wet . . . like our ancestor.

So what did you do?

I'll tell you what I did, littleness. I made the greatest mistake of my life, and left the gentle scented air of Faraway, wandering the whale-paths to see if I could find another great-fish to mate with. I wandered wide the world-over, but all I met were dead things – floating belly-up on the top or staring glass-eyed from below.

No surprises why.

*They were slain by the plague, the fever that burns me now. But it wasn't just the red-eye I found chasing me wherever I went, faster than the tide. The wet itself was changing. In places it became so thick it was hard for me to swim. Still I sang my song, hoping one day a mate would reply.

*But as my ancestor sang the world alive, I feared I was now singing it out-of-life. I swam through ice-fleets that had once been white rain-peaks on the land so high.

Wherever I wandered, the wet that had once been so pure tasted of metal poison. It is not just the creatures dying, you see, but the whole wide world herself. The sky, the wet and the dry look as if they will last forever, but they won't. Because I must tell you, I saw a terrible thing out there, the most terrible thing I have ever seen.*

The water is freezing, my skin is shrivelled, and my arms and legs are weak with paddling.

What . . . terrible thing?

She fixes me with her glittering eye again.

I cannot say exactly what it was, for I have never seen the like before. A thing that burned and dazzled in the sky like the surface of the sun itself . . . and scared me more than anything I have ever seen. If you do not find Faraway, if you do not stop these flames, they will consume you all.

She shudders, and her voice is weak.

*Then the red-eye came upon me, with shivers, shakes and weariness. And before I could find the whale-path home to Faraway again, a sky-storm so powerful and strong arose, and chased me – and I could not escape. I dived deep, trying to swim back the way I had come. But the calls of other great-fish that once guided me had gone. I was alone. The great-wet that used to be so full of creation was now full of nothing but rotting weed and man's knotted traps, entangling my jaw. Everything was silent. There was water everywhere, and not a thing to eat. My life-blood drained away.

High above me as I swam at night, the bright-dots shone in an empty sky. Hungry, ill and tired of this world, I bid the currents drag me where they wished. They carried me, as if I weighed no more than a fallen trunk, over crests tall enough to drown a mountain-peak. Riding a great wave I passed through man-gates of metal. Then my mind went dark, until I woke up here, calling out for help.

The whale must have been washed through the Amsguard by the storm when the squirrels opened the gates. She has been singing for so long I am tired and cold, my words faint in my head.

But why did you summon me?

I did not. I did not know whether anything still walked by these mud-shores, or if they were as deaded as the wet. All I could do was sing what was in my heart, hoping there were minds left alive to listen. And you came. My final words for you are these: I am the last great-fish that ever lived. My time draws to a close. This red-eye burns me from within. The world beyond your metal gates is also dying. Faraway is the only place that is not. I will never swim in its water again. Find our island, littleness. The world my ancestor sang into being is broken and dying. If nothing is done, in a few moons the terrible thing I saw in the great-wet will reach these shores. Your one hope is to find the place where it all began. Discover the secret of the great-fish's song and let the world begin again.

The whale pauses for a rattling breath. I realize my teeth are chattering. I've been in the water such a long time. But I don't get out. Not yet.

What's making this terrible fire? We're trying to rebuild the world, but we need to find a mouse first. She can help us. And even if I find . . . Faraway, what am I to do?

There is an exhausted sigh in reply. *If I knew the secret of the great-fish's song, I would not ask for your help now. But this much I can say: find Faraway, or there won't be a world left for you or your mouse.*

The unearthly music drifts away, leaving a breeze that whistles in the rigging of the ghost ships behind us. It is a new day, grey light spreading on to the water through a haze of morning mist. The water bubbles, as she breaches the surface one last time. I can see now, in the dawn, that her giant blue body hangs loose around her bones.

Then she dives again.

I take a gulp of air, plunging after her –

There is a trail of bubbles, a flash of red eye, a burning meteor sinking into the murk –

With that, the first and last whale I will ever meet – is gone.

PART 2: THE GLASS TOWERS

I swim back to the harbour wall in silence. My wet clothes billow out, weighing me down in the freezing water.

But it's not just waterlogged trousers which make my swim heavier. The last whale on earth – gone. An earth which, according to her, is now damaged beyond repair. And as if that wasn't bad enough, a terrible fire thing is coming over the ocean to consume us all. To destroy the whole world.

So even if we find Mouse and the Iris and recreate the animals that are lost, what will happen to us? As I swim back, heaving for air, the day is much brighter. I am so tired that I hardly notice the hands hoisting me out of the river, on to the dockside, where I collapse in a huge puddle.

A circle of faces peer over me. A stag. A girl with

curly hair. Another girl with mismatched gloves. And a wolf – who gives me an enormous lick with his tongue.

'Well?' demands Polly. 'What did the whale say?'

With a groan I roll over, turning my face away. Wet, shivering and miserable, I'm not sure I want to tell them that our whole planet is doomed. That our only hope of saving the earth – never mind rebuilding it – lies on a faraway island, which not even the whale who once lived there could find. Aida whips out a battery-powered hairdryer from her wheelie case and starts blasting my hair.

'That looks expensive,' says Polly.

'Oh, you know. Found it . . . somewhere.'

Polly tuts – louder than she needs to – and places something slimy and green in my hand.

'Go on, Kidnapper, you need to eat.'

It feels rubbery and smells of rotten fish.

Polly sighs. 'Please don't make that face. What do you think we were doing while you were swimming with your whale? I knew it had to be the beginning of another adventure, so this time I've thought ahead.'

She shows me one of the plastic bags she collected while we were clearing up the streets. I peer inside to see a mass of this slithery green stuff.

I gag. But Polly sticks her hand in and puts a small clump in her mouth. 'You were in that water for hours,' she says between chews. 'The tide started going out, and I found this on the rocks. It's a special seaweed you can eat raw. They call it hulse.'

I make a face.

'Don't be silly. Humans have been eating it for centuries! Everyone else can live on dregs of formula if they want, but we don't have to.'

Polly knows more about plants of all kinds than anyone else I know. Her knowledge of poisonous berries and their gross-smelling herbal-tea antidote cured my fever at Wind's Edge. She kept drawings and diagrams of so many flowers, leaves, petals, nuts and seeds in her notebook. The notebook that the Iris was also secretly stored in.

So I guess I should trust her on the slimy stuff. I stick a frond on my tongue and taste a tough, salty jelly. (Which isn't as gross as it sounds.) As I take another handful, the stag nudges me with his nose. *What will you do?* he asks. *Follow the whale's command?*

My shoulders sink. *How am I meant to find an island no one's ever heard of?*

A high-pitched voice interjects from the top of my head. *Yes. I've never heard of you so how am I meant to find your island?*

White pigeon, somehow I don't think it would be the best idea to send you off into the middle of nowhere to search for a mystery island.

For once he agrees. *Somehow I don't think that would be the best idea.*

So what do you suggest?

The little bird flutters down to my shoulders. He sticks his beak in my ear, as if he is confiding a big secret. *Why don't you send me off into the middle of nowhere to search for a mystery island?*

He somersaults in the air with a flurry of downy feathers and excitement at his own brilliance. As he does, the ninety-nine grey pigeons land around and on me.

Let us go, Wildness, they coo. *We cannot find a mouse hiding deep in a hole. But we can find an island in the sea. We will find Faraway for you.*

How are you going to find it without a map or any clues?

If there's one thing pigeons are good at, they chorus, *it's finding places. We listened to the whale's song too. Since the world is flooded, it makes looking for an island-rock much easier.*

What if you can't find your way back?

The one thing we are better at than finding places is finding our way home, say the grey pigeons.

I'm not very good at either, admits the white pigeon.

For once he might have a point. I can't expect one flock of pigeons to search the whole world's sea on their own, however good they are at finding places. So, closing my eyes, I call out in the animal tongue to others who could help.

To the starlings that flake off from the Facto chimneys, now sweeping in dotted swirls above our heads. And to the seagulls, redpolls and shrikes, till the sky is dark with overlapping wings.

Ooh yes, that's clever, isn't it, birds? squawks a familiar voice. One starling's feathers flash in the sun. Perched on the gable of an old warehouse, she grooms her chest, still bare in patches where her fellow birds punished her for being too bossy. Not that it has made much difference. *The whole *fill the sky with birds* routine – very commanding and dramatic, I must say!*

I am determined to ignore her this time.

Behind the warehouses and apartment blocks, the Four Towers are stark and bare again. I have to hope that the wild on the ground will keep the occupants trapped in their factory prison.

The steady beat of wings pulsing through the air makes a liquid sound, like a pumping steam piston. Over a thousand birds, waiting for me. The back of my neck prickles as I remember the first time the pigeons came into my room at Spectrum Hall. How frightened I was.

Birds of the new wild – you are the last flying creatures on earth. You have heard from the great-fish that the earth will give up on us unless we can find the secret of the whale's song.

Ooh, that doesn't sound at all good, does it? whispers

the starling to her flock. *The last flying creatures on earth? Bit bleak, don't you think?*

I pretend not to hear and continue.

The pigeons are ready to search the world's wet. But we do not have long. So tell me – who among your number is the strongest and fastest flyer?

They flutter around in the fresh morning air for a moment and then part, like dark curtains in the sky. Revealing, in the white beyond, a distant V-shape.

A V that gets much closer in a short space of time.

Not fluttering or flapping, but single beats of great wings that glide and dive –

The bird swoops on to the ground in front of us, his gleaming yellow talons digging in between the cobbles. The wolf recoils and even the stag takes a clop back over the stones.

It is easy to see why.

A curved beak sharp enough to tear any fur or flesh, eyes just as piercing, the sun flashing off them. The golden eagle folds in his giant wings and twitches his noble head, brown feathers ruffed up around his neck like a thick scarf.

I have never talked to this bird before, that I first saw circling in the sky above the Ring of Trees. I wait for him to speak, but he just stares at me with a steely gaze that makes me feel like skin and blood waiting to be torn apart.

So, Eagle, I start, *are you the fastest bird left?*

He ducks his head, scratching at his plumage. Then that stare again. *Reckon so.*

I don't know why I'm so nervous. *Are you the strongest?*

Strong enough.

Will you lead these others in search of the whale's island?

Could do.

And protect them as best you can?

If you like.

It could be dangerous. Storms, white rain . . . even the fire in the sky the whale mentioned.

The bird shrugs, in a birdish way.

You don't say much, do you?

The eagle jabs his beak at me, and I stumble back.

Don't need words much, he says.

With that, he flaps off into the air, a blur of golden feathers and claw. He circles the assembled flock, from starlings to pigeons, soaring high above them. He gives a shrieking call, and then is off, as if there were jet engines beneath his wings.

Then, without another word, the birds sweep after him into the sky, silhouettes against the pale light of day. I watch them with my hand shielding my eyes, until they are distant specks.

Come back quick, I say to myself.

A cough from behind breaks my thoughts.

'Kidnapper, where are your birds going? I hope

you know what you're doing, leaving Facto unguarded again.'

'Yes.' But I need more than two words to explain.

Looking around the dockside, I spy a weathered boathook leaning against one of the warehouses. I pick it up with my free hand, beckoning the others to follow me down the harbour steps, on to the strip of sludgy sand and hulse-splattered rocks exposed by the tide. Then, while Polly gathers more of the precious foodstuff, I attack the beach with the hook, scratching out letters, lines and symbols – until the whole shore is covered with the whale's story.

The sun is high in the sky by the time – dripping with sweat – I pause for breath, leaning on the pole. The girls read what I have written in the sand.

'What's this?' says Polly, pointing at something I've drawn, which looks like this:

I point with the stick to my drawing of the whale, and then thump my chest.

'That's not what a whale heart looks like, silly,' she replies, shaking her head. Then she grabs the hook from me, rubbing out the symbol. 'This is what a whale heart looks like. They're ginormous.' She sketches something which looks more like this:

'Ugh, gross,' says Aida.

'But it's the truth. The whale we saw has one so big you could crawl right through.'

At least, it did.

For a moment they are silent.

'The actual end of the actual world then?' murmurs Polly, her fingers tracing the letters on the shore.

I'm only half listening to her though, distracted by a low humming noise. It's hard to figure out where it's coming from.

'You mean that big flood only the beginning?' asks Aida. Then she turns, her eyes squinting in the light from the waves, as if she's just detected the humming too. 'So even if we find the Iris, this whale says there might not be a world left for all them animals and plants?'

I nod. The stag and the wolf stand with me, their faces set. Every prediction the animals made from their dream came true. Why should the whale's song be any different?

The world is dying, shrinking, flooding. A terrible burning thing is coming.

'So what are we going to do?' says Polly, standing up and interrupting my thoughts. 'It's simple. We have to find Faraway *and* the mouse.' Even raising her voice above the humming, which grows louder and louder, she makes it sound so possible and obvious.

But she's right. This city, this Island, this world – it's our home. If it's dying, we have to find the cure. If a fire is coming, we have to stop it. Although right now, the only thing definitely coming our way is the humming noise from the water.

We turn to face the river. I wonder if for a moment the whale has returned, but the whale didn't send a wake of white foam out towards the shore, lapping at our feet. The whale didn't have blinding bright headlights.

That's because it's not a whale.

It's a ship – heading right for us.

Shimmering across the sea, flood wrecks bobbing apart to make way, the prow sparkling in the sun . . . is a boat made of glass.

A transparent hull, the rippling light from the waves both reflected on and seen through it. The engine and the lower deck are also completely visible. Every working part looks like glass, or at least super-strong plastic. The bridge is the same, its glittering corners as blinding as a wall of mirrors directed right at the sun.

Above, silver crystal-shaped pennants flutter in the wind from a clear mast, and a revolving radio receiver slices through the air like a bar of ice. A transparent dinghy dangles over the stern.

I can just make out a name carved in swirling letters along the side of the boat.

75

THE GLASSCUTTER

The wolf shifts on the sand, trying to get a firm footing. *This is the second strangest fish I have ever seen.*

Then he jumps back, and we do too, as the strange glass fish runs aground, ploughing into the damp sludge. Polly grabs my good arm.

Together forever. Never to be separated.

But it is hard not to flinch as a transparent gangplank is flung on to the shore. A pair of sailors in matching grey uniforms run down it, wearing tiny shards of glass as badges on their chests.

I notice that not only do their clothes match, but the men are identical too.

Identical blond ponytails and goatees under their identical sailor's caps, with an identical glint in their blue eyes.

The twin guards stand aside and salute as a woman descends on to the beach. Her hair curves around her face in an ash-coloured helmet. She is so pale the blue of her veins shows through her skin. Hanging around her neck is a chain of multicoloured icicles.

She pushes the stag aside, who is too startled to resist. It appears that the icicles are shards of glass. They reflect my frightened face back at me from every possible angle.

'Come closer.'

Her voice is as hypnotic as the sound of the water lapping against her boat. I take a step forward. She stalks around me, a cape twirling in the wind, as she looks me over.

I do not like the smell of this pale creature, Wildness, says the wolf. *And remember, I am much better than you at smelling.*

Before I can reply, the pale creature's frozen face cracks into a smile and she flings her cloak wide open. 'Come and give Auntie Fenella a hug!'

'No . . .' I don't have an auntie, never mind an Auntie Fenella.

With two freezing hands, the woman grabs the back of my head and presses me into the folds of her dress, crushing my sore shoulder and making me gasp. I don't know what perfume she's wearing, but I can hardly breathe, choking on a scent that reminds me of damp snow.

'Poor boy,' she whispers, stroking and kissing my hair. 'You poor darling. So cold and wet out here alone on this deserted beach. What would your mother say?'

I think my mother would say, 'Get your freakishly chilly hands off my son.'

'Tommen? Timmen?' the woman snaps, letting me go so sharply I fall back on to the sand. 'Why are you standing there like statues? These poor children!' She clicks her fingers. 'Towels! Hot drinks! Some clothes that don't make them look like workhouse orphans! Chopitty-chop!'

Tommen and Timmen?

'From the northern countries originally. They make the best sailors. All those fjords. In fact, you could say they're the finest sailors I could afjord!' She laughs at her own joke. *'Afjord!* Do you see?' I give the biggest smile I can for such a joke, which isn't very big. The northern twins salute and march up the gangplank in lockstep.

'We're fine, actually,' says unfrightened Polly, and the woman smiles.

'Darling girl, of course you are,' she says, caressing her necklace. 'Because I'm here.'

'And who you?' says Aida, with a weapons-grade Aida scowl.

'Who me?' says Glass-Necklace. 'Why, child, I'm your Auntie Fenella.'

'I not got no auntie.'

'My auntie died a long time ago,' says Polly, folding her arms.

'No,' I say. This woman is definitely not a relation of mine either.

'Oh, but I am,' says Auntie Fenella. 'What do aunts do? They give you gifts, don't they?'

Tommen and Timmen have marched back down the gangplank and press frosted tankards of a hot drink into our hands. Not brown tea, but a creamy, frothy liquid, sweet and delicious.

'Formu-milk!' gasps Aida.

Artificial milk. A drink so rare and expensive none of

us has ever had it before – along with a formypop each, popped in our mouth before we can object.

'Aunts keep you safe and warm when your parents aren't there,' trills Auntie Fenella. The two twins materialize behind us with the biggest and fluffiest grey towels ever, drying my hair till it stands up on end. They drape one each over the girls' shoulders.

'And aunts,' she continues, propelling me along the beach, 'take you on lovely excursions to new and exciting places.'

Before we realize what's happening, we are being marched by the twins up the glass ramp and on to the boat.

Stag and the wolf look at me, confused. It's Polly who digs her heels in first, flinging off the towel and thrusting her empty tankard back into Tommen's hands. (Or Timmen's – I'm not sure.)

She stands at the bottom of the plank, her toad at her feet, both of them refusing to budge.

'Except you're not our aunt. And we're not going anywhere with you until you explain exactly who you really are and where you're taking us.'

Auntie Fenella arches one night-black eyebrow. 'Why should I? You're only children. Children should do as they're told.'

'Not these children,' says Polly, the colour rising in her cheeks. I'm beginning to feel safer and safer having her around.

The woman's ice face cracks into something that could be either a smile or a snarl. 'Very well. We can do this the easy way, or the hard way.'

'Easy way,' says Aida, through a last glug of hot Formu-milk. Polly scowls at her.

'As you wish. The easy way is this. My name is Councillor Fenella Clancy-Clay of the Glass Towers Council. I am an official representative of the citizens who live in the towers across the water.'

She stares at me for a moment, as if she can read the forest of thoughts pinging up behind my eyes.

'Hmm,' says Aida, rubbing her chin. 'I lived in this city a very long time. And I ain't never heard of no Glass Towers Council.'

The councillor looks down her nose at the girl in the mismatched mittens and filthy sneakers, her hair sticking up in eighteen different directions. The girl who lived on a rubbish tip.

'Well, you wouldn't have, would you?' she sneers.

'What that meant to mean?'

'It means never you mind, you're all coming with me. Who knows what could happen to three children on their own out here?' The councillor touches Aida's shoulder, her hand like a white spider deciding whether to pounce. 'The water is so deep and unpredictable. I would never forgive myself if you, you know . . .' She glances at the murky river.

'No,' I say. I don't.

'Do you want me to spell it out?'

'He means no, we can't go with you,' says Polly. 'We need to find—'

'Don't tell her!' yells Aida. 'We don't know who she is or who she work for.'

'Don't tell me what?' says the councillor. 'No secrets from your Auntie Fenella now.'

'You don't understand,' says Polly, digging her heels deeper into the damp sand as the twins try to propel her up the gangplank. 'There's a terrible fire coming, and we have to stop it.'

'Naturally. Where is this fire and what's causing it?'

I hang my head.

Aida speaks for me. 'Anyone's guess. We got to find this island first.' She cups her hand over her mouth immediately, realizing her mistake, and starts backing down the gangplank, but the damage is done.

Fenella grabs her by the wrist. 'What island?' she asks, a glimmer of curiosity in her eyes.

'I told you!' Aida tries to pull free. 'We have to go discover.'

But Fenella doesn't let go. I've had enough of this. Aida is right. We have a mission to complete. *Wolf! Stag! You have to help us.*

At my command, the wolf leaps forward and tugs at Polly's sleeve, pulling her in one direction while the twins try to drag her in the other. The toad hops to and fro between them both, bellowing encouragement. The stag charges at the boat, horns lowered.

81

Unperturbed, Councillor Clancy-Clay sighs. 'Shall I tell you what I see?'

We ignore her, but she carries on anyhow.

'Three young children, putting themselves in very dangerous situations, your parents nowhere to be seen. Children with scant regard for the law – which, incidentally, bans animals from this city.'

Fenella reaches for her necklace, and twists off a bright green glass shard. She holds it up to the light briefly, before chucking it down between the stag and the wolf. It sparkles on the beach like an emerald washed up by the tide. As we watch, it melts away on the wet ground, dissolving into a mist, which curls up around my animals, making them choke and splutter.

Wildness, gasps Wolf. *Why is it suddenly night time? I can normally see better than anyone in the dark, but right now I can't see beyond my nose.* He lets go of Polly, who shrieks as the twins drag her up on-board, the toad following fast behind. The wolf starts to stumble around in circles, looking like he no longer knows where he is.

'Monster!' says Aida, but Fenella grabs her again. Both of her wrists this time, and hard.

'Three young children who think this is merely a game – with imaginary fires and made-up islands – when this is a very serious situation indeed.'

Stag! I call. *Get away from that mist.*

My great stag takes two steps forward up the plank.

Wildness! His voice is blurry, like someone who's just woken up. Then he too begins to stagger around like the wolf, both of them bumping into each other as if they are blindfolded. I try to leap over the side, only to find that my ankles are now bound with plastic cable.

The engines of the glass boat tremble into life, and the silver pistons whirr beneath our feet. The boat powers back into the water, sending a huge wave over the blinded animals which washes away the whale's story in a single splash. I can't bear to look.

Instead I follow Fenella's gaze across the Ams towards the glass towers of Premium, clouds swimming across their glossy squares. Her hands grip the crystal deck rail so tightly I worry it might shatter.

'Your adventure is over, children,' she smiles. 'The grown-ups are in charge now.'

I turn away from Councillor Clancy-Clay and run down the deck of *Glasscutter* to the other end. Except, with one arm in a sling and my ankles bound, it's technically more of a hop-shuffle. Pigeons can waddle faster, but I don't care.

At the stern of the boat, leaning over the icy railings, my view is obscured by curling clouds of mist, closing up behind us as if we were leaving not just a riverbank but the whole world.

Desperate for any sign of movement that shows me the stag and the wolf are still alive, I try and squint through the haze. But with every churn of the giant propellers beneath me, they get further and further away. With them recede our family, friends and any chance of finding the mouse. I'm not sure this 'Faraway' is the kind the whale meant. I thump the glass railing with my free hand, hoping it might snap.

It doesn't, but my hand nearly does.

'Oh, come, come,' says a voice behind me. I whip round, boiling with rage, to find Fenella standing there on her own. She doesn't have either of her twin sailors. I could charge, I could lash out, I could . . . But as if she sees what I'm thinking, she toys with the necklace of coloured glass shards hanging round her neck.

'Glass is an amazing material, don't you think?' she says. 'Humans have been making it for centuries, and yet – as with so much we have been doing for centuries – we're only just beginning to comprehend its potential.'

I stamp the deck. The only potential I'm interested in is the one for this boat to fracture from top to bottom in a thousand pieces.

'We can see straight through it and use it to see things close up. It can show us to ourselves. Glass lets light in, but can also measure light and even turn the world bright.' She nods towards the twinkling glass towers. 'We use it in everything, from the smallest computer chip to the walls of the skyscrapers behind me. We know enough about this amazing material to build a boat this strong . . . or a necklace this delicate.'

I begin to get a bad feeling in my stomach about why she has this boat, and who paid for it. There was special glass in my window wall at Spectrum Hall, that kept the temperature the same all the time. A glass roof like an upside-down boat to protect against the virus. The glass towers of Mons where Polly's parents were arrested by Facto.

She dazzles me with a whiter-than-white smile.

'I can see you're impressed. Take my necklace, made of dissolvable glass. It seems magic, but it's only technology. Doctors invented this material a long time ago, to hold bones together after operations, and dissolve into the body once the wound had healed. I simply found a way to accelerate the chemical process. Enough surface contact with moisture and each one will disintegrate, releasing a different . . . surprise.'

Animal-blinding surprises. Maybe a boy-killing one too. Who knows?

'Oh, come, come! Don't give me that look! Your Auntie Fenella isn't a common culler, thank you very much! Your precious animals are just drugged for a while. Then they'll get their sight back and find . . . a place better for stags and wolves than a glass boat, I suspect.' She gives a gritty laugh. 'So stop sulking and let me explain why you're aboard.'

Councillor Clancy-Clay spins on her heels and I shuffle back to the front deck, where my friends and their guards stand in a semicircle, backlit by the sun-reflecting bridge. An early-afternoon breeze drifts across, bringing with it the coolness of the deep waters that surround us.

She turns to the others. 'The expression on his face, poor boy. He thinks we might do something horrid to him.' She runs bony fingers over her necklace. 'As if your Auntie Fenella ever would.'

Struggling with my cable-tied ankles and bound arm I try to lash out at her, but Tommen and Timmen step in perfect formation between us, blocking me.

'On the contrary, children, we brought you here because we need your help.'

'Real funny way of asking for it,' grumbles Aida.

'The people I represent spotted you on the beach through their cameras. They asked me to invite you to join them the easy way, which you declined. So I had to fetch you the hard way.'

'Why? What did we do to you? We're just children, as you keep telling us,' says Polly.

As *everyone* keeps telling us. But I'm not really listening any more. I'm thinking about the people who can spy things going on in the city through cameras. Who ask people to build towers and roofs and necklaces and boats out of glass.

For the first time there's emotion in Fenella's voice, a tiny glimmer of heat warming her icy gaze. 'For six years we endured the virus, the dead animals, the curfews, the food shortages and the . . . formula. Trust me, no one is more grateful to you for finding a cure.' She gives a hiccup of a laugh and continues.

'Then, as if we hadn't been through enough, those vermin running rampant through our city, the power cuts, the damage, that wretched storm and the floods.

Again, we are very grateful for everything you children did to save us from the worst of those disasters.'

'Yes,' I say, but I don't mean it. The boat pitches gently as it speeds over the river, and we sway side to side as we watch each other across the deck.

'Which is why we need your help now more than ever.' Fenella sounds desperate. 'There are exciting plans ahead for this city, but we need to persuade the citizens that they are the right ones.'

'I still don't see what that has to with us, Mrs Clancy-Clay,' says Polly.

'Councillor Clancy-Clay, please,' corrects Councillor Clancy-Clay. Her smile disappears for a moment, before returning bigger and whiter. 'Because you stopped the animal attacks and saved us from the floods. You are the future generation, the ones whom our plans . . . will benefit the most.'

She strokes my head, as if she's blessing me.

'And you are going to tell the citizens of this city the truth. You listened to nature. Now our people will listen to you. Come with me, Kester Jaynes, and tell them that humans have an exciting future ahead.'

In a world that the whale told me is going to be destroyed? There may be just half a metre of glass deck between us, but it might as well be light years in terms of what we think.

Tommen and Timmen begin uncoiling piles of rope, as the boat slows to a putter and starts to wheel around.

'We don't care for your plans, whatever they are,' says Aida. 'We got our own.'

'Yes,' says Polly. 'We can't help you, I'm afraid. We are already very busy saving the world.'

'Yes,' I add. The toad gives an extra burp of agreement, puckering his lips up at the councillor.

The last trace of a smile and any glimmer of warmth vanish from Fenella's face, which once more becomes the model of an arctic shelf.

'That is most disappointing.'

'Are you going to lock us up if we don't?' asks Polly, as the sailors throw the ropes off the side in tight, coordinated moves. 'Because I must warn you – we are very good at escaping.'

'Yes,' I add again.

Councillor Clancy-Clay puts a hand to her chest in shock, as if we'd just stabbed her with one of her own icicles.

'Lock you up?' she chuckles. 'That's positively the *last* thing I want to do.' Reaching inside her cape she produces a pair of sparkling pliers. 'Diamond. The strongest glass on earth,' she explains. Then with three short snips she has released us from our plastic ties.

I survey the uniformed sailors, the councillor's poison necklace and the river all around, looking for an escape route. Nothing. We exchange glances, the kind that say, 'Whatever we do, not yet.' Glances that, I hope, fake aunts are bad at noticing.

89

'You mean you're *not* going to put us in prison?' says Polly, sounding disappointed, as the boat bumps gently into the glass towers' harbour wall.

'Put you in prison?' Fenella gives another tinkling laugh. 'No, sweet children – I'm putting you in hair and make-up.'

I have jumped off a cliff and nearly drowned in a waterfall. I have been shot at, almost burned alive, trapped underground and savaged by a vicious dog. But *hair and make-up*? This is the single scariest thing I have ever heard in my life.

No sooner has the *Glasscutter* bumped up against the glass towers' white dockside, than I lean over the boat's railings, preparing to jump . . . when Polly grabs my arm.

'Kidnapper,' she whispers. 'Remember what we said?'

Together forever. I know. 'Yes.'

Aida points to her wheelie case full of stolen booty. 'And I ain't jumping off no ship with this. So wait.'

'Besides,' says Polly, 'who knows? If we help her, perhaps she might be able to help us . . .'

91

Before she can say more, Timmen and Tommen frogmarch us in quick time down the gangplank, Polly clutching the toad in her arms, followed by Aida, her case bouncing behind her. The white flagstones, which once must have looked polished and new, are stained with grime, weeds straggling between the cracks. And rising up above them, the buildings I have seen so many times from afar, but never this close.

The Glass Towers.

'Children!' sings Fenella, clip-clopping across the muddy quartz slabs. 'Come along! I have a surprise for you . . . It's going to be such fun, I promise!'

She disappears into the large revolving doors at the bottom of the first tower, and the twin guards push us after her. The inside is not what I was expecting. The floor of coloured glass tiles is dirty and cracked, our reflections only just visible. The toad blinks and recoils at his. Shafts of light struggle to squeeze in through window panels caked with dust, and the large atrium is full of gloomy shadows.

But if the glass tower looks like a derelict ruin, it doesn't feel like one. There are people everywhere. If Premium has sometimes felt like a ghost city since I got back, there's no danger of that here.

Families fill every square inch of the floor, huddled in groups, their eyes sunken and hollow. Fenella seems not to give them a second glance as she picks her way towards a long reception desk. She exchanges a few words with the sullen-looking attendant sat behind, dressed in the same grey uniform as our guards.

We look around. The only things not made of glass are the vast fake trees sprouting up from wells in the floor, filtering the light through clouds of plastic leaves. In their shadows we can see a pair of children taking it in turns to lick out the last few drops from a formula carton.

The Glass Towers, where many Islanders came to live when the red-eye struck, in the mistaken belief that the virus could spread to people, and that living under glass would protect them. Now, like so much else, they seem close to collapse.

'What a horrid place,' says Polly. 'Why does anybody want to live here?'

'Cos there is nowhere else to,' replies the girl who lived on the rubbish heap.

And she should know.

The tower dwellers come and go, slouching in and out of the wheezing glass elevators that serve this see-through ants' nest. We crane our heads to see yet more people sitting on the edges of transparent walkways, peering through double-glazed windows, curled up on benches.

The strangest thing, though, is right in the middle of the atrium, far above our heads: what looks like a giant glass bell. It hangs in the air without any visible support, just shaking a little in the dry air-conditioned breeze.

But of the many things to see here, there is one vital thing missing.

'There's no way out,' says Aida, clearly thinking the same as me. Apart from the way we came in, and that's guarded by Timmen and Tommen.

There's a shout from the reception. Fenella, her glass necklace glinting.

'Oh, children!' she calls. 'As I said, we can do this the easy way . . .'

I don't wait for the rest. My head spins from sunken-faced children to glass lifts to massive indoor trees and, tucked in between the colossal trunks, I spot . . . a door, just open a crack.

A door that could lead anywhere. But anywhere is better than this fake forest of plastic and glass. I glance over at Timmen and Tommen, admiring themselves in the glass walls, stroking their blonde goatees – and sidle through the crowd towards the door. The others follow, weaving in between the trees and people.

Slamming the door shut behind us, we find ourselves at the top of dimly lit stairs. I start running down, the others clattering after me. I know they are full of questions, and so am I, but we have to escape. There is a mouse to be found, and a whale's call to be answered.

I run in big leaps down the steps, hitting the sides as I round each corner, hoping that this will lead somewhere useful, somewhere that isn't . . . a locked door.

A door that is not only locked, but double-chained and

padlocked shut, no matter how much I rattle it. We wait in the darkness, listening to the sound of our own breathing. I touch the watch around my neck, hoping there might be one last gasp of power left in the light, but there isn't.

'Why is that strange woman pretending to be our aunt, do you think?' whispers Polly. 'And why does she want to put us in make-up?'

'I don't know, but no make-up ever going on me, that for sure,' says Aida.

Polly laughs, and then stops, catching her breath as we hear a door creak open. We freeze.

The door opening is followed by a light, gentle noise.

The sound of someone slowly and carefully coming down the steps after us.

It doesn't matter who can hear us now. I rattle the chain till it rips the skin of my palms, banging my fists against the door.

Polly grabs hold of my elbow. 'Together,' she whispers.

'Forever,' says Aida, grabbing my other hand even tighter.

'Yes,' I whisper in reply, letting go of the chain.

The steps get faster, skittering over the stairs as they grow nearer. There's only one set of them, which rules out Timmen and Tommen. They sound too light to be Fenella's heeled boots. In fact, as I shrug the girls off for a moment to listen again, I realize they sound too light to be made by a person at all.

These aren't footsteps, they're claws on concrete.

Claws, I realize, that I've heard on stone before. Along with a familiar panting breath, getting closer and closer, until . . . There, coming round the corner, glowing in the shadows, is a large white head.

One I hoped I'd never see again.

The head with two black dots for eyes. The last time I saw them was on the Amsguard, collapsed in a dripping puddle of blood and torn fur. A Dark Wildness defeated, stripped of his power – Littleman's artificial metal jaws swept away by the waves flooding the city. Then the birds flew me to the estate, followed by the new wild along the ground . . . but Dagger disappeared.

I thought maybe the floods had swallowed him. I was wrong.

Hello, dog.

He nods but doesn't speak. We stare at each other. Before I can say anything else to him, the woman we were trying to escape from comes steaming round the corner. Fenella brandishes a black leather lead and a torch, which she shines in our eyes.

'Or,' she says, not missing a beat, 'we can do this the hard way.'

She flicks Dagger on his haunches with the lead, and the dog opens his mouth. His metal jaws have gone for good. And in their place are rows of teeth so bright we can see our faces in them.

Jaws made of glass.

We're cornered.

Fenella raises the lead. Dagger grinds his glass teeth, putting dogs grinding glass teeth right to the top of my worst-sounds-ever list. All three of us take an involuntary step back towards the chained door. Then something very unexpected happens.

Polly's toad leaps from her arms and squares up to Dagger.

Dagger growls and opens his fake jaws, very real drool dripping from their sparkling tips.

The toad's eyes bulge, and his lower lip trembles. But he doesn't budge.

For a moment, even Fenella looks unsure about what might happen next.

'Oh, Toad! What have I said about picking your battles?' says Polly, scooping him up again so he rests in her arms, glowering with fury at the dog.

(As far as I know, Polly has never said a word to the toad that he can understand, and he's never spoken – to her or to me. In talking-animal terms, he remains what Dad calls 'an enigma'.)

'I don't think you've met my new pet,' says Fenella, regaining her cool. 'I found him wandering alone in the streets after the floods. He was so adorable I couldn't resist – could I, darling little Crystal?' She leans forward and squeezes his fat neck. The dog once known as Dagger remains stony-faced and silent.

'He not called Crystal, he called Dagger,' says Aida, rolling her eyes. 'And I wouldn't do that, if I you. He don't like that, not one bit.'

'Nonsense! He's my dog, and he's called Crystal. Inspired by the sparkling set of gnashers I gave him.' She leans forward and tickles his chin. 'So I can do as I please, can't I, my darling?'

Briefly something passes behind Dagger's eyes, before his unfriendly gaze returns.

'Dagger,' says Aida.

'Crystal,' says Fenella, not smiling any more.

'Isn't!'

'Is!'

'Isn't!'

'Is!'

'Now listen!' says the councillor, standing up again to her full height. 'He's my dog. I found him! I rescued him! I replaced his teeth. I gave him the name Crystal. And if you don't come with me right now, I shall order him to tear your little throats out.'

She squeezes his neck again and Dagger growls, lunging at Aida, making her shrink back against the locked doors. Polly shields her toad under her top.

I don't recoil though. I'm not scared of Dagger any more. I'll never be scared of him ever again. *You're not anyone's dog, are you?* I say to him. *You weren't Littleman's, and you're not Fenella's. You're not a pet, you're your own animal.*

A light flashes behind his eyes, before the dog with two names is snapping at our heels and chasing us up the stairs behind Fenella.

'No time for hair and make-up now, I'm afraid,' she sings out. 'We'll have to face our guests in the Vitrine just as we are.'

The Vitrine turns out to be the huge glass bell we saw hanging in the atrium between the twisting fake trees. We approach it along a walkway that looks as if it's suspended in mid-air.

Dagger snaps at our heels, making us walk faster and faster. The toad leans out of Polly's arms and bellows at him.

'Chopitty-chop, children,' says Fenella, as she strides ahead to the Vitrine entrance. Timmen and Tommen are waiting for us in front of two grimy glass doors. Just as the councillor looks about to fling them open, she spins around and plucks Polly's toad out of her arms, ignoring his burps of protest.

My friend lunges after her only animal companion. 'Hey! He's mine. Give him back.'

But Fenella wags a glossy fingernail at her. As if she is handing them a filthy rag – instead of the most loyal amphibian you ever met – she passes Polly's friend to Timmen. Or Tommen.

'Consider it our insurance policy,' says the councillor. 'Behind these doors are some friends of mine. Important ones. Which makes them the most important people in Premium. And as Premium is the biggest megacity left in the world, it makes them the most important people in the world. Are you with me so far?'

I haven't liked any of the important people in Premium I have met. None of us has. But we nod, Polly not taking her eyes off the toad.

'Good,' Fenella purrs. 'Because these friends of mine have a very special project they need your help with.'

'The only friends we helping right now are a whale and a mouse,' says Aida.

'Don't be absurd. What about your own city? The people of Premium trust you, since you stopped the sea flooding and the animals rampaging. So my important friends want you to persuade them that their new project is a good idea.'

'What project?' demands Polly, raising an eyebrow.

'No spoilers now,' says Fenella. Her eyes narrow. 'Do what I say and speak when spoken to, or the frog gets it.' She draws a line across her throat.

'No.'

'Excuse me?'

'No,' I repeat, glancing at the others.

'You heard him,' says Aida. 'What do we get in return?'

Fenella shrugs. 'Your precious froggie staying alive, for one thing. Plus I don't ask Crystal to shred you to pieces, or Timmen and Tommen to lock you up in one of our secure glass cells. Deal?'

At the mention of his new name Dagger growls menacingly, but it's hard to tell whether it's at us or his latest owner.

She turns to the doors again, but Polly puts her foot in the way. 'You know that's not fair. We're helping you, so you've got to do something for us in return.'

Fenella tries hard to smile at Polly. 'Child. That's not how it works. I'm in charge around here. These are my towers.'

'Fine,' says Polly. 'We will be so rude about your friends' stupid project that you won't believe your ears.'

The ice lady is not impressed. 'You don't care what happens to your little pet?'

We turn to look at the toad, who is giving Timmen the longest lick on his cheek with his tongue, while Tommen strokes his head.

Their boss sighs, and squeezes her hands so tight they go even whiter than they were. Her voice drops a notch deeper. 'Once again, I offer you the easy way. And once again . . .'

'We take the hard way?' says Aida with a smirk.

'You took the words right out of my mouth,' snarls

Fenella, and in a single move twists off a sapphire shard from her necklace, shoving it under my nose. I try to pull away, but I can't. Whatever is inside wafts up my nostrils, smelling of vinegar and bleach, making my eyes water and the back of my throat itch.

She does the same to Polly and Aida, before the glass icicle dissolves in her hands and she claps them dry.

I get ready to lose my sight, or to stumble over, but if anything I'm more awake and alert. Before anyone can say another word, the toad dives for cover as Timmen and Tommen grab the handles of the mirrored doors, flinging them open, and Councillor Fenella Clancy-Clay marches us into the chamber beyond.

The room is large and echoing. Darkness seems to hang from the walls, which once must have gleamed and shone. Tatty grey curtains are dragged across tall windows, blocking out the day. Broken glass crunches underfoot, Dagger waltzing between the fragments with ease. A chandelier overhead fizzes with a flickering low light.

I wonder if this is the main assembly hall of the Glass Towers. If so, it has not been used for a while.

Perspex chairs are stacked in piles around the edges, some covered in dustsheets. But three are set up in the middle of the empty room, behind a transparent desk. The furniture looks lonely and bright in the fierce glow of a studio lamp, whose cable snakes away into the shadows. A large blank ultrascreen fills the back wall.

The light is so strong, right in our eyes, that I can't see who is behind it. From the muttered whispers I know there is more than one person. Spots fly before me as I try to peer beyond the glare into the gloom, but trying to look makes me dizzy, and I stumble – Polly grabbing my arm before I fall.

Perhaps the contents of the sapphire shard are taking effect. I want to run and hide, but the mirrored doors have swung shut behind us, Timmen and Tommen standing guard with their most serious matching stares.

Fenella sashays ahead, talking to the unseen people behind the light. 'Gentlemen! Here we are.' The gentlemen in question say something which I can't make out. She presses her hand against her chest and makes a sad face. 'I know. It's desperate, isn't it? Those brave little smiles. Those awful clothes.'

She pauses for a moment in front of the desk, basking in the studio lamp's rays as if she is soaking up the sun after years indoors. Then she turns and guides us into the chairs, smoothing our hair and producing a small compact from her cape, to powder our faces.

It feels hard to resist, like I'm no longer in control of my actions.

There is a jug of water on the table. Fenella pours us each a glass but the toad knocks one over immediately and splashes about in the puddle.

Dagger comes to lie at our feet under the desk. I can't tell if he is there under Fenella's orders or his own initiative. He flashes his crystal teeth at us before resting his heavy paws on Aida's shoes.

I fidget on the hard chair, the heat from the lamp making sweat trickle down my neck. I turn away, trying to see through the gaps in between the curtains. Beyond that glass lies the other side of the city, where our family and friends are looking for a mouse. Four Towers, where Facto are, trapped inside by my wild. Premium's far shore, where we could be waiting for the birds to return with news of Faraway.

Ahead of us, the last things we need: shadowy figures, and a lady with a poisonous glass necklace. I try to get up but feel glued to my seat. The others too are struggling to stand. We give up and link hands under the desk, but even this feels harder than it should.

Togever. Forether. Why is it getting tricky even to think the words?

Fenella plants herself in front of the desk and addresses the people behind the lamp.

'Gentlemen. Here are the children you requested. They were exactly where you said they would be. And I think you'll find they are only too ready to help you.'

She gives a tinkling laugh as she says this. Why is it funny? My mind feels foggy. I notice the others looking strange as well, their heads sinking. I sit up, taking deep breaths, the room cloudy and sharp at the same time.

'Help. You. How?' asks Polly slowly, as if she too is having trouble forming words.

'Why, dear child, by saying that you approve this message.'

There's a murmur of appreciation from behind the light. For some reason the sound makes my stomach somersault. It doesn't matter. I'm not approving any message. I open my mouth, but no word comes out. The drug trapped in the melting glass is muddling my thoughts and movements.

'What. Message?' says Aida, sounding as drowsy as I feel.

'Trouble speaking, my dear?' says Fenella. 'It's a rather marvellous shard, this one. I'll show you. Try repeating something I say, like . . . "My name is Aida and I am the dumbest girl in Premium."'

'My name is Aida and I am the dumbest girl in Premium,' repeats Aida automatically. Her eyes say otherwise, but she has no choice.

'For a brief, precious while, you will say just as I say. Can't science be magical sometimes?'

At least I can't speak.

But as if she read my mind, the councillor turns to me. 'Do you like animals, Kester? Say no.'

'No.' I said it before I thought the word. At our feet Dagger growls. I try to explain to him in the animal voice that that's not what I think, but even that seems blocked.

We're drugged and trapped.

'What I say, you say. And soon you will be saying it on every ultrascreen.'

It's not the drug from the shard making me sick, sending chills spreading across my body. There's only one way to access the screens. After we had trapped Facto in Tower 1, the Waste Mountain Gang hacked into their network to broadcast the truth about them. The gang tried the same thing again later, but the system was blocked from the inside.

The system designed by Facto.

They built her towers. She found us through Facto cameras. This is going out on Facto ultrascreens. Fenella is rapidly turning into the worst aunt ever. She turns to me with a flash of white teeth. 'The only slight problem is, I'd much rather be on the screen with you than behind the camera. So I've asked some old friends of yours to lend a hand. Would you like to meet them?'

All my old friends are on the other side of the river looking for a mouse. I don't want to meet any of her friends.

'Say yes,' whispers Fenella.

I try to shake my head and say no, but instead I end up copying her.

'Yes,' I say.

I want to send the jug of water crashing over her, but my free hand hangs uselessly by my side.

'Marvellous! I thought so. And here they are.'

Two people move out from the shadows and into view.

One skipping, one tapping. We shrink back as they come into the light. Old friends indeed. One in a floppy sunhat, and one on crutches.

Littleman and Captain Skuldiss have escaped.

Parp! Parp!

Aida puts her hands over her ears at the sound of Littleman's horn. Not even Fenella's drug can stop that reaction.

'Come, come, my lovely,' says Littleman, dancing around behind us in his baggy shorts. He somehow looks younger and older all at the same time. 'I thought you'd be pleased to see your governor.'

He was the one who commanded the Waste Mountain Gang, until he betrayed us to Selwyn Stone, who paid him to get the Iris. At least they haven't got that yet.

As far as I know.

'You. No. Friend,' mutters Aida, grimacing.

'I don't think that's a very nice way to treat someone who has come here all the way from Facto, is it, Miss Aida

True?' says Fenella. 'They had to use that grotty escape tunnel too, which hasn't been touched for years. Oh yes,' she says, seeing our faces. 'Mr Stone built these towers, remember. Full of all sorts of surprises, they are. Now say hello politely.'

'Hello politely,' says Aida with a scowl.

Before Fenella can reprimand her, a cold crutch cracks on the desk, making us jump. 'Well! This is a nice caboodle and how do ye do. So glad you could join us. We're going to make a home movie, my ickle ninknonks. Mr Littleman is the award-winning director, with me the big honcho producer. And you are going to be the big stars of the show!'

Captain Skuldiss grins at us. He looks tired and thinner than before, but the voice of Facto's chief culler is horribly unchanged. 'Your antics with them beasties has only accelerated my employerman's plans. And you did something very naughty.' He raps the table with his crutch again. 'You told General Public some awful lies about us. Big stinking lies they were.'

Polly shakes with the effort of trying to reply, but she can't fight the drug.

'Mr Stone is about to reveal his big top-secret project, the work of a blooming lifetime, would you believe? He needs the world to trust him and to believe in him. So! You will kindly undo this mess you made and tell the good peeps of Premium the truth, please. How kind we are. How good we are. How our hearts are made of gold and all things nice.'

I reckon the Captain's heart is made of something black and horrid.

Fenella parts the curtains to glance out of the windows, and draws her cape closer across her chest. 'How long do we have?'

Skuldiss checks a watch built into his crutch. 'Not long. Come along. Mr Director, to your position, if you please!'

Littleman ambles back to the shadows, his shoulders shaking with excitement. Skuldiss hops over to the lamp, so his face is in shade. We watch as one silver crutch emerges from the gloom, extending into the fuzzy head of a microphone, as the other reveals a blinking revolving lens.

'New techno improvements, my child monsters!' he chuckles. 'Multimedia crutchies – what do you say to that?'

I say these people are crazy. Nothing Selwyn Stone has designed can be protection from what the whale foretold. We are in danger. The world is in danger. Why can't they see? I have to show them. But the shard's mesmerizing drug is so strong, as powerful as a magic spell.

A red light flashes at the end of the camera crutch. The lens flickers as it zooms in and out, finding focus.

'Ready when you are, Captain Skuldiss,' calls Littleman from the shadows.

'We are good to go, Mr Director,' replies the Captain. 'Councillor?' he says, with a weird purr to his voice.

Fenella sweeps in front of us, basking in the crutch camera's gaze.

'Are we recording? Excellent.' She smooths her hair and clears her throat. 'Good evening, citizens of Premium. This is Councillor Clancy-Clay from the Glass Towers. Apologies for the disruption to your ultrascreen service. Welcome back. The news is this: everything is going to be fine. Here are some special young people to explain why. Please welcome Kester Jaynes, Aida True and Polly Goodacre!'

Fenella swishes to the end of the desk. The two crutches swivel towards her. 'Hello, Aida. In a moment we're going to reveal Mr Stone's brilliant new plan to save the world. I believe you said, "I am very excited by this idea. Facto are the best."'

We don't even know what the idea is. But as if she is sleepwalking, despite trying to resist the drug as best she can, Aida says, 'I am very excited by this idea. Facto are the best.'

'Marvellous!' Fenella is on to Polly, asking the same question, and Polly also says, 'Facto are the best,' but with closed eyes, pretending it isn't happening.

Then it is my turn, Skuldiss thrusting the crutches so close they nearly poke my eye out.

I clench my fists, trying to fight the toxin.

'Ladies and gentlemen, I do apologize, our guest of

honour is a little shy,' announces Fenella to the camera, brushing her glass necklace. As she does, she twists off another shard, clutching it behind her back. A warning.

'So I'm going to ask him one more time. Kester Jaynes, the boy who can talk to animals, hero of the hour. I believe you are excited by Mr Stone's new idea. You have made up over your past differences, you deny all the lies you spread about formula and the virus, and you too think Facto is the best.' I stand up, desperately trying to resist. Fenella smiles at me so tightly I think her cheekbones might snap. 'Just one word, that's all we're looking for. I believe the answer you want to give is *yes*.'

And my mouth begins to open . . . the word forming in my throat.

I can't. We haven't come this far to become mouthpieces for Facto. I'm straining so much, trying not to speak, that I'm shaking.

Which is when I notice that *everything* is shaking.

The upturned beaker sitting in the toad's puddle on the table, is vibrating like there's an invisible bee trapped under it. The toad leaps on to Polly's chair. Then it's not just the glass shuddering but the desk too. The chairs bounce around underneath us across the floor. I'm finding it hard to stay upright, never mind speak, because now the whole Vitrine is swaying.

Above, the crystal chandelier is making so much noise I worry it will come crashing down on our heads at any second. The beaker shudders one last time, before rolling off the desk and smashing on the floor. And, with a great rip, the tatty curtains slump to the ground.

'We are too late, you wretched glass-face,' says Skuldiss to Fenella, turning to the window. 'You took too long finding these here urchins. Mr Stone can wait no longer. This old planet can wait no longer. The experiment has begun.'

Littleman sighs. 'Pity. I was rather enjoying that.'

Fenella doesn't reply. Like all of us, she has turned to face the window wall of the Vitrine, staring out at the silvery water outside and the dark horizon beyond. The sky is getting darker by the moment as it fills with a cloud of buzzing insects. My insects. The bees, dragonflies and butterflies of the new wild flung into the air – but by what?

It's not just the insects. The streets are once more filled with animals. It's the night the earth rose all over again. But this time they're not attacking. They're running: wolves and deer falling over one another, squirrels leaping from signpost to street lamp. They don't seem to be heading in any clear direction. They're stampeding.

I try to call to them, but they can't hear me from across the river.

Then I see what they are fleeing from. Because there, swelling up between the Four Towers like a giant balloon, is a vibrating dome of polished steel. There are no windows, no doors, no markings of any kind. It shudders for a moment, and then stops, as if it has always been there – as if it isn't the most unnatural thing I have ever seen in my life.

As the steel dome settles into position, the Vitrine begins to return to normal. The window wall is no longer vibrating, although the eruption of the dome has left a spider's web of hairline fractures across each corner.

My insects disperse to who knows where, the sky clears and the river keeps on drifting by beneath us. A crowd of people has now gathered on the white dock, alongside the crew who were mopping the transparent deck of the *Glasscutter* – all watching the dome that has appeared on the opposite bank.

There is no more movement, no explosions, no lights, just a vast steel dome where minutes ago there wasn't one. It could be a massive tick, feeding off the skin of the city, sitting there, waiting for something to happen.

Councillor Clancy-Clay, using a squirt of spray from a maroon necklace shard, rearranges her rumpled hair back into a helmet of perfection. 'Now,' she says. 'Where were we?'

Before anyone can reply, the ultrascreen behind her head flickers into life, showing a pale head on a dark screen. A face that makes my scalp pinch and my heart kick-box my ribcage. The face I never wanted to see again, the eyes that haunt my nightmares.

Selwyn Stone is back.

Suddenly I find it hard to focus on anything. The shock of the dome's arrival and Stone's return have stirred me from my drug-induced trance, but everything still feels sluggish and blurred. In the background, Stone begins to talk about our video-message, thanking us for our brave support, but I can't focus on his words. Our captors gather round the screen, their voices now a muddled babble in my head. Polly and Aida sound to me as if they are underwater, and everything moves slowly.

Through this drug-filtered haze, only one sound cuts through, making me sit up and listen. The sound made by the white dog turning his wide head to me from under the desk, his eyes dark and cold.

Your wild are in danger, he says. *Go to them. You will need to follow me if you want to leave here alive.*

116

It is hard to believe what I'm hearing. I try to reply to him, fighting the last of the toxin in my system. *Thought you . . . hated us. We . . . won.*

He sighs. *I despised humans for what they did to us.* He glances at the flood-smashed city outside the window. *Think I made my point.*

Don't . . . you belong to Fenella now?

I belong to no one! She gave me shelter, food and new teeth when there was nowhere else to go. He flashes his jaws, just to remind me how sharp they are. *Don't get any ideas, boy. I will never forget how you humiliated me. But I am still a dog, and I can hear the cries of your wild across this fish-road – even if you can't. They were my wild once too, remember. If you will trust me, I will lead you to them.*

I don't have time to explain to the others. Dagger turns and braces himself, looking towards Tommen and Timmen. Our enemies are distracted, Captain Skuldiss leaning on his crutches while he watches Stone on the ultrascreen. Littleman stands behind him, jiggling from foot to foot, while Fenella fiddles with her shards. It appears the sudden way the silver dome arrived, like an earthquake, has shocked even them.

Which gives us our chance. The new wild are in danger. We haven't a moment to lose. Taking Polly's hand, I squeeze it tight. 'Together,' she whispers, scooping up the toad. 'Forever,' says Aida.

Now! I say to Dagger.

With his crystal teeth bared, the white dog charges at Tommen and Timmen, who leap out of the way in opposite directions simultaneously. He barrels through the doors and we follow him out of the Vitrine, ignoring the cries from Skuldiss and his accomplices. We race along walkways, thumping downstairs and into the atrium – still crowded with people. Every single resident seems to have wandered out to stare at the ultrascreen, blocking our exit.

Never have I known a species so expert at breeding. Where do you all come from? mutters Dagger, darting between legs as he weaves towards the revolving doors. We fight our way through after him, pushing at elbows and even crawling on all fours to get past the crowd to the exit.

'I am afraid those children's kind endorsement was the good news. Now comes the bad,' says Selwyn Stone's voice, booming out of speakers all around us. 'The world is dying.'

Tell us something we don't know.

'I apologize for my lengthy absence. Our best scientists have been studying data from our satellite cameras and research stations across the globe. I wanted to confirm the results before talking to you.'

Yeah, right, I think, as we break free of the crowd, piling after Dagger into the revolving doors of the Glass Tower. Nothing to do with us exposing your lies and trapping you in your creepy kingdom.

This way! orders the white dog, racing off across the bright pier towards the city centre.

We might be escaping from the Glass Towers and Facto's clutches, but there's no escaping Stone's voice or face. The sparkling quartz harbour is thick with crowds, standing around as if they are also drugged, gazing at outdoor ultrascreens. These once carried news bulletins and ads but now show only the face of the man I hate more than anyone in the world, his voice pouring out of loudspeakers hung from street lamps.

'I understand that we don't agree on every matter. I gather you were told awful lies regarding Facto and myself. History must decide whether I chose the right course of action. I believe I did what was best for our country.'

Polly almost throws the toad up in the air with frustration. He gives an indignant burp. As well as he might at a man who killed all the animals on purpose, so we'd have to eat his formula.

Dagger leads us through the wide streets of the centre, where Stone's face is projected on to the sides of office towers. People are everywhere here too, spilling out of doors, jamming every pavement and corner.

As we barge through them, I notice a large crowd dressed in dirty clothes full of holes, hunger carved into their faces. They walk with a slow and shuffling pace, trying to get closer to the screens. If I don't recognize the people themselves, I recognise what kind they must be.

119

'Outsiders!' says Polly as we push past them.

'Yeah, and what of it?' says one, turning round, a tall man with a scruffy beard, his raggedy jacket hanging off his scarecrow frame. 'We ain't got nothing now. Them storms flattened what little we had and flooded it for good measure. So we've travelled south to this hellhole. All we want is some food and shelter.'

I guess there isn't even any hulse in the Quarantine Zone. I don't want to imagine what they might have been living on.

The other refugees next to him pick up his words and shout at the screen. 'Food! Shelter! What do we want and when do we want it?'

'Food! Shelter! Now!' comes the reply from the men and women huddled together. I scan the crowd for any sign of a blonde woman smoking a cigar. But there is no sign of Ma, the farmer from the Quarantine Zone who tried to cook my wild, or her heavyset accomplice. I wonder if they even survived the storms. Oblivious to my thoughts, Dagger races on and we follow, leaving the Outsiders behind.

'We now face the greatest challenge ever to be confronted not just by any one country, government or company – but by the entire human race. The science is conclusive. Oceans now cover most of the globe, but those seas can no longer sustain life. Their water is too acidic, the temperature too high. There is a dangerous build-up of methane gas beneath the world's seas. The land surface that remains above sea level beyond the boundaries of this Island is burned into desert.'

'He obviously hasn't heard of your Faraway island, has he, Kidnapper?' says Polly, as we career round a sharp corner and down an alleyway after the dog.

Either hasn't heard of or doesn't want to tell us, I think. I try to push nightmarish thoughts of pigeons drowning in acid seawater or roasting alive in a desert from my mind. But so many animals are risking everything for us. My rat and the General on their secret underground mission. The stag and the wolf stumbling around the beach, drugged by Fenella.

Stone's voice drones on, and when I next glance up at a screen it's filled with pictures from the satellite cameras he mentioned, capturing what he describes.

'I have tried to keep you safe on this Island, the last home for humans on earth. I have managed our dwindling resources – food, space, water – as best I can.'

Aida clears her throat loudly at scenes of Facto handing out formula to starving crowds from the backs of lorries. Somehow I never saw those trucks for real, just the people of Waste Town scavenging the rubbish heap, living off pink – a cut-price, dangerous version of formula.

'Where 123 got to?' she mutters as she pounds the streets. 'Could really do with a bike right now.'

But there's no sign of the boy with the Mohican or his gang. We keep on running, past more faces. Types I recognize. Children our age in clothes I have not seen for a while. The grey trackies and trainers of a Facto school, marshalled by wardens. I don't spot a Maze or a Doctor Fredericks though, just a series of hollow-faced kids. Their heads hang low with exhaustion as they shamble along, guards prodding them on with their sticks.

If Factorium can't even feed or keep safe the children in its own schools, what hope have we got?

'That time is now at an end. Our modelling shows that the storms and floods of the last week are set to return any moment, at a far greater ferocity. The climate can no longer be relied upon to stay favourable to human existence on this Island.'

If Dagger was nearly wiped out by our struggle on the Amsguard, whatever Fenella has been feeding him has returned him to his full strength and more. As if powered by the knowledge of our guaranteed destruction, he races ahead. The dog bounds through the last of the puddles, shooting through the legs of spectators glued to the screens, and up on to the damaged remains of the bridge.

Wait for us! I call out, but he pays no attention.

'Premium survived the last storm. The other three Island cities were not so lucky. Even now, their citizens are fleeing their flooded homes, marching across the Quarantine Zone to join us. They come in search of shelter we can no longer offer and food supplies that are non-existent.'

I guess a few strands of seaweed aren't going to feed this many people. Aida pulls in her cardigan tight around her. *He should try Waste Town. We always got room.*

It's growing much colder. The sky has gone from orange to a pale grey. Premium's bridge is broken but not impassable and we tread carefully across strips of exposed stone, sheer drops into the water on either side. Dagger trots ahead as if he was strolling through a park, rather than a path not much wider than him. I follow, walking sideways, my fingertips just touching Polly's behind me. The light is fading and we are silent, concentrating on where we place each foot, while Stone's voice rings out from the one loudspeaker left on the bridge.

'No doubt many of you have alternative ideas of what our future will be in such a changed world.'

A faraway island. A metal dome. Who knows what any more?

'Our scientists investigated every possibility, from building homes underground to scouring the earth for other possible places to live. But none of these allow for an expanding population, produce enough food or guarantee the quality of life we once enjoyed.'

With a sigh of relief, I see the end of the bridge approaching, and leap over the final gap after Dagger, back on our side of the river at last. He turns down the road we were helping to clear up only yesterday morning.

'I therefore conclude that life as we understand it, for all living creatures, will soon no longer be possible on this planet.'

We're skipping over the puddles in the dusk, guided by the digital flicker of Stone's face reflected in them. Before we know it, we are once more in the shadow of the Four Towers. Rising up between them, the steel dome. It appears even bigger from here.

'Is it the top of something?' wonders Polly. 'A giant's helmet, or maybe the lid for his saucepan. It looks amazing.'

'Don't give me no giant nonsense,' scoffs Aida. 'It dangerous and weird.'

In a way they're both right. It looks amazing and dangerous at the same time.

'Which is why,' says Selwyn Stone, 'we have been working on the incredible feat of engineering you just witnessed.'

The picture changes to show him standing in a long metal tunnel.

'Welcome,' he says, with a small bow, 'to the future of mankind. Welcome to the ARC.'

PART 3: THE FUTURE IS NOVA

Then, suddenly and softly, it starts to snow.

We hardly notice, now transfixed by the screen, stopped dead in the street. As we watch, Stone gets up from his desk and walks along the tunnel into a great steel chamber filled with light and space. The camera follows him, drawing us into the belly of the beast. He stops by a network of walkways leading off to thousands of white pods that cover the walls.

'This, ladies and gentlemen,' he says, gesturing to the pods, 'is what we call the Advanced Relocation Craft.'

Just as Dagger sat in front of the ultrascreen in the Waste Mountain, transfixed by pictures of the Amsguard, so he now squats on his haunches to watch. Polly places the toad on the ground beside him, as the snowflakes pile up on their heads. Aida rummages in her case and pulls out a stray woolly hat that she scavenged earlier. I begin to regret Dad wrecking my scarf to make my sling. We group together, the light of the screen casting long shadows behind us on the whitening ground.

Whatever I think of Stone or Facto, if I had a hat (and right now I wish I did), I would take it off to them for the ARC. It's the most amazing thing I've ever seen.

'Maybe this what Mum discovered,' mutters Aida, looking at her feet.

Maybe.

The classified Facto research project she uncovered that cost her her life. The secret project Stone mentioned in his library of stuffed animals, the strange noises I heard in the basement of the Four Towers. Everything does seem explained.

Well, almost everything . . .

The dome that nearly shattered the Vitrine is, in Polly's words, like the lid of a giant's saucepan. A saucepan full of pods that – Stone explains – can support any life form on earth. 'Each one,' he boasts, 'can deliver nutrients, air and water to every kind of creature from a man to a . . . stag.'

Something tells me he didn't choose that word by accident.

Stone shows us plans of engine rooms, rocket-propulsion engines, fuel stores and high-tech navigation systems. This craft can move, but to where, he doesn't say. The screen glimmers in the dusk with high-definition pictures of tubes and wires, pulsating lights and instrument readers, medical bays and research labs. I wonder if these are the same secret labs that created the red-eye, and what that could possibly have to do with constructing a giant spaceship.

As Stone explains each element in detail with his echoing voice, I am conscious that we are no longer alone.

Creeping out from the gloom of the abandoned side streets around us are the wild who fled when the ARC erupted.

Deer, wolves and foxes pad over the deepening drifts. I wonder if they had any idea something so strange and powerful was taking shape beneath their feet while they stood guard. With a soft flutter, the butterflies and bees return as well, clustering for warmth on the furry backs of those better suited to this weather.

I look around at hundreds of animal eyes in the night in a circle around us, each a mirror of the pictures moving on the screen. The shadows cast by the animals' ears and horns stretch out behind them across the snow.

Their faces are expressionless. I can talk to them, but will I ever see the world as they do? I see pictures of scientists, gadgets and spaceships. I'm not sure I'll ever know what those things truly look like inside the animal heads surrounding me.

Then a nudge to my hand reminds me that I have more idea than some. My wolf, alive and damp to the touch. Fenella wasn't lying about that at least.

You're all right! I hug him tight, rubbing my face in his ice-flecked fur.

That magic was the worst kind ever, he says. *I still feel asleep. It was the great-wet washing over us that made us stand. Then of course I tracked our way back here through this white rain, because I am the best at—*

He is interrupted by a crunch on the snow behind us. There is the stag as well, bowing his horns. His eyes are half-shut, but he is here. I hug his warm flank. *We worried we would never see you again.*

No chance of that, Wildness. The woman's magic was weak.

I don't suppose you saw any sign of the mouse on your way back, did you?

He shakes his head. I am about to ask the General what he has learnt when I remember he wasn't with the others. He is on the secret mission with the rat. A mission I ordered when I had no idea the ARC lay beneath Facto.

I shiver and cross my frozen fingers so tight they might snap.

Stone's voice draws me to the screen. 'So, that is the ARC. But where is this amazing spaceship going to take us?' He gives a sickly smile and I feel he's looking right at me, even though he can't be. 'The answer is here.'

Spinning on to the screen, not a ball of glass or steel, but one of rock and water and air, swirled with blue, grey and white like a marble.

A planet. One that looks like ours, but isn't.

'Wow,' says Polly, eyes wide.

'We started to build the ARC in preparation for this day a long time ago. But we never knew where it might take us. The reason I have been so silent for so long is that we were waiting to confirm this exciting new discovery.'

'Liar!' yells Aida, chucking a snowball at the screen.

'Last week we finished our tests and I am today able to confirm a scientific breakthrough. The ARC will be the first ever vehicle truly capable of interstellar travel. For the first time we have the fuel power and technology to travel to a distant planet, a destination that can sustain human life. A planet in the orbit of a star just under 500 light years from us. It has breathable air, water and land to live on. We have named it Nova.' His jaw hardens, and the camera closes in. 'I believe Nova is humanity's only chance.'

By now, the whole street is full of not just animals but people too, huddled in blankets against the snow. I wonder if the waterlogged streets have begun to freeze over yet. The screen gives off so much coloured light I almost expect it to be warm. It's not. Someone tries to start a fire with bits of wood in an empty bin, but it only smoulders.

Stone goes on to explain the various calculations they've used to work out how we can live on Nova. There are graphs about rainfall and temperature on the screen, which don't make much sense to me.

A heavy hand falls on my shoulder and gives it a squeeze.

'Hi, Dad,' I say, without turning round.

'Kes. We thought we'd, you know . . . lost you again.' There's a catch in his voice as he says this. 'Speaking of which, no sign of your . . . I'm sorry. We searched everywhere – the park, the Culdee Sack, the streets in between . . . everywhere you said she might have, you know . . . Mr and Mrs Goodacre must have looked under every bush in the city.'

'Professor!' says Polly. 'We've got so much to tell you. There's this woman with poisoned glass shards and a glass boat and she's working for Selwyn Stone, and they forced us to make a video, but Dagger is good now and he helped us escape.'

Dad glances at the new addition to my wild with a frown. 'Did they? Did he indeed,' he says grimly, stroking his beard. I'm just relieved that he didn't see the video. 'And what else did you learn about, you know . . . this Nova business?' He jabs a blue thumb towards the screen.

'Only that they wanted us to persuade everybody to go along with his plan,' says Polly, shivering.

'We'll see about that.' Dad takes his coat off and drapes it over her shoulders. 'Oh,' he adds, 'that reminds me. Mrs Goodacre thought you might, er, need this . . .' He digs around in his pocket and pulls out the tatty rug from my bed in the flat. Except it isn't a rug any more.

A brand-new scarf, after my last one became a sling.

It's checked rather than striped. I tie it round my neck as tight as I can. *Thanks.* He musses my hair and I frown. I'm too old for that now.

Then the Goodacres are there too, and they've brought hot mugs of weed tea. Everyone's talking about the ARC and Planet Nova, and I realize everyone's proper excited about the prospect of a whole new earth. A planet with clean air and water, with room for us all to start over.

Everyone apart from me, that is. What's to stop us repeating the mistakes we made on this one?

Something hits me hard in the chest, and I glance at a ball of snow slowly sliding down me to the ground. From across the way, Aida laughs behind her hands. 'Why such a serious frown, snowman?'

I start rolling some ammunition of my own along the ground, one-handed.

Wolf comes bounding up behind and nearly knocks me over. 'What is this game, Wildness? Can I play? I bet I will beat you all, whatever it is.*

You can try! I say, chucking the snowball at Aida, and he goes racing after it.

The wild relax, and don't mind when the people from the houses bordering the road come up to pet them. Since we broadcast the truth about the virus, no one is frightened of touching animals any more. (Although luckily no one tries it on with Mother Wolf.)

It feels like we're at a party that we weren't expecting. Raised voices, laughter on red-cheeked faces, eyes gleaming, animals and children running around in the snow, everyone imagining what Planet Nova could be like.

'Do you think they'll have jungles and mountains, Professor?' Polly is tugging at Dad's sleeve.

'Well, I don't know for sure of course, but . . . it's very, you know.'

I'm silent. I still don't get how running away to a new planet we know hardly anything about is better than fixing the one we've got? We could do it if we only tried.

For the first time ever, the only creature who seems to feel the same way as me is . . . Dagger. He sits alone, bathed in the blue light of the screen, silent as usual, jaw clamped shut in determination.

Are you OK? I ask.

Watch, is all he says.

He keeps on watching, like he's searching for something. So I do as well. I study the screen as the 3D computer models of Nova fade away. We are back with Stone, standing in a lab surrounded by scientists in white coats working at desks covered with banks of microscopes and test tubes. There are plants under lamps, bubbling experiments and pulsating light monitors. I begin to wonder what kinds of animals and plant life are going to be on this planet. Will it just be the ones he brings from here, my wild, or . . .

Then I see what Dagger's looking at.

In the lab, on a white desk in the corner. In among

the test tubes and plant shoots, a glass tank with a few wood shavings scattered along the bottom. And creeping accidentally into shot, the one thing on earth you would need to create life on a new planet, because of her precious cargo. Scrabbling at the sides, but trapped all the same.

The mouse we have all been looking for.

Before I can tell the others what we have seen, there's a commotion behind us. The deer and wolves, startled, withdraw into a circle around what appears to be a white volcano. For a moment it looks as if another dome might be erupting from underground.

A much smaller one.

It turns out to be a pile of snow, shooting up into the air from the middle of the street. As it lands with a soft thud, I see the pile came from a manhole cover. And emerging out of the hole is something as black as the snow is white, almost unrecognizable underneath a thick layer of soot. But how could I ever forget those eyes and that tail?

Rat!

I run to him, brushing the dirt away with my sleeve

as gently as I can. He lies on the ground, his body bent in exhaustion, shaking, his eyes staring into space.

What happened?

The rat groans and mumbles something, turning away from me. I carefully pick him up and lay him across my legs. Polly hurries over, taking off my dad's coat– freezing though it is – and drapes it over him.

'The poor thing. Where's the cockroach? I thought you sent them to look for the mouse together, when we were on the flat roof.'

I did, but the General is nowhere to be seen. The rat makes a gurgling sound. By now everyone is in a silent semicircle, watching. Mrs Goodacre picks up a lump of snow which she stirs into her boiling cup of tea, cooling it. She hands the mug to me, and the rat takes a few feeble sips.

He closes his eyes for a moment, and begins to speak. *Friend . . . dear friend. Thought . . . I might never see you again.*

The stag glances at me. For the rat, that would be his worst nightmare. He has sworn never to leave my side, and he has risked death more than once to keep that oath.

Don't be silly, Rat, I say, stroking him, *I would never let that happen.*

Thank you, dear friend. He takes a few more sips of snow tea. I can feel his tiny heart beat a little stronger. *But you have not seen what I have seen.*

*Did you find the mouse? Where is the General? *

He raises a small paw. *Please, dear friend . . . too many questions. All in good time. I do not know if I will be able to answer every one. I am only strong enough to tell you what I saw.*

We wait while a coughing fit racks his whole body, his tail slapping against my leg. Finally it passes, and with a deep breath he begins his tale.

After you sent us off, me and my new friend for life the General, we did as you instructed. By cover of darkness, we entered one of these man-made ground holes. It lay just outside the four dark tall-homes, where you thought we might find the mouse.

Dagger and I think we spotted her on the screen.

For a moment the rat's eyes go wild with fear. *Dagger? Please tell me I misheard you, friend.*

He is no longer our enemy, Rat.

I call the dog over, but he stays at a distance, watching us with his beady eyes. He may no longer be our foe, but whether he can be called our friend is a different matter. Maybe he never will be. Perhaps that isn't important any more.

If you say so. The rat does not sound convinced, but waves a filthy paw at me. *Now, where was I? Ah yes, the ground holes . . . We entered as the sun set, first the cockroach, followed by myself. He was as impatient as you are, complaining that I was making him slow or didn't know where I was going. You can imagine.*

I can, and smile at the thought.

*We called out for the mouse, but no reply came. Instead, we sometimes heard confused cries from the new wild above, keeping guard and thinking we were trying to talk to them. We had no trail, no scent to follow, only our own wits. The cockroach was very sure of which tunnel to take at every turn. I am afraid that, although we are the very closest of friends, we did exchange bitter words on the subject. He paid very little respect to a rat's natural sense of direction when it comes to the Underearth.

*The iron walk-upons we crawled through got hotter and noisier. They led us far deeper into the ground than I had ever imagined, and the cries of the new wild faded away. Instead, our heads rang with human machine noises, roaring and growling, as if we were entering the den of the most ferocious beast. I was very brave and never jumped with shock or worried for our safety, but this did not stop the cockroach calling me a coward with every second breath.

These noises grew louder and louder, screams and wails that sounded like they came from the centre of the earth. As the cries grew, so did the heat, and we realized we had strayed into the veins of the mechanical creature itself.

I heard similar noises in the Four Towers, when I was trying to escape, I said.

The rat nods and continues. *I spied a bright patch of light at the end of one of these veins, and against the cockroach's wishes, we headed towards it. The light came in through slats, letting air into or out of the tunnel, we couldn't be sure. My whiskers quivering, I peered through these vents at a shiny floor, human feet thumping past with the occasional flash of those long white flapping skins you sometimes wear. Beyond them I could make out a platform, bearing a glass box. My rat heart jolted as I saw that, inside the box, was the mouse we sought. Your mouse. Never before has a rat been so relieved to see one of those, I can tell you.*

He pauses for breath and laps up some more cool tea. *If only I had heeded the cockroach's warning. I am so sorry, dear friend. He was so bossy that I stopped listening. I should never have done that. He was such a good pal.*

Was? It takes everything in my power not to grip the rat with both hands and shake him. *Tell me. Tell me what happened.*

I can sense everyone staring at us. The animals and Dad can hear every word. Aida, Polly and her parents can tell from my expression that the news is bad. All of us willing the rat to continue, I know, but frightened of what he might say next.

It was the dancing, dear friend. I didn't understand the dance. That's a peculiar tradition of those country mice, which I knew of but had never seen for myself. The cockroach tried to warn me, but it was too late.

He shudders.

*I'm sorry, Wildness. I should never have gone in

140

there, but I was trying to help. You had told me to rescue the mouse. We called to her, and she replied, although we could not hear her words clearly though her glass prison. Despite my friend's protests, I squeezed through the bars and into the room, scuttling between the humans towards her.*

You brave rat.

No! No! Foolish, stupid rat. The closer I got, the more she danced, whirling like her life depended on it. The cockroach barked at me to return. I dodged falling feet, followed by shouts as their owners became alerted to my presence. Then I realized what else was in the room. There was not just a mouse in a glass box, but everywhere I looked there were animals of many kinds in cages of metal and glass. Some poor souls connected to wires, some with their fur shaved, some had been . . . He closes his eyes, grimacing. *They were not all there. There were parts missing, and even . . . parts where there should be none.*

Dad and I exchange glances.

And too late, like the stupid worthless creature I am, as I reached the base of the mouse's glass cage, I realized what she was trying to say.

He looks up at me, pleading. *You have to understand, it all happened so fast. The gloved hands reaching for me, the cockroach flying out of nowhere and nipping them, he himself caught and trapped as I dived back between the bars. I fled from that place of utter darkness into the

141

only darkness I can cope with, the lightless ways of the Underearth. And as I ran, I at last knew what the mouse's dance was. A dance of warning, telling us to stay away. A dance of every living animal's greatest fear, especially rats and mice.*

My friend shrinks back into himself, his eyes alight with terror. *A Dance of Human Experimentation.*

Later that evening, back in the safety of Aida's flat, we huddle round the one heater, which gives off as much warmth as a cup of tea. At least Polly's hulse harvest from the shore gives us something to eat beyond hot weed drinks and watered-down portions of formula.

Then, our energy partly restored, and with Dad interpreting, we try to make sense of the rat's story.

I put him in my bed, wrapped up in my new scarf, and keep darting back and forth to check he is all right while we plan. He is fast asleep, his fluttering whiskers the only sign he is still breathing. Dad thinks he is just suffering from exhaustion, but tonight I am so scared of losing anyone else I don't dare leave a single thing to chance.

The stag, wolf and his mother are with us in the flat.

Gathered outside on the walkway are the other creatures of the new wild, eyes peering in from the snowy darkness.

Dad is furious, punching his palm. 'Typical of the man . . . offering something with one hand . . . doing that with the other.'

The rat was too weak to tell us any more about Stone's experiments. But he was sure on one point – which was that the mouse no longer had the Iris data balled up in her cheeks. They were quite empty.

For a moment we are so dejected that if our snow-dusted shoulders sank any lower people could ski down them. Then Aida claps her hands.

'Come on! Why this misery lazy lumping around?' She nudges me with an elbow that is sharp enough to be a prohibited weapon. 'Tell them, mister leader of the pack, tell 'em what we know.'

So we do.

First, away from the ultrascreens and the crowds, my friends finally explain in detail everything that happened after we left the stag on the beach, including Councillor Clancy-Clay's attempt to use us for propaganda.

'Democratically elected, eh?' says Mrs Goodacre, a fire in her eyes. 'Not by me she wasn't.'

In my animal voice, I ask Dad to translate what the whale told me, and explain why I sent the birds on a mission.

Mr Goodacre strokes his nose. 'So let me get this

straight. Facto's scientists and this whale of yours are agreed on one thing – whether from floods, food shortages or this terrible fire thing the whale told you about, it's coming our way fast.'

'What is?' says Polly.

'The end of the world as we understand it,' he says.

Silence falls, the only sound the faint fizzing of the electric heater at our feet.

'Right,' says Dad. 'Well, that's got things off to a, you know, cheery start.'

Mr Goodacre holds up a long finger. 'Perhaps, Dawson.' It's always weird when someone calls him by his first name. I forget sometimes that he's a real person and not just Dad. 'But, thanks to these brave children of ours—'

'And animals,' says Polly.

'And animals – there are at least some options.' Each one summoned by a stroke of his nose. 'For example, we could join Mr Stone's ARC and head for a new life on this Planet Nova.'

'I think going into space could be exciting,' says Polly quietly.

'What, with that monster and his disgusting experiments?' spits Dad.

'But he has the Iris, the mouse and the cockroach,' replies Mr Goodacre. 'The only way we're going to rescue them is by getting on-board. We can't prevent Stone going into space, can we? So perhaps we should be the ones who stop him being a monster in a new world.' He flushes and stops, folding his arms.

Mrs Goodacre touches his hand. 'I can see where your mind is headed, my lovely,' she says, 'but what's the other option?'

'Well, I suppose we could hope Kester's birds discover this Faraway place, that it exists and is not a fairy tale. It seems we only have two choices.'

'Or we could,' muses Dad, rubbing his chin, 'chance our luck and try to survive the end of the world just as we are.'

All of us turn to stare at him. He holds his hands up. 'It was only a, you know . . . thought.'

But it's as if he's pulled the stopper out of a jar, letting a cloud of trapped words out. Everyone jumps in, shouting about the best thing to do. We should break into the ARC and rescue the mouse, or just wait for the birds to return. On and on till they all talk themselves into and out of every option a million times.

All apart from me.

I'm just sitting there repeating one word, until he listens.

Dad.

DAD.

DAD!

He stops in the middle of his argument with Mr Goodacre and turns round to look at me, shushing the others.

146

'Yes, Kes, what is it?'

I sigh. *You haven't found out what we all think yet.*

'My dear boy, we must know everyone's opinions on the matter, well . . . backwards by now.'

But we don't. We haven't asked the most important creatures in the room what they want to do. *What about the animals?*

The stag, his head crooked in the low flat. Wolf, nuzzling my hand, his mother's soft almond eyes studying us both. Dagger sits at Aida's feet. The toad splashes in his tank of damp soil. Many others wait in the shadows outside. They've been quiet during our conversation so far. Which only reminds me more of the General's absence – he wouldn't have stood for this.

I turn to them.

You heard what the whale sang. The end of the world is coming. We can't agree on how to save it. The rat told us what happens to animals who enter the ARC. You are the animals who survived the berry-eye, who found the Ring of Trees and sought the safety of the Underearth. Tell us what we should do.

They look at the stag. Even though I am their Wildness, he still speaks for them. He steps forward into the circle of humans. His horns spread out beneath the light fittings, throwing twisted shadows against the walls. Then he does something I've never seen the stag do before. He slumps. His head lowers, and his eyes cloud with sadness.

I wish with all my heart, Wildness, that you had not asked me that.

I don't understand. *Why? You were Wildness before me, you made decisions, you chose Guardians, you found sanctuary. You believe the dream; you knew the world was changing before we did.*

He shakes his head. *I implore you, do not ask me that question.*

Now it is my turn to act taller, and straighter. *I could never stop you asking difficult questions, so why can't you answer mine?* I go to him, but the stag shrinks back.

In the indoor light of the flat, his wet nose, his long eyelashes, his thin legs – he is more fragile than I've ever seen him, even after he was shot by cullers in our garden. If I push any more, he could break.

Because if I give you the true answer to your question, the answer you seek, I fear it will . . . His voice trails away. Everyone is watching us, my face burning.

What? Help us? The end of the world is coming, great Stag. What does your dream say? You've got to tell us.

That's just it, you see, he says. *That's all the dream says.*

I don't get it.

The dream of the animals tells us that the end of all things is approaching.

So did the whale, so did Stone. How does the dream predict I will stop it? You need to tell me. You see, I'm not afraid any more, Stag. I take a step closer. *Don't you

148

remember? I saved the last wild. I stopped the dark wild and brought them into the light. Whatever your dream says I must do, we can do it. You were the one who told me to believe in myself. So why don't you believe in us now? We can go to Faraway, we can stop Facto, we can rescue the mouse, we can do anything. But you need to explain what the dream says. Tell me!*

The words pour out of my head. I hear my voice rise to a shout without even meaning to. The animals he once led to safety are watching him; the humans I saved are watching me. For a moment, we are frozen, held in time.

I swear I can see wetness brimming at the corner of the stag's eyes. I don't think animals can cry, but if they could, he would be. *That is what I am trying to tell you, Wildness. It doesn't.*

It must say something. Tell me the last lines. Tell me!

It is just a dream, Wildness, a song we sing to ourselves over generations, and every song must end one day –

Tell me.

He looks to Mother Wolf. *He has to learn sooner or later,* she says, a new softness to her voice.

The stag nods. Then once more, he begins to hum. And the creatures in our flat and waiting outside begin to hum, filling the cramped rooms with noise until it seems the roof will lift off. Perhaps for the last time, their dream pictures rise into my mind.

*Then! Let the waters cover the earth once more.
Let the sun turn the sky bright with flame
Let the ice cover the land which is left
And so ends our dream, as it began.
In darkness and in silence.
The silence of the end.*

With that the final dream picture rises into my head. Except it's no longer one of floods or an exploding planet. I almost wish it was. Because the final picture is just emptiness, with the same rib-stabbing feeling of loneliness I had in my dream.

Stag was right. The animal dream ends with the end. Of everything. There is no hero who saves the day, no magic solution, no last-minute escape. Our earth is going to destroy itself and, according to these animals' dream – whatever the whale believes about her island – there is nothing I or anyone can do to stop it.

That night I don't need a dream to make me feel cold and alone. The window in Aida's flat doesn't shut properly, freezing wind whistles in through the gaps and the only warmth in the room comes from the rat, snuggling up to me under the thin sheets.

While he snores, I lie awake, staring at the cracks in the ceiling, one thought going around and around in my head.

The stag was wrong.

Telling me the truth doesn't make me weaker. I'm not sure yet what it makes me. I suppose it wasn't a total surprise. The dream pictures that rose into my head as the animals sang around me – of a world flooding, burning and going black – were pictures I had seen before.

In my own sleep. That darkness, emptiness and loneliness – I dreamed them.

It was an animal dream, a dream I'm growing less and less scared of. I'm becoming more like my wild in ways I could never have, well . . . dreamed of.

I don't feel strong though. I'm not sad, I'm not cross; it's as if a weird calm has washed over me.

Because windows that don't shut properly can be fixed. A cracked ceiling can be repaired.

I know now what I need to do.

I keep my thoughts to myself at first and let a few days pass. Each one begins in exactly the same way. We drink our weed tea and eat our rationed formula breakfast – with added hulse – in silence. There is no need for anyone to speak; they are thinking so hard that the sound of their brains whirring can almost be heard above the slurping.

The knowledge that the end of the world is near focuses the mind.

Then, on the third morning, I finish my breakfast as quickly as I can and head out on to the balcony, wrapped up in my new scarf, to find some air . . . and the stag. He stands pressed against the low wall, sniffing the freezing sky.

Once a wild stag on the walkway of a housing estate would have seemed strange. (Especially standing next to a wolf.) But when we're looking at a gleaming spaceship that just rose out of the earth, designed to transport us to another planet, it could be time to re-evaluate what 'strange' means.

That's all we do for a while though. Watch. Watch the snow-fringed dome sticking out between the dark chimneys, trembling as if it might take off at any second.

What will you do, when the end comes? I ask the stag. We haven't really spoken since the night he revealed the end of the animal dream.

He looks startled, as if he hadn't noticed I was there. *Does it matter? It will be the end. There is nothing we can do.* For the first time, my old friend sounds afraid.

It matters to me.

Mother Wolf speaks instead. *You may speak our tongue, child, but you are not privy to all our secrets. When the winds blow in ill news, be it a plague or a storm, there is an ancient tradition we follow.*

A wave of tingles creeps up my neck. *Which is?*

Her eyes flash. *What animals have done since time began, when disaster approaches.* She licks her lips. *We run.*

I don't understand, until I remember TV pictures I once saw of wildlife fleeing a forest fire. The stag waits for me to put the puzzle together.

You didn't lead the wild away from the berry-eye, did you? I ask him.

I guided them as best I could.

153

That's not the same thing. You ran, as far from the plague as you could.

We are not cowards.

I didn't say you were. You ran until you could run no further. You sent the birds for me. What else could you do?

He doesn't reply, making me feel I have to fill the silence.

I saved us before. I can save us again.

There's a noise behind us. Dad has been listening, his hands wrapped around a mug of weed tea.

Kes, we know you want to help. We all do. But what if the animal dream tells the truth? Much as we hate him, perhaps Mr Stone's ARC offers the best solution – maybe we do all need to find another planet.

I can't even bear to face him. My own dad. *But it won't be all of us, will it?* I point to the toad, skidding over the top of an ice puddle by the front door. *What if there are animals he doesn't want? Or only wants for experiments? Even people he doesn't want – what happens to them?*

We cross that bridge when we come to it.

There are no bridges left to cross! Of any kind. The flood washed them away. Whatever is going to happen, it's going to happen soon. Shouting at my own dad. I don't think Mum would approve, and I'm glad for a second that she's not here to see this . . . before hating myself for even thinking that.

Polly steps out, clutching the watch strap around her

neck. 'Whatever Kester is suggesting, Professor Jaynes, you should understand that we're with him.'

Mrs Goodacre pokes her head round the door. 'Dear? I think this time we should listen to the Professor. You've been brilliant, but it's time to do what we say. And for goodness sake, will you all come in? You'll catch your death.'

'I don't have a dad. Or a mum – thanks to that crazy across the road,' says Aida, squeezing out between her and the door frame, shivering in a T-shirt. 'I don't listen to you. And she stays with me.' She grabs Polly's hand, who reaches for mine. I complete the circle and together we stand in the snow.

Dad, I say. *Not all of us think moving to another planet that might or might not be safe is a good idea. This is our home. We want to stay here. Can't we fix it together?*

His face crumples. He speaks to everyone. 'I want to live here too, son. But this planet won't be habitable for much longer. Everyone's agreed on that. Even the animals agree with us for once. There won't be anywhere to live. This Island could be flooded again any day now. Or worse, if your whale is right.'

I shake my head. *There is one other way.*

What?

One that depends on the noise I heard as we began arguing. The sound I have been waiting for for days. A distant fluttering, accompanied by the sight of dots

155

hovering over the dome of the ARC, turning into a beating of wings that now fills the sky above us.

At last, the birds are back.

They are fewer in number than when I sent them off across the ocean. Exhausted, missing feathers in places, scorched in others. Dirty and shattered as they are, they make way for one huge bird to strut between them.

The eagle. He stares over his hooked beak, looking us up and down. I still don't know whether he wants to help me or eat me. We watch with bated breath as he picks his away in silence across the balcony, lost in thought.

Well, he says eventually, followed by another long pause. *Found it.*

You found Faraway?

Might have done.

Where is it?

Far away.

Can you guide us there?

Could do.

Will that be dangerous?

Yup.

One of the grey pigeons hops on to my hand.

Except it's not a grey pigeon. I recognize those pink eyes, even under layers of soot and dirt. The white pigeon's voice is cracked, broken and has never sounded more serious.

*Wildness. You have no idea how dangerous. We have

flown through winds so fierce they turned us upside down. Through white rain, where in places the air was so cold some of us dropped stone dead like hail from the sky. Including your bossy friend.*

I don't understand. Looking around, both Polly and Aida are still here. The General is trapped in Facto. And then, spying the bedraggled flock of birds behind the eagle, their once glittering plumage scorched and filthy, I realize who he means. Their heads hang low, and they are without a leader.

A creature who once tried to lure us to our deaths.

And who has now fallen to her own, trying to save us.

The starling.

We were never really friends. I ignored her the last time she tried to speak to me, at the harbour. Yet in the end she was prepared to sacrifice her life for a mission I sent her on.

I am growing more determined than ever about what we need to do.

The white pigeon continues. *The cold was not the worst thing either. We also saw clouds of fire . . . we had to fly the fastest we have ever flown to escape – and not all of us did.*

The pigeon is speaking normally for once. He must be delirious.

I'm sad for all of those we have lost, not just the starling, and I know I should wait a moment, but I can't

157

help it. The words burst out – *You did find it though, didn't you – the whale's island?*

He nods solemnly. *I can confirm we didn't find the whale's island.*

I give him a stare.

The bird shakes his head, scratching it with his wing. *The great-fish was right, Wildness. It exists. A rock in the great-wet. It has not flooded or been burnt. There are tropical tall-homes on the shores bearing strange fruit as bright as the sun.* He somersaults in my hand. *Faraway is a real place.*

I turn back to the others, triumphant. The white pigeon hasn't finished though.

But it is also a place that is properly far away.

I don't care. *That's probably why they called it that.*

Dad is moving towards me. *Now, Kes, just because your, you know . . . found this Longaway place . . . I don't want you getting any . . . foolish ideas . . .*

But the whale said we could save the earth if we found it. Perhaps we could use the Iris to restart the world there.

The stag stands next to Dad. *I am not sure the great-fish meant that exactly . . .*

Well, too bad she's no longer around to ask. I touch the watch on my neck, and hold my hands out to Polly and Aida, who take them.

'Let's all calm down. I'll go and put the kettle on . . .' begins Mrs Goodacre, but her daughter waves her away.

158

'We don't want any more tea, Mum. We want to find Faraway.'

'Don't you see? We gotta do something,' says Aida.

'If we work together, we could all get on board the ARC, couldn't we?' says Mr Goodacre. 'Every option has its dangers, but crossing the world's sea in search of a fantasy island—'

'But, Dad,' says Polly, 'it's not a fantasy island, you see; the birds found it. Besides, you can see nothing will stop Kester going. He has that look on his face. We promised we would go with him, and I never break a promise.'

When Polly puts things like that, it's hard to disagree. The tip of Mr Goodacre's nose glows pink and I can't tell whether it's with anger or pride.

I turn to my wild, who are huddled together behind the stag and Mother Wolf, looking fearful. It's not the same when they're . . . ordinary animals again. I want them to be my friends, forever.

Well. Who's with us?

My wolf steps forward. *I think I will be better at finding this island than a few stupid birds.*

We already found the island, insolent wolf, say the grey pigeons.

I will be better at finding it again, he says.

And leave your pack once more? says his mother, but she doesn't try to stop him. She is too weak. They all are. Until this crisis is over, the animals have a truce where they won't eat each other, and the formula supplies are running out. These wolves have lived on roots and berries from city wastelands for too long.

Come on, I say. *Is there anyone else who wants to join us?*

Polly's toad goes to her without a sound. Aida claps her hands, and Dagger waddles over. There is a noise from the bedroom, and my rat staggers out through the door, still filthy from his underground escapade.

You're not well, I begin, but he struggles into my arms, as if to prove me wrong.

A friend for life is never not well enough, he mutters before closing his eyes once more.

But not this time. Not on this journey. I give the rat one last hug before passing him to Dad, who cradles him in his arms. *And besides, you would be sharing the trip with Dagger,* I whisper.

I suppose it is for the best then, friend, he murmurs, before drifting back to sleep.

So this is our party. Three children, a flock of scatty pigeons led by an eagle, a wolf, a silent toad and a dog with crystal jaws who might or might not be our friend.

Just a few feet of snowy walkway divides us from the grown-ups and the older animals.

Right, I say, *we are the only ones prepared to find another way to save the earth? Yet again, it's left to us to sort out your mess –*

It's not that simple, mutters Dad. His massive frame blocks the path to the stairs, his arms folded. There is no

160

trace of a smile on his face. No crinkling at the edges of his eyes.

Are you going to try and stop us?

Dad's voice is clear and strong for once, no hesitation, no trailing off, speaking so everyone can hear.

'Six years ago I lost your mother. Then Facto separated us. We had just reunited when you and Polly both disappeared. I agreed to the mouse hunt on the strict understanding that no one strayed far from this flat – and see what happened! Now you want to find this island miles away . . . It's unacceptable. I won't wait and worry any more, Kes.' He enfolds me in his arms, even though I resist. 'If the end of the world is coming – I want us to face it together. So, yes, I am going to stop you.'

We're divided. Aida rolls her eyes, and Polly sticks out her lower lip. The Goodacre parents side with Dad. (Literally standing next to him, while they usher us back inside with stern faces.)

Even my wild can't agree. The birds that made it back from Faraway call from the window, urging me to follow them before it is too late. The stag refuses to take sides. He has been suspicious of the whale from the start, perhaps because she sings a different song to his. But he also seems resigned to his fate somehow. Mother Wolf only wants her son not to leave again so soon, like Dad.

I wish the General was back here, and not trapped underground in Facto. He would bark some sense into us. As I shut my bedroom door for the night, the rat dozing on my pillow, I realize there is one thing I could try.

Summoning up a long-buried memory.

I hate to. I have done so well. I really tried, Mum, on my own. For six years I tried not to think of you, because it was too painful if I did.

My friends were right though. I always try and do everything on my own and I'm as tired of that as they are. So I flop next to the rat and allow myself to remember Mum. I don't have a photo or a letter. Just what's left of the watch around my neck.

I untie it and hold it in my hands, pressed tight against my chest.

Closing my eyes, I think back. Mum's image is faint and fuzzy in my mind, a hologram projected from very far away. Her hairstyle keeps changing, and sometimes she's in a cardigan, then a T-shirt, sometimes she's smiling, now she's frowning.

That's typical of memories, isn't it? They're never clear and sharp the way a photo is.

It doesn't matter. It's still Mum.

I realize she can't actually speak. She's not here, and wherever she is, it's too distant for talking. Yet at the same time, if I speak to the fuzzy, clothes-changing picture in front of my eyes, I can hear her voice in my head. As if I knew her so well, a bit of my brain can guess her reaction. I tell her everything: about the mouse's capture, the whale's warning and Dad's decision.

'Dawson loves you very much, Kes,' says the

Mum-voice-in-my-head. 'All he wants is to keep you safe.' Classic Mum.

'But the whale was right. You have to believe me. You weren't there – you didn't hear about the terrible burning thing. We can save this world, I know we can, if only Dad would let us.'

'What do you mean I wasn't there? I'm always there, you daft noodle. Don't tell me you forgot what I said?'

No. How could I? Lying in her hospital bed she told me she wouldn't be coming back home. But then she said she would also be there forever. I didn't understand what she meant at first.

'And what's more, did I tell you not to go? I only said your dad was trying to keep you safe.' Her image wobbles, like the signal is getting weaker. 'You must do what you believe is right.'

I sit up in bed. 'Does that mean I can go?'

'You're thirteen, Kes. You have to decide for yourself now.' The fuzzy face folds into a soft smile. 'But promise me you'll take enough warm clothes.'

I stretch out my arms as if she was there –

But she's not. She's gone. And no amount of thinking hard can bring her back.

It's only as I'm stuffing my pillow under the sheets later, to look like a sleeping dummy, that I realize . . . I was talking like other people a moment ago. It was to a memory of Mum . . . but it was, all the same, *talking*.

*

We move as quietly as we can through the dark kitchen, trying not to wake the snoring figure of Dad on the sofa bed. Aida wheels in her suitcase full of flood booty. Polly puts a few things in her bag, like the seaweed supplies, but leaves the formula for the others. Then, sliding open a drawer, she takes out a blunt-looking knife.

Just in case, I guess.

I travel light. Only a broken watch and my new scarf.

We can't help waking the stag, who watches us in silence. As I unhook the latch, trying not to let the chain rattle, I catch his gaze.

You don't think we should go, do you?

He sighs. *I hope you find what you are looking for. We will still be here when you return.*

Let's hope so. I glance towards Dad. *Can you tell him?*

The stag nods. Then, without another word, I close the door and our party sets off through the snow, the birds flying above our heads in the night sky. They will lead us to Faraway – but first we need a way to get there.

And I know exactly where to find one.

An hour later, back down on the white harbour by the Glass Towers, in the smoky moonlight, the *Glasscutter* looks like a ghost ship. We can see right through her from the now deserted docks. Only the mast and grey mooring ropes stretched tight over the water give the boat's existence away.

A breeze ruffles a silver flag hanging from the masthead.

Aida looks around, shaking her head. 'We crazy to even come back here!' she hisses. 'What if Skuldiss and Littleman still there? That woman with her freaky drugs. If they find us . . .' She shivers.

I glance up at the mist-shrouded skyscrapers behind us, hoping that Fenella isn't at the window, fiddling with her poison necklace.

Polly understands. 'We promised, Aida. We do everything together. We might not always be able to stay in Premium, you know.'

Aida jabs her finger at me. 'Maybe! But that doesn't mean we make a fool plan to steal a glass boat to find a mystery island!'

'Why do you always disagree with everything? I like adventures.'

'Why you always agree with everything? I different to you, OK? You very pretty and nice, with your big country house. Fine. This your adventure. But this my city. I don't want to leave without a real good reason.'

But Polly isn't listening any more. She is climbing up one of the mooring ropes, the toad poking out of the rucksack over her shoulder.

'You nuts!' whispers Aida. Then, scowling, she follows her.

Dagger, the wolf and I watch them swing and wobble their way on to the deck.

How will you get up there, Wildness? asks the wolf. *Are you going to crawl like a rat as well?*

He is answered by Polly and Aida heaving the glass ramp over the side. It lands with a crash on the wharf before I can catch it. We freeze – but nobody runs out of the towers.

I loosen the mooring, and then the animals and I hurry up the gangplank on to the *Glasscutter*. While the girls haul in the ropes and the ramp, we try to find our way to the bridge in the gloom. We keep bumping into sharp edges we can't see, or walking into invisible glass barriers, but no alarm sounds.

Finally I find a set of stairs in the middle of the deck. Dagger scrabbles on the smooth steps, and the wolf skids back to the bottom twice, as their claws fail to find a grip. I haul them up by the scruff of their necks, and we enter the ship's bridge. In a glimmer of moonlight I can just see a revolving chair, a table of electronic maps, and banks of phones and radio receivers.

I slide the large tiller between them back and forth, but nothing happens. Next I run my hands over panels of buttons and switches, hoping one will send the boat glowing and humming into life. Again, nothing.

'Can you make it work, Kidnapper?' asks Polly, tumbling into the room behind us with Aida.

Not yet.

'Have you got the key?' she says, pointing out a large ignition socket on top of the steering column.

'Looking for this?' says an icy voice from the doorway.

She steps forward, her necklace of evil jangling lightly against her chest, the dark shadow of her cape billowing in the breeze. With skin as pale as the moon itself, her lips painted black – it's Fenella.

The councillor holds up a shard in her other hand, which flashes red, buzzing loudly. 'On our little trip earlier, I didn't tell you about one of the boat's most advanced security features. Pressure-sensitive alarm glass. One unauthorized step on board and this starts vibrating around my neck like you wouldn't believe. Super-clever, just like me.' There's a glint in her eye. 'So you want to steal my boat to find this island of yours, do you?'

'That was the plan,' admits Polly.

'Oh, I do hate it when plans don't work. That must be *so* frustrating for you.'

'You not going to help us get to Faraway then?' says Aida, almost sounding relieved.

'Oh yes, let's help the revolting ragamuffin who stole my dog. *Not.*'

Dagger growls, and Fenella flinches, clutching at her necklace. 'Naughty boy, Crystal.' She pats her skirt. 'Come on, come to Mummy. You know you want to. Come on.'

But the dog with two names doesn't move.

'He not yours,' snaps Aida. 'I didn't steal him. He came with us because he hates you.'

'Nobody hates me,' says Fenella with a shrug, twisting another shard off her necklace. 'I'm your favourite aunt, remember. Now, who wants to be drugged first?

'You have to listen to us. If we find what we think is on this island, we won't need to go on Mr Stone's spaceship to another planet,' says Polly quickly.

The councillor's eyes narrow, cross-hairs focusing on a target. 'Why? What's so special about this island?'

I look away. The girls are speechless.

Fenella gives a honking laugh. 'I knew it. No idea. You want to take my precious boat miles across the sea to find some mystery island, and you can't even tell me why? Never in a trillion billion years.'

Polly stands her ground. 'The last whale in the world told my friend that if we find this island we can save the planet. My friend believes the whale, and we believe him.'

'And that good enough for us,' concludes Aida. 'It no more crazy than sending us all into space to a faraway planet.'

Fenella isn't budging. 'You're even more deluded than I thought.'

'How you going to stop us?' says Aida.

'Yes,' says Polly, standing shoulder to shoulder with her. 'How *are* you going to stop us?'

Dagger and Wolf circle the councillor, growling. Fenella shrinks back against the steering column. 'Call them off! Or I'll . . .'

'Or you'll what?' says Aida, stepping forward.

'Or I'll do this,' she snarls, and twists off a purple shard, sprinkling the contents over the ignition. It smoulders as the acid burns the metal beyond recognition. The air fills with a sulphurous smoke, making us cough and our eyes water. My animals retreat, whimpering.

For a moment we stare at the ruined dashboard. Fenella brushes a hank of hair off her forehead and runs a hand over her shards. 'Now. Are you going to come with me, or do you need more persuading?'

'Fine,' says Polly. 'If that's what you want, Mrs Clancy-Clay.'

'Yes, it very much is what I want,' says Fenella. 'I knew you'd see sense in the end. And it's *Councillor* Clancy-Clay.

'Sorry, *Councillor*. Would you mind helping us carry something back to the towers?'

'My pleasure.'

'Good. In that case you can take him,' says Polly, and she thrusts her toad into the woman's hands.

I'm not sure who looks more surprised at first, Fenella or the toad. Aida and I are looking at Polly like she's gone mad. The councillor grimaces at the creature, as if unsure whether to drop him or throw him back to her.

He closes his eyes, as if he was going to sleep.

And then . . . the strangest thing happens.

The toad begins to change colour.

Councillor Fenella Clancy-Clay turns the whitest she's ever gone. She grips the toad, like she can't let go. Her hands and then her arms begin to shudder. Her hair quivers and her eyes start to roll upward as a drool of spit slides down her chin.

As she slumps to the ground beside the steering column, the toad jumps free, landing at Polly's feet. We stare at him, his normal green slowly returning. He gives a satisfied croak.

'Did you know he could do that?' Polly asks me.

'No.'

'Didn't you?' Aida asks her.

'It was a guess. A lot of toads excrete poison from their skin. It's their secret weapon against predators.'

'And she was one mean predator aunt.'

'Exactly. It also means we need to be more careful with you in the future, don't we?' says Polly to the toad, opening the rucksack on the floor for our secret weapon.

'She dead?' asks Aida, prodding the councillor with her foot. The toad gives an indignant croak from the rucksack, and Polly shakes her head.

'I hope not . . . but she should be out long enough for us to make our escape.'

'So now what?' says Aida, with a glance at the still-smouldering ignition. 'This boat ain't going to no island in a hurry. What a shame.'

I stand at the top of the bridge stairs, staring into the dark shrouding the stern.

'Well?' she nags. 'Is there a Plan B or can we go back home now?'

Aida isn't getting out of our adventure that easily. Because there may just be a Plan B.

The transparent dinghy is still where we first saw it: dangling from the *Glasscutter*, near the stern.

'You gotta be kidding me,' says Aida, as we peer over the crystal railings.

'It's a boat, isn't it?' says Polly.

'Yeah, if you want to get over there, maybe.' Aida points to the far bank of Premium. 'But as for crossing the world's sea . . .'

She shakes her head, but helps us untie the boat anyhow, which lands with a soft slosh in the water. I help

Polly climb in, and then pass the toad in her bag to her, followed by Aida and her case, then Dagger.

Put me down! he roars as I scoop him up under one arm, but he has tumbled into the bobbing dinghy below before he can resist. The young wolf is trickier because of his size. I tie him up in a rope, looping it around his waist and the railings to make a pulley, before carefully lifting him over the edge of the ship.

I do not care for this new game, Wildness!

I try to lower him in gently. But he is too heavy now and I can't hold him . . . The rope whizzes out of my hand and he lands in a heap on top of the others, nearly capsizing the boat.

There are fits of giggles and growls. Finally I jump in.

It is a tight fit: us, animals and luggage.

Even if the General was here – and I wish he was – there wouldn't be much room for him. But we have bigger problems.

'So, I admit, we got a boat,' says Aida, picking up two mini-oars between her feet. 'How we going to get there though?'

She wheels the tiny paddles through the water, making loads of noise and spray, but not moving us very far. To make matters worse, as I wipe the drips off the sides of the dinghy with my sleeve, I see that, like the parent ship, it has a name engraved on the side. Only this one is worse.

Much worse.

The boat meant to be taking us all to a mystery island to save the world, is called:

THE GLASS BOTTOM

Polly and Aida collapse in laughter again as I point the words out.

I don't see the funny side. The sky is beginning to turn grey with morning. Who knows when the last morning will be? In a week? Tomorrow?

A shadow slides over us. The eagle circles twice before landing on the edge of the *Glass Bottom* with a graceful swoop. He stares hard at the girls rowing, then back at me.

You following us in this?

That's the idea.

Hmm, says the eagle. *It'll take a while.*

Any other suggestions? I say, shivering as I get soaked by the splashing oars.

Don't go anywhere, he replies, powering into the air again.

That won't be difficult, mutters Dagger, watching the great bird glide over to the middle of the river.

The pigeons hover around us. *We found some friends out in the big wet,* say the grey ones. *Perhaps they can help you. We should warn you though, they're quite strange.*

I should warn you, your friends are quite strange, says the white pigeon, balancing on one leg in Aida's curls. She shoos him away, and we squint through the morning mist in the direction of the eagle.

At first, I can't see anything.

Then something bobs up from the water beneath him. My frozen heart leaps. I imagine that the whale has returned, that she might still be alive, but . . .

'It's too small,' says Polly, sounding disappointed.

She's right. And, there are three things bobbing.

Three rubbery, bulbous shapes bouncing around in the water, like they are on springs. I gasp as they leap out, clean into the air, twisting as they do – making the eagle rocket out of the way. They dive and spin over one another, acrobats from an underwater circus.

'Baby whales?' asks Aida.

Whatever they are, they're heading for us, and fast.

Now jumping, now speeding through the water, only fins visible above the surface, till we are surrounded.

Three grey snouts poke out of the waves. It's the weirdest thing, but they seem to be smiling.

Except we're not, says one.

Excuse me?

You think we are, to use a human word, smiling. It's a common mistake. Owing to the curve of our lips, your brain translates a permanent physiological feature as a temporary expression of amusement. We don't show that emotion facially. It's all in our mind. In fact, we share a similar problem, because our enlarged auditory cortex . . . she pauses, and looks at her friend. *They do say cortex, don't they?*

The other grey snout nods.

*Our enlarged auditory cortex gives us a greater

power of hearing, instead of sight. It's what you would call sonar. So, for example, right now I can hear every single organ in your body. Your heart, your lungs, your liver, even your brain. The sound waves generated inside my bulbous head are this precise second bouncing off your insides, giving me a complete three-dimensional, if sadly monochromatic view.*

I feel embarrassed, as if I'm naked, and pull my anorak tighter.

So I can hear that you are hungry and tired. But I'm not going to let it distract me. Just as you are going to learn not to be distracted by our "smiles", because a very long journey awaits us.

I've never met any animal like these.

That is correct, says the second one. Can their sonar read minds too? They're freaking me out. *We are a species known as dolphins, with a brain-size-to-body-mass ratio that makes us one of the most intelligent creatures alive. We have a computational capacity that far surpasses your tiny human mind. This may come as a surprise when you learn that we evolved from your wolf companion's ancestors.'

His eyes light up. *Wolves of the sea!* he murmurs.

Indubitably, says the first one. *Now, I understand you prefer a naming convention for identification purposes, so you may call me Dolphin Alpha 1, or Alpha for short.*

Therefore, by logical extension, says the second, *I am Beta.*

The third dolphin hasn't said a word yet. *Is this one as weird as you both?* I ask.

They glance at each other, and it might be my imagination, but I could swear there's a flicker of embarrassment in their eyes.

This, says Alpha, *is our younger brother. He is still in training.*

By equally logical extension, he is called Gamma, says Beta. *But I regret that his faculties are not as developed as ours.*

Dolphin number three narrows his gaze. When he speaks, he doesn't form whole words but spluttering noises.

He sounds like a propeller.

Alpha quivers in the water. *We learnt words from the scientists who came to study us before the plague arrived. Most unfortunately, Gamma here was more interested in their boats and machines, so he learnt his language from them.*

Gamma makes a ship's horn noise. Twice.

That's quite enough of that, younger sibling, thank you. Now, are we to comprehend from these feathered vertebrates that you seek the subcontinental land mass colloquially known as Faraway?

I do.

That would be illogical, says Beta. *It's a journey fraught with certain death.*

Gamma gives an emergency siren whoop.

The water out there is dying, says Alpha, as if

she was telling me the time of day. *It has record levels of acidity, very little active sea life and extremely poor oxygenation. The wave formations are distorted, the air pressure unpredictable, and we have seen many terrible things.*

Terrible things.

Tick tock, tick tock, says Gamma. *Tick tock.*

This is not a recommended environment for children or their . . . land-based companions, sneers Beta. *We have only survived because our supreme intelligence has enabled us to logically locate the last remaining food sources in clean water.*

I'm beyond caring any more. Any option we choose feels impossible, whether launching into space towards a planet we know nothing about or sailing across the ocean to an island for reasons we don't yet understand.

Do you know the whale's song? I ask the dolphins.

Every creature that has ever swum in the sea knows it, says Alpha.

But do you believe we could renew the earth on Faraway? Do you know if it has anything to do with our lost mouse?

That would require us believing in an unproven mythical assertion, says Beta. *Whether you will make a parallel concrete scientific discovery of the kind required to save this biosphere is unknowable. And we do not know anything about the rodent to which you refer.*

'Whatever you're talking about, there isn't time,'

interjects Polly, whose teeth are beginning to chatter. 'Just find out if they can help us.'

Ignoring her, the dolphins swim round the sides of the *Glass Bottom*, exploring it with their snouts.

I had no idea glass was so versatile, says Alpha.

Gamma says, *Attention! Attention! This vehicle is overloaded.*

It is indeed a curious substance, says Beta. *Do you know whether the chemical vapour deposition still retains its original optical properties?*

I've no idea what you're talking about, I say, getting impatient. *Please, just answer my question – can you help us find Faraway?*

The two dolphin sisters nod. I'm convinced they're smiling at each other, laughing at us.

We're really not, says Alpha. *I assure you we are deadly serious. We will help you find the whale's rock.*

I advise traction motion in a singular direction, says Beta.

Heave! Heave! adds Gamma.

I am ready to tear my hair out. *You may be the cleverest animals in the world, but please, can you shut up and help us out?!*

A rather unnecessary display of emotion, says Alpha. *I suggest you take some deep breaths to stop yourself releasing stress hormones. Simply hand us the ropes coiled by your feet. We'll tow you.*

And they do.

The three dolphins start pulling the *Glass Bottom* down the River Ams, heading towards the world's sea. They are strong and steady, powering ahead, the ropes firmly gripped in their jaws.

Polly and Aida begin sorting the flood flotsam they scavenged earlier into small piles. They go through Aida's case, finding:

3 damaged umbrellas
a selection of hats
the contents of someone's bathroom cabinet
1 plastic bag of squirming hulse
bottled water

Wolf wrinkles his nose at these, especially the seaweed. *I

wonder what fish tastes of,* he says. *It could be the best thing I have yet to ever eat.*

I don't want to remind him that there might not be any creatures left to eat in the ocean. The wolf skids around in the wet see-through bottom of the boat, trying to get a grip. But his claws can't fix on the tough rubber. No sooner has he found somewhere to sit, than we bump over a wave, tipping him forward or back to the other end.

I am the worst ever at riding the wet, he says miserably, curling up in the corner, his tail dripping.

But, Wolf, I say, *I reckon you might be the first ever wolf to set sail in a boat.*

His ears prick up. *The first of my kind to ride the wet?*

I nod.

You really think so, Wildness?

We will always remember you for that, I promise.

He sits up straighter and licks his chops. *I am the *first ever* wolf to ride the wet,* he wonders to himself.

It is at least more comfortable than the last time we were in a river together. Polly watches him for a moment, then twists away, hiding her face. I want to say something nice about her cat, her animal friend who lost, but of course I can't. It is not just Sidney we are missing now either. The brave mouse and cockroach, trapped in Stone's laboratory. My rat, recovering in Aida's flat and . . . for the first time since I met him, I am setting off on a journey without the stag.

With fewer animal friends, I wish I could speak to the human ones on this boat. I just seem to have . . . forgotten how.

But at least one of us has never been happier. At the stern a small puddle has gathered, in which the toad splashes around like it is a home from home.

The two girls perch on the raised prow of the boat, the wind in their faces, Dagger peering out between them. Aida sits with her arm resting over his back. He doesn't appear to mind. If he has any of the wolf's worries, he doesn't show them, just wrinkling his nose now and then at a flick of freezing water from a dolphin's tail.

It is either the journey ahead or the freezing temperature, but my nervy imagination is playing tricks on me. For one thing, I keep thinking I can hear the steady chug of another ship, behind us. Yet whenever I turn round there is just empty morning mist floating above our wake.

Chug chug chug.

Do you hear that, Wolf?

Hear what? he says, paws up on the sides, leaning over the edge and gripped by the endlessly churning foam of our wake.

The eagle and the pigeons soar ahead, leading the way. They are sometimes so far above us they appear nothing more than pen marks on the blank sheet of sky.

Occasionally the white pigeon will call out a helpful remark, like:

Don't worry, the wind is against you,

or,

The worst is ahead of us now.

As the lights of outer Premium flash past along the banks, the city falling away, Polly turns to me. The rushing air has sent curls blowing over her face, and her cheeks are flushed. For a moment, she looks like a stranger again, the girl in a big house, with a cat and a gun. She touches the watch strap dangling round her neck. 'Will we find it, Kidnapper?' she asks. 'Do you think we'll discover the secret of the whale's island and stop the fire?'

What I think is that I have never agreed to anything more INSANE than persuading three dolphins to drag us on a tiny dinghy out into the world's sea towards a mysterious rock, which *might* contain the secret to saving the world.

So I just say, 'Yes.'

'I agree. You always do what you promise. I wouldn't go with you unless you did.'

She catches my gaze and I look away, confused and embarrassed.

Right now I want to speak more than I ever have for six years. And it's harder than ever to work out what to say.

The spray from the river is landing in cool little prickles on my face. I can smell drains and taste salt on my tongue. We pass empty gasworks and forgotten jetties, shingle shores piled high with rusting metal sheets, and even an ancient watermill. In a leafy inlet, its clumsy wooden wheel still creaks round.

'Stop being so soft, you two,' says Aida, mussing Dagger's head with her mittened hand. 'We got a problem. A big one.'

Polly and I follow her gaze. Dagger is suddenly sitting bolt upright.

As we round a bend, passing a flooded building site, the columns of the Amsguard rise ahead out of the river. Nine concrete pillars built to protect us from the world's sea. With nine giant steel gates, which are all shut tight.

Gates which keep out the very ocean we need to reach, and which this river now bashes into, hurling exploding balls of froth at the shovel-shaped barriers. The barriers look even bigger from the water than when we were standing on top of them. They are automatic, opening at scheduled times to regulate the flow and height of the river. I have no idea what that timetable is, or if they are still working after the dark wild's attack.

Dolphins! I call. *What lies ahead?*

Some kind of primitive flood-defence system, says Alpha, *constructed from galvanized steel and high-performance concrete. My sonar is detecting hydraulic pistons activated by off-site satellite signals.*

Beep beep. Whoosh. Psssch! says Gamma.

But is there a way through?

That is a negative, says Beta. *Unless this craft is also a submersible.*

184

That is also a negative.

I ask the birds if they can spot anyone on the platform or in the control box.

Don't reckon so, calls back the eagle. The pigeons join in, disagreeing on the best way forward, the white one confusing the issue as usual. Gamma begins to make a noise which sounds like a boat crashing into a wall, and still the dolphins pull us towards the gates, which now block out the whole horizon.

Dagger stands up, the wind blowing his ears behind him like miniature flags. *There is no way,* he says. *I studied this monster of metal and stone on the old-young man's picture screen. The fish-road can only pass through if the gates are opened up there or from the dark towers.*

The early morning turns to night as we come under the shadow of the Amsguard. I drop the ropes, and the dolphins stop pulling, but it makes no difference; the waves churning at the gates suck us towards them. Our dinghy begins to spin, and we hang on for our lives, the toad trembling behind Polly's legs and the wolf lurching up and down in the seesawing boat, muttering to himself *I am the first ever wolf on the wet and the best . . . the first ever wolf . . .*

The dolphins pull back as the waves lob us ahead.

We apologize for any inconvenience to your journey that this may cause, says Alpha, bobbing up by my side of the boat, *but due to nine giant satellite-controlled flood barriers not opening on demand, we are experiencing severe delays.*

The water is bone-cracking cold, we're soaked to the skin –

Polly clutches at me, and I take her hand –

The boat buffets the gates, sending us sprawling on to the floor. I cower as low as I can, closing my eyes, waiting for us to be tipped upside down or hurled against the concrete pillars.

We surge forward again, and I brace, expecting to be dashed to pieces, when I hear Gamma doing another impersonation of hydraulics. I'm about to finally lose my temper with him, but Polly nudges me.

'Look, Kidnapper.'

And I do. At the white gates, stretching into the sky above our heads, that begin to groan and turn, slicing through the water, sending us eddying back.

They're moving.

The Amsguard is opening for us, right on cue.

'It's a miracle,' says Polly.

The gates keep on opening, blades ploughing through the foam, until with a final shudder they come to a halt, at ninety degrees from the pillars.

Beyond them, between the columns, lie pink light and distant clouds over the horizon. I pick up the clammy ropes, and the dolphins take up the slack, drawing us under the long shade of the Amsguard.

Cold, wet and shaking, we huddle together for warmth

as we slice through the big waves, which lap over one another like liquid scales of green. Every slap of water against our hull is magnified a thousand times, echoing against the concrete walls.

Then, with one final pull, we are through. The dolphins slow their pace, catching their breath. The boat drifts for a moment on the calmer sea beyond.

It is hard to believe that this eerie, flat sea – drawn as tight as a sheet – produced the tidal wave that engulfed our city.

But it is even harder to believe what just happened.

Aida turns around and squints at the Amsguard. The sky is lighter and brighter out here, reflecting into our eyes off a much larger surface. 'That not right,' she says.

Polly is puzzled too. 'Why did that happen, Kidnapper? Did the birds find a way to work the Amsguard?'

Not that I know of.

'The dolphins?'

If only they were as clever as they sounded.

'Then how come the gates opened bang on cue? Do you think it was on schedule?'

Aida snorts. 'Girl, you talking about a city where steel domes explode out of nowhere and wild animals stampede in flooded streets. I don't think anything happen "on schedule" for a while. Everything about this stinks. We should go back now.'

'We always have to consider every possibility,' says Polly. 'It could just be a coincidence.'

'What, that now they closing too?' says Aida. 'That also a coincidence?'

With a drawn-out groan, the steel scrapes against the stone as the oversized gates begin to close. We watch in silence as they once more seal up the Island against the water we are drifting on. It takes forever – until, with a final wash which sends us bobbing further out into the open, the Ams and everything we know disappears from view.

'Well. No way back now,' Aida says, looking downcast.

And stretching ahead of us is a watery plain that nobody from Premium has seen for a long time: huge, flat and empty. An ever-moving place of unknown dangers.

The world's sea.

PART 4: FARAWAY

The white gates of the Amsguard reflect the early morning sun into our eyes, making it hard to see the pigeons circling above.

On either side scrubby cliffs form the edge of our Island, with a sheer chalky drop. I shudder, remembering the precipice below Spectrum Hall. No doubt thinking the same, the pigeons who saved me then swoop down from the Amsguard, covering us, the boat and even the wolf – who tries to swipe them off with his paw.

That was the easy part, say the grey pigeons. *Now we have to see if we can find Faraway again.*

Finding Faraway again has to be the easy part, says the white pigeon.

I clock the one bird who hasn't landed, his great

shadow soaring over the ocean. *Can you find the way again, eagle?*

Maybe, comes the muttered reply.

Then he rockets back into the distant sky. The dolphins pick up the slack ropes, and we are off again, churning across the water. It takes us a while to adjust to the pitch, but at first the sea is smoother than the river. It feels as if we are speeding across a big outdoor swimming pool.

The wolf is happier than before, paws up on the prow next to Dagger, his tongue hanging out, as the fresh sea breeze ruffles his fur. The toad is doing something toad-like in the shade, involving some tiny and unlucky flies which have come buzzing into the boat.

'Right!' says Polly. 'Who wants a seaweed snack?'

We help ourselves. Even the wolf has a portion. Then Polly ties the bag in a knot. 'That's it. We have to ration ourselves. Who knows when we might next see land or food.'

No one disagrees. We are used to the idea of rationing.

'Hang on, I bought stuff too,' says Aida, delving into her case for a special cream which she tells us to rub all over our exposed skin, along with three white floppy sun hats.

Sun hats I have seen before.

'Bought?' repeats Polly.

'From Littleman's spare supply.' She smirks. 'I borrowed them a while back.' We stare at her. 'He not going to need them now, is he? Not with all that snow.'

192

Then she produces the umbrellas, which we wedge between the slats of the *Glass Bottom*'s see-through floor, providing some shade.

'And where did those come from?' asks Polly.

'Hey! Stop judging me,' snaps Aida. 'So I nick stuff. You like to travel, I like to stay home. Now you want sunstroke or not?'

I try to make peace between my friends, but it's hard with just two words. They fall silent, sitting deliberately on opposite sides of the boat, not looking at each other.

It is so quiet out here. Just the waves lapping, Dagger and the wolf panting, a gust of wind occasionally catching one of the brollies.

The dolphins pull hard –

Toad turns round and round in the same puddle till I go dizzy watching him. My friends doze, curled up in the corners.

Sun and clouds pass fast overhead –

Then before we know it, we are far out at sea.

Our guides are strong. They don't ever let up, towing us away from our Island until it is nothing more than a smudge on the horizon.

The minutes turn into hours, and the hours become days.

We are voyaging further than any of us has ever been from home. Drifting along in a world of blues and greens, taking it in turns to keep watch and hold the dolphins' reins, living on seaweed and some bottled water that Aida just happened to 'find'.

'No one else wanted it. Premium not exactly short on water right now.'

The nights are spectacular. I have never known darkness so big, like it has swallowed the whole world. What the whale called bright-dots light up the black canopy, and once or twice there are plumes of phosphorescence glowing in our wake.

Sometimes I am convinced I can hear a buzzing in the sky behind us, like the distant drone of a plane.

Buzz buzz buzz.

But the birds don't report anything unusual, focused on finding the way ahead, dropping down on to the dinghy to roost at night. The buzzing might just be in my head of course. The open sea does strange things to your mind. The strangest thing, though, is the smell. The world's sea stinks. And I mean *really stinks.*

'Like eggs used to when they went off,' says Polly, holding her nose.

'It not so bad,' says the girl who once lived in the Waste Mountain.

We can see the smell too. Every now and then there's a bubbling pop and clouds of funky gas explode out of the ocean. Sometimes the bubbles are small on the surface, and sometimes they erupt like mushroom clouds, with squelching noises, showering us with tepid, stinking water. The boat rocks from side to side, and we grip the edges to avoid falling in.

'The sea is actually farting,' says Polly after the third time, and then we can't ever talk about the bubbles again without laughing. This sea has the worst indigestion ever.

During the days the sun sits high above us, and we swelter under Aida's stolen umbrellas. I let my hand trail in the water as the dolphins tow us. It should be cool but it feels like a warm bath.

I must inform you that is not advisable behaviour, warns Beta. *I can sense your every move from here. The deep is not safe.*

But I thought that the whale said everything – apart from you, and a few glowing things, it seems – had died.

*Regrettably, that is *almost* true.*

You mean there might still be living things out here? Should we call for them?

In the Forest of the Dead, where the animals had gone for their long sleep, there were meant to be only bodies and bones. But it was where I found most of the wild I brought to Premium. It was even where I first met Dagger.

I would not recommend that.

Yanking my hand out of the water, I study the waves instead. Beneath my own drifting reflection are deep shifting shades of aquamarine that go on for miles under us, silent and empty.

It's not that I don't trust the dolphins, but I try calling

out all the same. The whale said the sea was lifeless, but I haven't yet been anywhere where *nothing* else was living.

Hello? Is there anyone out there? If you can hear me, we're going to Faraway. Then, once we've stopped the terrible burning thing, we're going to rescue our mouse and bring back all the friends you've lost.

No reply comes apart from the waves slapping at the side of the boat. And the words of a very angry Alpha.

Please! If we are to escort you to your destination in safety, we must insist that you do not draw attention to our presence in these waters.

They are starting to slow down. They must be tired.

'Look, Kidnapper,' says Polly, peering over the side. 'Seaweed.'

That's not exactly surprising in an ocean.

'You aren't looking,' she says, reading my face. 'Loads of it.'

More food, perhaps. I look over. There is now a mass of greenery all around the boat, but it's different to the rubbery stuff in Polly's bag. This looks like the top of a submerged tree.

Underwater treetops have sprung up all around us. We're sailing over an oceanic forest canopy. The dolphins have to go very slowly, so that neither they, the boat nor the ropes get tangled in the twisting knots of dark green, which want to attach themselves to us at every moment.

Eagle! I call up to the sky. *Can you see how far the seaweed goes on for?*

196

Yep.

Well, can you tell me?

Sure thing.

Which is . . . ?

Everywhere.

What do you mean?

Them tall-home tops go on forever. Ain't no end to it from up here.

We are surrounded by waving fronds of giant seaweed that fill the whole ocean in every direction. Polly reaches down and snaps a strand off, examining it.

Can these wolves of the sea find a way through, Wildness? asks the wolf, pawing the rubbery stems.

There is a route, but we have to proceed with care, says Alpha, lowering her voice. *They can detect the slightest movement or sound.*

Who's they? I ask. *The seaweed?*

She doesn't reply.

I tell the others to be quiet. We sit as still as we can. The underwater undergrowth is so thick now that the dolphins are straining to pull us, as if they're dragging us through mud rather than water.

Then Aida says, 'What's that?'

I look to where she's pointing, but I can't see anything at first, just the endless horizon and the clotted weeds that surround us like a spreading bloom.

'No, there!' she says again.

And – I see it.

There is something caught in the tangle of green, several boat lengths to the west of us. Something colourful, bobbing, twisting . . . making a noise.

Squeak. Squeak.

'It's alive!' says Polly. 'And trapped too, poor thing.'

I knew the whale had to be wrong! Of course there are things still living in the sea. There is no reason for the dolphins to be so scared. Focusing my mind, I call to the cheeping thing that bounces in the water.

Hello? Are you OK? No reply comes. The animals in the Forest of the Dead were frightened at first too. *Don't worry, we'll help. Alpha, Beta, tow us over there!*

The bobbing thing cries more loudly.

SQUEAK. SQUEAK

I must caution against it, begins Alpha, but I've rescued enough animals not to be put off by a neurotic dolphin.

It won't take long. I command you.

This is most illogical, mutters Beta, but they wheel around towards the trapped animal, pushing aside the seaweed fronds.

Birds! I yell up. *Can you get any closer?*

There's nowhere safe for them to land, but they swoop down as the poor creature is swallowed under the surface for one heart-stopping moment, before bouncing up again.

SQUEAK.

It's yellow, cry the pigeons, taking a quick look and

198

then zooming off before they are enmeshed in the weed too. *A yellow bird.*

Then the bird disappears from view, and this time stays hidden. I listen desperately for one more squeak.

Hurry! I urge the dolphins. *It might be drowning!*

They plough on, calling to one another as they do, getting tangled in the seaweed, but they follow my command all the same, dragging us deeper and deeper into the forest.

I lean out of the boat as we approach. *It's OK. We're here, we're friends.*

Polly holds on to me, Aida holds on to her.

Wolf looks suspicious. *If this is an enemy, I will give it the hardest bite ever!*

Waiting for another squeak, I rummage around in the twists of weed. *Don't be frightened. We're here to rescue you.*

Then my fingers touch something. Something hard and . . . *plastic*.

My hand dripping with water and weed, I pull up a . . . duck.

But not a living one.

A battered, yellow plastic duck, with a painted orange bill and only one eye.

I squeeze it.

Squeak. Squeak.

Aida bursts out laughing. 'That the only animal left in this whole ocean? A toy duck?'

I wish I could find it as funny. Wolf sniffs the duck and jumps when I squeeze it again, which makes the girls laugh, but not me.

I'm afraid it is not the only thing out here, Wildness, says Alpha.

What do you mean?

They're here. Her voice sounds strangled and scared. *They heard us.*

Which is when I see them. Wafting up through the seaweed, floating to the surface, all around. Translucent pads of purple and pink, each one the size of a small car, swollen tentacles drifting across the surface, crackling with electricity.

Not plastic, not toys, and all too alive for my liking.

Jellyfish. *Giant* jellyfish.

For a moment, no one speaks or even dares move. The sun is high in the sky, and the birds won't risk coming any closer.

'What is these? Monster brains?' says Aida.

I'm not sure what they remind me of. Rubbery alien domes, every colour of the rainbow, drifting in a fringe of tentacles that completely encircle our boat.

Alpha instructs her sister and brother not to move. *Not even one flipper,* she says. *The shock from a single tentacle will send you plummeting straight to the ocean floor.*

Bzzz! Bzzz! says Gamma, sounding scared.

If the dolphins can't move, neither can we. And worse than that, in our race to rescue a plastic duck, the boat has become trapped. It lists steeply to one side, snared by dark

201

green matter wrapped around our rudder. Water slops in at a steady rate. We shuffle over to try and rebalance the dinghy, but the weed rope's pull is too tight.

'The only way out is to cut the seaweed,' says Polly. 'Which means someone has to go in the water.'

Suddenly everyone is looking at me.

'Can't you talk to them, Kidnapper? Can't you tell them to go away?'

I don't know. I've never talked to a creature before that didn't have eyes or a face, like there was a person inside that I could connect with. Well, perhaps not a person, but a living thing with feelings, memories and a voice. These are blobs of jelly. If they didn't move or sting, they could be plants. And yet . . . I try to listen for their voice. They must have sensed me calling for the duck.

As if someone has flicked a switch, my brain is instantly full of thoughts. Not mine: colours, images, sounds, a rush of data, pouring in. There's no sense at first, as if the monster brains around us are talking all at once.

I try to speak to them. *Do you need help? We are friends.*

The only reply is another jumble of noise broadcast into my head. Then, very faint at first, the crackling static forms a kind of sentence. Just like the water snakes at the whiterforce, or the whale, it seems these underwater creatures have their own strange way of speaking. Their sentences are as unformed as their jelly bodies.

No help. No friends. Our water.

We're on our way to find the whale's island – Faraway. Do you know where that is? We're sorry if we're trespassing by mistake—

Not friends. Our water. Sting.

It would be great if you could not sting, and let us—

Sting. Sting.

With a squelchy lapping, the jellyfish float closer. Gamma begins to make non-stop buzzing noises, and the three dolphins cluster together, their snouts poking up as if they are preparing to dance in formation.

'They're trying to get in the boat,' says Aida, using one of the umbrellas to flick a tentacle off the side of the dinghy.

Our water. Not yours. Sting. Sting, come the waving voices.

Dagger barks at them, but he and the wolf can barely stay upright in the wobbling boat, never mind attack a shoal of giant jellyfish. Polly takes my hand. I notice that she's trembling, and it's not from the movement of the water.

'You have to go in, Kidnapper. You have to untie us from the seaweed.'

Aida picks up the plastic duck from the bottom of the boat. 'We'll distract them with this. And put them birds to work too.'

They're right. We can't stay here and hope they'll go away.

I can command most animals, but these underwater blobs seem beyond my reach. I give the pigeons my instructions, and mime to Aida what I want her to do.

She nods, understanding, while I shuffle towards the rear of the boat. It is dragged down by the seaweed, the ocean trickling in. In the water there are blooming thickets of blubbery green and a single small crescent of water not yet invaded by the jellyfish.

The sun is high over my head and as much fun as having a laser aimed right at my scalp. I take off my sweaty sun hat, handing it to Aida, before kicking off my damp trainers. I stuff them in the driest corner I can find, along with my socks, and dangle my pale white feet over the edge.

Finally I touch my stained, fraying sling. I will need both arms down there. I untie the scarf and gingerly exercise my healing arm. It is still swollen and scarred, but not as stiff as it was. Perhaps days of doing nothing in the sun has helped.

Polly hands me the stubby knife she took from Aida's kitchen. 'It's all we've got, I'm afraid.'

I hold it between my teeth so at least I look like a pirate, even if I don't feel like one.

Are you sure you do not want me to dive in and attack these wet bugs for you, Wildness? says the wolf, to a snort of derision from Dagger.

Aida touches the plastic strap around her neck, as

204

does Polly. I pull off my T-shirt and touch the watch face, hot and sticky against my bare chest.

'Together,' says Polly.

'Forever,' says Aida.

I squint up at the sun, so white, so blinding, circles within circles of fire. And hate myself for bringing us here. To the middle of an ocean that spreads out for miles and miles without end in every direction, including beneath us. A sea that is as toxic and lifeless as the whale said, rubbish floating on the top, only weeds and ghostly jellies below. And now we're entangled, surrounded, sinking . . . because I believed a whale's song.

We could be at home with our parents. Or rescuing the mouse from the ARC. I wish the stag was here to advise us, and that Dad was here to help. I wish it wasn't just us trying to save the planet on our own.

'Hey! Stop daydreaming,' says Aida. 'We're sinking over here.'

She picks up the duck, pulls her arm right back and hurls it into the sky. We watch it tumble and turn in the light, and land with a splash about fifty yards away. The jellyfish tremble and then drift towards the bobbing toy, muttering, *Sting! Our water now! Sting!*

Now is my time. I hold my nose, and –

I am in, eyes open and blinking.

Everything changes.

The water smells and fizzes.

I tread water at the top of a huge oceanic jungle,

stretching beneath me into bottomless green black. Ahead of us, at the front of the boat, the dolphins huddle together.

Don't worry, says Alpha. *Your diversion is working. The jellies follow shock and vibration. Hurry now. We will keep lookout.*

Bubbles streaming from the corner of my mouth, I swim to the knot of weeds wrapped around the rudder. They are elastic, hard to cut, but I try. I saw for as long as I can, freeing one, which peels away, spiralling into the abyss beneath.

A leaf falling to the forest floor.

Then I am up, gasping for air, in the bright world above. It is like swimming in soup down there. My ears full of water, I half catch Polly asking a question about how long this will take. I glimpse the eagle diving for the duck and dropping it elsewhere for the jellyfish to follow.

Then I am under again, slicing again. Another strap pings free, and the boat rises a little.

More air. 'It working, don't stop!' urges Aida.

Down a third time, and another slimy chain is severed.

Up, the duck decoy retrieved and dropped further still –

I dive yet again. Only two final strands now. The thickest and the toughest. And something moving towards me in the water.

Bzzz! Bzzz! shrieks Gamma.

I must advise one free-swimming gelatinous non-polyp phylum has strayed from the shoal, warns Beta.

I'm about to ask what on earth she's talking about, when I glance up and nearly expel all my breath as I see my first jellyfish close up. No eyes, no face, no mouth, a ball of translucent skin, flapping into view from the depths.

Have to chop faster, slice harder.

Electric charges that tingle even from this distance, tentacles searching through the acidic, foul-smelling murk, folds of watery flesh, waiting to envelop me –

The second last strap gone, just one remaining. I have to buy some time.

Why? I scream in my head, as I tear and rip at the seaweed. *Why are you attacking us? We're your friends!*

For a moment the creature stops moving towards me, and I receive the crackling of disconnected words, a pulsing, mesmerizing beat. It's hard to get much sense from the shoal when they all speak at once, but I can just about understand this one on his own.

Yes. Friend. Human friend to us.

So why are you still coming to sting me?

Human destroyed world of wet. Look around. All empty. Used to be so much colour, so much life. Whale, shark, fish, crab, bug. So many enemies to jelly. Now only fake duck, weed and dead bodies crumbling into water – this good for us.

One. Last. Knot of weed. Why won't it cut?

I still don't get it. If we helped you, why would you harm us?

My hand finds it is cutting only water as the last strand snaps in two.

With a slosh the boat rights itself above me.

Several things happen at once, in underwater slow motion. First, I stick the knife between my teeth and shoot to the surface, imagining I'm a missile, a fuel trail of bubbles.

With a dizzying series of deep pulses throbbing in my skull, the nearest a jellyfish could get to a roar, the massive blob propels itself towards me –

This our water now. Our water. OUR WATER. Human must die.

I break the surface, blinking and gasping for air –

The hands of my friends reaching and heaving me over the side –

I roll into the boat on my back –

A single glistening tentacle curls out of the ocean, a whip that flicks flat against my face. Into my eyes. And the world disappears.

I have no idea how long I lie there unconscious, how many hours or days. Time seems to have both stopped and stretched into an infinity. One moment feels like a week.

At first there is darkness, then only pain. Skull-burning, eye-piercing, face-blistering pain, which shudders in waves through my body. Or that might be the boat pitching.

I can't tell, because I can't see.

Seriously, I mean I can't see at all, as in blind.

It's a struggle to open my eyes, but even when I do, the blackness doesn't lift. My brain processes images that aren't there instead: swirling kaleidoscopes of jellyfish colours and fizzing tentacles. There are bolts of light, exploding stars, what feels like broken glass being pressed into my eyeballs.

209

I feel the warmth of the sun rise over my head and set behind it, over and over. In my fever I also think I hear a helicopter buzzing in the sky, but it must just be the last of the water in my ears.

Sickness rises and falls as the boat pitches and heaves, not helped by the sulphurous fumes all around. Perhaps the dolphins are speeding through the seaweed forest as fast as they can. Perhaps we are being tossed on waves.

I don't care. I toss and turn myself, unable to find anywhere comfortable or dry to lie. Lukewarm seawater splashes over me. The lick of a wolf-tongue.

From time to time, hands touch me, checking my pulse, or pressing something damp to my brow, or something slimy over my eyes. Warm breath and dangling watch straps graze my cheek.

Sometimes a plastic bottle of tepid water is pressed to my lips, which let a trickle in, or fingers try to squeeze some hulse into my mouth.

But somehow I've gone right off seaweed.

My hearing goes completely, my waterlogged ears making their own sounds instead, like when Dad used to hold shells to them on the beach – many years ago. Without sound or sight, my brain fills with dreams of electric tentacles that wrap themselves around my thoughts, dragging me back down, my mind sinking into the cloudy depths below.

*

I reckon the sun has passed over my face and disappeared at least eight times, when without warning my hearing suddenly returns – with a sonic pop.

It's LOUD.

I can hear the wolf's every pant, every slap of a wave against the boat, every hop of the toad. Dolphins ahead, discussing currents and thermals. Pigeons calling to one another high above, only they're too far away for me to hear properly. I think it sounds like they're talking about wind, but that could be my fevered mind playing tricks.

The sounds make me nauseous again and still I'm blind. I pass in and out of consciousness, drifting in and out of someone else's conversation.

Two girls, whispering at the other end of the boat. They sound tired and worn down.

'You reckon we ever gonna find it, this island? We can't live off seaweed forever. And we running real low on water.'

'I'm sure the birds and dolphins will get us there, if Kester thinks they can.'

'Then what?'

Sun roasting my face. The skin around my eyes scorched and peeling.

'You have to trust him, Aida. I know he can be annoying. Especially when he never explains what he's saying to the animals or what is inside his head. But everything works out in the end.'

Aida grunts. 'If you say so.'

My arms and legs feel swollen and weighed down, impossible to move. No way to even let them know I'm listening.

Nothing to stop Aida. 'You understand it won't be like this forever, right?'

'What do you mean?'

'This three-friends-forever deal.'

'I'm afraid it lasts at least until we find the whale's island and the mouse, and save the world from this terrible fire in the sky.'

'OK, so we saves the world. And after that?'

'Well . . .'

'Then what? Life go back to normal? We pretend none of this happen? You in your castle, me in my rubbish heap?'

'It's not *really* a castle . . .'

'It not *really* a rubbish heap either.'

Polly doesn't reply. I can hear her scraping something into a bucket.

Aida snorts. 'Wish I could be cool as you.'

'What do you mean?'

'Imagining everything will last forever. The world. Friends. Because it doesn't. I know it doesn't. I thought Mum and I would be forever, but . . .' She falls quiet for a moment. The umbrellas creak in the breeze. 'It just the way life is. Things have to change. And not always for the better. One day you grow up and you learn. Three of us in a boat on the sea, with animals, looking for a paradise. This never happen again, understand? This not forever. This only now.'

Then silence, a breeze across my face, cooling my burning skin.

'Well, in that case we should make the most of it, shouldn't we? Come on, let's dress his wound.'

The boat rocks as they stumble back to this end, every step a shockwave of pain up my spine. I am inflamed and blown up, a balloon of a boy. More slimy things are laid over my eyes.

'It may have trapped us, but we're lucky this seaweed also soothes his burns,' says Polly. They must have cut more while I was unconscious.

'Hmm,' says Aida. 'Well, we lucky that *I* borrowed this ointment from one of them flood houses.' She smears something that smells of the old days and grazed knees around my cheekbones.

'It's not a competition, you know.'

'Ha! You keep on believing that.'

I'm too wiped out to be embarrassed. I wonder if I can communicate to them by flickering my eyelids, except even that feels painful. And my eyes are covered in seaweed and cream.

I try wiggling my fingers and toes, but if my friends notice, they don't say so. There is the sound of an umbrella whooshing up into the air, as they try to give me extra shade, the brightness on my face fading.

Right now I cannot communicate in any way with the humans on this boat.

This is a problem. A serious one.

Because right now I can hear other voices in my head, warning me. The pigeons, from a way off, ringing through the fuzzy clouds of pain and nausea.

Wildness, the air is changing. You must prepare your craft – wind and rain are coming. And we mean big wind and big rain.

Prepare your big wind! says the white pigeon.

Not funny. Not good. I take a deep breath and try to sit up, but if my nerves are still connected to my muscles, they appear to be on strike.

The girls sound within touching distance if I could raise a hand. But they are busy chatting away again, looking out for the island and not paying any attention to me.

There must be clouds ahead. They must have spotted those at least.

Storm a-coming in, says the eagle, the boat shaking as he lands on it, claws locking on to the side.

'I wonder why the birds are landing on the boat,' says Polly, accompanied by the soft flurry of pigeons all around.

'They probably tired from too much flying,' says Aida.

No, no! We need to batten our non-existent hatches, we need to splice a main brace – whatever that is – we need to prepare!

214

Wolf. My own words sound faint in my head. *Wolf.*

I am so hot, Wildness, I want to take off my own fur.

Don't worry, you are about to get wetter and cooler than you can imagine.

I don't understand.

A cough shakes my chest. A liquid I don't want to think about leaks out of my inflamed eye and down my cheek.

Did you hear the birds? There's a storm coming. You need to warn the girls.

But I cannot talk to them. Neither can the toad or the dog.

Fat drops of rain land on my forehead.

My stomach lurches as the boat surges up on a sudden swell, the ocean rippling underneath us.

Message from the navigation deck, says Alpha. *As the birds have informed you, we are entering a fast-moving area of low pressure, with a spiralling network of strong winds and heavy rain radiating outwards. I gather you call these weather events hurricanes.'

Immediate preparation for turbulence is advised, advises Beta.

'Shall we put another umbrella up?' Polly asks Aida.

'Go away, dog,' says Aida to Dagger. 'Stop tugging at my sleeve. What you want?'

The rain becomes fierce, and I sense a wind too, riffling the surrounding sea. The *Glass Bottom* starts to judder, like a hidden onboard motor has sparked into life.

I don't want to be a wolf on the wet any more, says my wolf. *Can you make it stop?*

The rain is lashing now, soaking me through, washing seaweed and cream off my face. It sounds like a hail of bullets hitting the deck. There's a fresh blast of wind and a crumpling noise behind me, something folding, twanging and whipping free –

'The umbrellas!' shouts Aida.

Waves slam down, and for a moment I feel like I'm underwater again.

'Hold on,' screams Polly. 'Everybody hold tight!'

This is more powerful than the storm of storms, says Dagger, as if he's admiring it. *So much greater.*

Then there are no more words. If only I could see what was going on. The wind is screaming around our heads, trying to rip them off, tearing everything apart –

Another wave, salt water pouring down my throat, I can't stop it –

Dolphins calling, something about losing the rope –

Our boat swings up – was that the wheelie case I heard fly off?

The dinghy swings back down, water churns around and around.

Tilting us up, a swirl of feathers and fur, biting, clutching.

Now we must be under the ocean.

We rise and fall in mountains of water. You haven't known falling like this, falling that never ends, dropping like your guts are going to spill out of your belly. No one to catch you, nothing to break your descent, just a great force sucking and squeezing the air out –

UP!

Which should be a relief, but is more frightening because it's so fast and it doesn't hold back if there's half a smashed boat or a dog in the way. Whatever's throwing you around doesn't care, it's going to yank you up regardless.

Water falls from the sky. Water everywhere. Instinct kicks in and you gulp as much air as possible, before a breaker forces you under again, a school bully in the swimming pool with his hand on your head.

Some bully, some pool.

I have never, not anywhere, not in a fish-road, on top of a whiterforce or at the Amsguard, experienced such power.

Under again, eyes open but unseeing. How long can I survive this?

DOWN

UP

Breathe!

DOWN

A collision with a set of paddling furry legs.

UP

Breathe!

DOWN

A slimy thing touches me, maybe a toad, maybe not. Where are the birds? Where is our boat?

UP

Breathe!

There is a piece of our boat. (Even though I am still blind I know this, because the piece is dripping and jagged, and it whacked me in the head.)

DOWN

Blood billowing out in sticky clouds, right in my eyes.

I am not sure if I will come up again.

Now I sink, clothes ballooning around my ears.

A snout touches my toes.

Emergency evacuation procedure initiated, says Beta, pulling at my scarf with her beak. *Commencing underwater rescue, phase 1.*

That's when I lose it, and we . . . fade to black.

Water laps at my feet. The air feels warm and gentle. There is no driving rain or stormy wind. Instead, just a smell. A floating, honeyish one. The kind that suggests it might be safe to open your eyes.

As I wake up, I'm amazed to discover I'm lying on something solid. I imagine I must be back at home or on the tiny bed in Aida's flat. Except I don't remember the sheets being so damp or so gritty.

I try to move and end up flopping.

But I'm still blind. I see only blackness again, a fuzzier black than before. Purple round the fringes, a few dots of light here and there. If you want to wake up fast, I can recommend the dawning realization that you might never see again. Not your friends. Polly's raised eyebrow of disbelief. Aida's electrified stare. The stag's fur or the General's stripes. Dad.

I just wish I could see.

You do realize it's night-time, right? says a voice from behind my head.

Who said that?

Oh, you know . . . Now the voice is to my left. It seems to be moving without making any noise.

No, I don't know. What do you mean, it's night-time?

Well, when the big fiery ball sinks beyond the sea, and the bright dots come out above, we call that night round here. It's pretty cool.

I rub my eyes, still so sore and tender. But I now get that the purple-fringed blackness might be . . . a night sky.

Time to sit up.

That hurts.

Blurred and painful it may be, but I manage it and I can make out two things that might be my legs, my trousers ripped into shreds, gentle waves washing over them. My hands feel bruised and are caked with sand.

I'm on a beach.

Twisting around – which isn't a good idea – I squint through my puffy eyelids. I'm hoping to catch sight of a girl or a wolf but can only see a wall of darkness.

Yup, that's the thing about night, it's not great visually, says the voice. *Especially round here. Our nights are, like, super-dark. It's pretty cool.*

Now the voice is on my other side.

Who are you? Show yourself.

No problem, dude.

The speaker whisks over the sand, moving so fast I barely glimpse it. Especially at night. Especially with swollen eyes.

I can make out a creature about the length of my forearm, including a skinny tail. Colours swim before me – pale yellowy green, black speckles and stripes. I see the gleam of his eyes studying me from something raised out of the white sand – a rock or a log? – while a long tongue flicks from side to side out of his mouth.

You're a lizard.

Yup, I guess so, he says. *Pretty cool, huh?*

Except not one that speaks like I expected a lizard to.

So, where are we?

We're hanging out on my favourite beach. You cool with that?

It seems that 'cool' can sometimes also mean 'annoying'. I shuffle round to face him, taking deep breaths and trying to ignore the shooting pains in every part of my body.

But at the same time, as I feel the sand beneath my fingers and the honeyed scent in my nose, a thought surfaces in the mush that passes for my brain right now. It pulses and grows stronger with every moment, making my throat dry and my stomach jumpy.

Can I ask . . . are we on an island known as Faraway?

Hmm, says the lizard, musing. *Faraway? It's a pretty

221

cool name, I guess. I have heard it called that before, but it's not what we call it.*

*What do you mean, *we*?*

Hey, no worries, plenty of time for that . . . So, how did you come to be all washed up, if you don't mind me asking?

I start to tell him, but as I begin remembering the events that led me here, they start to crash over me as powerfully as the waves of the world's sea that flung me here in the first place. The memories pile up in my mind, until, before I can even explain a word to the waiting lizard, they topple over, plunging my mind into darkness.

I wake again some hours later, the purple sky reddening around me. A new day begins. My vision still blurred and painful, I can now just make out what looks like a leafy jungle fringing the sparkling white beach ahead of us.

A new day. My first without Aida and Polly for a very long time. I touch the battered watch face around my neck, wiping the sand off. Untying it carefully, I peer at my own dim reflection. I don't know what else I'm hoping to see. That perhaps, by magic, the faces of my two friends will reappear behind my shoulders, with big smiles, reassuring me that they haven't . . . that we're still together forever.

But as the cracked screen stays blank, my heart and shoulders sink deeper than any wrecked boat ever has. I think I've found the island we were all looking for, only now it is just me, alone in the middle of the world's sea, miles from anywhere and anyone I know.

There's a sharp twinge in my ribs, and I cry out. It's like the pain I felt in my animal dream. The pain of being left alone. It can't have come true already.

I clutch the damp watch tight in my hand and wish the most I have ever wished to hear a friendly voice – from an enthusiastic wolf, or a moody dog, a silly pigeon, or . . . a strange green lizard on my shoulder.

Wow, that's a pretty amazing story, he says.

I start, and he leaps back on to the sand. *But I didn't tell you anything! I passed out again . . . didn't I?*

Oh yeah, cool, maybe you did. Maybe I just made up my own story to fill the void. I find myself doing that a lot out here.

Perhaps I'm not quite as alone as I thought. We sit in silence for a while, listening to the morning waves brushing gently against the shore.

The lizard cocks his head at me. *So . . . what next? Maybe hang out here for a while, enjoy the view?*

No! I don't want to hang out anywhere. I had . . . some friends. I need to find them. And anyway, why do you talk like that?

Like what, dude?

Like, I don't know, not how I thought a lizard would sound.

Oh, gee, I dunno how a lizard is meant to sound. He

thinks, whisking around in the sand. *Hey, do you know what my voice reminds me of?*

I shake my head.

A while back, when I was real small and learning to speak, we used to get these other human visitors. They came in brightly coloured clothes and took lots of what they called photos, with flashing lights that made me jump. They made a real mess of the place too. But come to think of it, they talked just like I do! Do you think that might have something to do with it?

I sigh. *Yes, I do.*

Wow, that's so cool. The lizard sits watching me, and I can see his heart pulsing away under his scaly skin. *I, like, never thought about that before. That's awesome, dude.*

No problem. My eyesight is beginning to slowly return. I need to find the others. *I had some friends, who I'm hoping might be on this island too. Will you help me find them?*

He blinks. *Sure. Cool. No problemo.*

I try to stand up, and fall over straightaway, stumbling in the soft sand. Everything swims before me – surf, beach and jungle.

The lizard is suddenly in front of me. He's fast. *Do you know what might be cool? Why don't we look for your friends on this beach first?*

I glance to my left, and then my right. With my impaired sight, all I can see is the emptiness of a deserted beach, the jagged shadows of rocks at either end. *There's nothing here.*

Nothing? says the lizard.

Nothing.

Gee. Are you sure? I mean, how big are these friends? Cos things can get caught in rock pools.

Big enough not to get caught in a rock pool. You do realize one of them was an actual wolf, don't you?

A sand-coloured wolf, maybe?

I have no idea if lizards can read human expressions, but if they can, this one just experienced my best YOU HAVE TO BE KIDDING ME face.

*Or maybe we should dig a few holes and see if they're hiding *under* the sand?* he muses. *That would be *mega* cool!*

Right. I've had enough of this. I pick myself up, take a second to get my balance and start tramping over the beach towards the scent of the jungle. Like magic, the lizard is perched in front of me again, his tail ticking.

Hey, buddy, what's the rush?

I've told you. I need to find my friends. We need to save the world.

Coolio. It's just that I . . . wouldn't go in there if I were you.

Why not?

Oh . . . because that would be kinda . . . uncool.

I don't care.

As the sky lightens, I can see the line of giant trees

ahead of me have leaves the size of my head. The sweet scent is so much stronger here. I push one of the rubbery branches aside.

Majorly uncool! warns the lizard, sounding very unrelaxed now, appearing on the branch and skittering around in agitation.

Why do I get the impression you're trying to stop me going in here?

Me? Stop you? No way. That would be, like, a total downer.

I let the branch spring back, and he darts off on to the forest floor. The sounds of the sea fade, as I take my first step into . . . the jungle of Faraway.

This island must be much bigger than it looked from the beach. The jungle goes on forever. I don't know where I'm going, and after half an hour of pushing through identical leaves and branches, I couldn't tell you the way back either.

If I was lost before, now I'm *really* lost.

And the creature that I thought would be my guide really isn't helping. In fact, if anything, it's the opposite – like he would do anything to stop me going any further.

He keeps whisking just under my feet, getting in my way. Finally he puts himself right in front of me, so I nearly trip over him. *Hey, do you know what? I was thinking *this* bush looks pretty nice. Why don't we chill here for a while?*

It's so humid that sweat is dripping off my forehead.

And eerily quiet too, with green stretching away in all directions. I can't see or hear where the shoreline is, or make out any sign of a path, clearing or anything that might make me feel a little less completely lost.

I listen for any sign of my friends, human or animal, but the only sound is the rustling of the lizard's tail against the bush.

*Listen, I thought you were going to help me find my friends. But why do I get the impression you are trying to stop me?'

He gulps. He actually gulps. *No reason,* he whispers.

It really has gone dark in here. Much darker than I thought it would be from the outside. I gaze up at the tangled canopy above our heads, only letting tiny spots of early morning sun in.

Why are you whispering? I whisper back.

The lizard's eyes widen. *Am I whispering?* he whispers. *I'm not whispering.*

I shake my head and do the only thing I can – which is to continue deeper into the island jungle, swiping aside palm fronds, pulling off sticky creepers, stepping round strange rubbery plants that smell of rotten rubbish, all the while the lizard leaping ahead and trying to delay me by any means possible.

Check out this leaf, it's so cute.

and,

Wow, I dig this light through the trees, isn't it neat?

The more he tries to stop me, the more I push on, not

228

caring where I'm going until finally the lizard shrieks –
Hold it right there!

I pause, leaning on a branch hung with swags of moss.
My hair hangs in my eyes, limp with sweat. *Why?*

Because of him.

Who?

I look up.

And I see who he means.

Yes. That might be a good reason to stop.

Or run?

Or RUN!

As we hurtle through the undergrowth, I'm trying to
make sense of what I've just seen. I only caught a glimpse
through the jungle leaves, but a glimpse was enough.

Bright eyes, staring out from a face dried brown by
the sun. White hair cropped short, and what looked like
a tattoo of a thorny rose curving down one side of his
neck.

And a tie. No shirt, but a ragged, faded tie around his
neck.

'I'm not going to give you another warning,' he roared
after us. 'Get off my island. Now!'

That wasn't what made us run through. What made
us run was the giant, sharp spade clutched between his
tattooed hands, raised high above his head.

The spade that comes splintering down on the branch
between us as I ducked between his legs, the lizard

shooting after me. I hear him yank it straight out again, without a single grunt of effort.

I crash through the jungle as I imagine dinosaurs must have once done, trampling and squashing wherever I go. Yet there isn't a sound behind me. If he is chasing us, he is as silent as a ghost.

You might want to watch your head there, calls the lizard from above my head. *That thing is kinda toxic.*

There isn't time to see what he's describing, but I duck under a red flower shaped like a jug with sticky thorns jutting out beneath. So many kinds of plants, trees and bushes, as if this jungle was a plant, tree and bush emporium.

We pass pink blossoms so small they could be nothing more than confetti scattered on the ground, and flowers big enough to hide a bus behind. Things like bananas, only bright purple. Tree trunks thicker than the pillars of the Amsguard, and thin, whippy ones that spring back and whack you in the face. Everywhere I put my feet, I'm squashing something beautiful – a crisp white orchid, a paper-thin fern dripping with crystal dew. My hair, face, hands and every inch of my shredded clothes are covered with a dusting of luminous green pollen.

The sticky air is making me short of breath, and I'm slowing down. Now and then I keep hearing what sounds like a slip of air squeeze past me, and turn around, but there's no one there.

Can you see him? I ask the lizard as I sprint, while he leaps from branch to branch above my head.

Relax, enjoy the scenery, he says.

I can't relax. I can only run.

Light filters through the jigsaw-shaped pieces of greenery ahead. I stumble towards it. There is one last shallow ditch to cross, which I leap over – and something tight yanks against my shin.

A wire.

I sprawl on my face, on to hard dusty ground. The heat of the day burns my back. All the shade of the jungle has vanished. We must be in some kind of clearing. Blocking my view is a speckled lizard, waving his tail.

OK, so now you've stopped running and you're just going to lie on the ground. That's cool, except—

The spade slices into the dirt right in front of my nose.

I glance up.

A man in desert boots, torn shorts and a tie, the sun behind him blinding. 'I warned you,' he says, tugs the spade out of the ground, and raises it over his head –

'Stop!' calls a voice from my right.

'Drop it right now!' says another, from the left.

They're alive. My friends are alive.

The man holds the spade high in the sky, sweat dripping off his arms on to the ground. He doesn't flinch. But right now I care just a little bit less about him and his shovel. Because my friends are alive. I am not alone on this island.

Polly comes closer, holding a glowering toad under

her arm. 'Don't hurt him, please. We've come so far. To save the planet, you see.'

'This is my island,' says the man. 'No other humans allowed.'

'Who says?' asks Aida, taking a step forward from the other side of the clearing, casting a big shadow. 'You ain't in charge of everything.'

'I am here. No other animals either,' says the man, but he doesn't move.

My friends are filthy, their hair bedraggled, their clothes in rags like mine, and they are dusted in luminous green pollen like me – but they are alive. Polly cradles her toad in her arms. He looks parched and shrivelled.

'That a real shame,' says Aida, 'because we got more.' She puts her fingers in her mouth and gives two short, sharp whistles.

A dog whistle. Then a whistle for a wolf.

Dagger trotting out of the undergrowth, scratched and now more a luminous greeny dusty white, but alive, his glass teeth glinting. And behind Polly, my wolf, limping but also still breathing. They both crouch low around the man, ears back and growling. The man grunts and whacks the spade into the ground inches from my nose.

Third time lucky, says the lizard. *That, like, never happened before. Normally he goes straight for the chop. Pretty cool.*

The man turns to Dagger and the wolf, and even though they're still baring their teeth, he doesn't look scared.

He squats in front of them and speaks in a very quiet voice. Not like how I talk to them, inside our heads, but talking all the same. He holds out his hands for them to sniff, which they do. He breathes on them. Everything he does is steady and calm. To my amazement, instead of leaping on him, the two are soon licking his hand.

Wolf! I call. *You're meant to be protecting us. What did he say?*

I don't know, he replies. *It wasn't how you talk to us, Wildness, it was different.*

It was normal human speech, but he was kind, says the white dog. *He was kind.*

Yes, says the wolf. *That's it, he was kind.*

Even the toad softens his frown.

Spade-man finishes petting the animals and stands up. I try to get up too, but I can't; the tripwire is wound tight around my ankles.

'Together forever,' whispers Polly, darting across and – with massive effort – yanking the spade out of the ground, holding it in front of her.

'That might not be for very long,' hisses Aida.

The man studies us and, shaking his head, pulls a large knife out from the back of his shorts. Not just any old knife though.

A machete.

And raising it high in the air, he strides towards us.

I frantically scan what lies behind the man with the machete, trying to see if there is anywhere to hide or run to. Some bamboo huts, a water pump and piles of some round green fruit . . . If this truly is the whale's island, it is not as deserted as she thought.

Behind the camp is a hill. A low, dumpy hill.

In fact, hill isn't the right word.

It's a hump. A lush, overflowing hump. But a hump all the same. It reminds me of something; I just can't put my finger on what. The more I stare at it, the stranger it seems to be.

The man sees me staring at the hump-hill and stops, lowering the machete for a moment. In the bright sunlight I now see his whole body is covered in swirls of the thorny tattoo and what might be white war paint. What with the tie and shorts, he is the weirdest-looking man I've ever seen.

But there is also something familiar about him.

He jabs the blade in our direction. 'How did you even find me?'

Polly gabbles, trying to play for time. 'We weren't looking for you. The whale told us about the island. Then the dolphins pulled us on a boat guided by the eagle, but there were jellyfish and a storm . . .'

'And you expect me to believe that?'

'It the truth!' blurts Aida. 'What, you think we walk here?'

'There is more than one way to get to this island,' mutters the man, marching over to me. This is it. I'm about to yell to the wolf to stop thinking he's kind, when with a swift slice of his knife he's cut the wire around my ankles.

That was not what I was expecting.

I stand up, rubbing the blood back into my legs. He jabs at me with the blade. 'Go and join your friends, over there.'

I hobble over, the girls take my hands and we hug each other. They are so frightened, and it's all my fault. I shouldn't have dragged them on this stupid adventure to this madman's island. But Polly just touches the watch strap dangling round her neck, and for a moment I don't feel so guilty. The dog and the wolf trot to our side.

Spade-man turns the knife in the sun. 'You can tell me

235

any story you want. It makes no odds. There's nothing for you here, understand? I haven't let another human being stay for seven years.' He pricks his thumb with the point, a bubble of bright blood welling up. 'Not that they haven't tried. They just don't last very long. The only reason you're still alive is the fact you're children and I've got a soft spot for these handsome beasts of yours. So however you got here, you've got to leave again.'

'Not until we find why the whale sent us here,' says Polly.

'What happens if you don't?'

'The fire will come and the world will end, and everyone will have to leave earth in Selwyn Stone's spaceship, that's what,' says Aida.

It's like she's set another tripwire off, only in his mind. In a split second he is behind her, pressing the blade against her neck. 'How do you know that name? Did he send you? Are you his spies?'

Aida's dark skin has gone paler than I've ever seen it, a single bead of sweat rolling down the side of her head. 'Everyone know that name. He run the Island.'

He keeps the knife tight against her bare throat.

'Send us? He tried to stop us coming here to start with,' says Polly. She seems unruffled, but then I remember she was the girl who first greeted me with a gun aimed at my stomach.

'Prove it,' snarls the man.

'We don't need to,' she says, pointing to me. 'Our friend

Kester is the person he hates most in the world right now. Ask anyone.'

There isn't anyone to ask, but it doesn't matter. He pulls the knife away and stares hard at me, while Aida stumbles back, rubbing her neck. I have no weapon. Wolf moves in between us with a low growl.

'That's impossible,' says the man quietly. 'There is another whom Stone despises more than you.' His eyes burn with a new fierceness, a fire sparking behind the black twists of tattooed thorns. 'Me.'

Our world is ending. The sea is dead, the land is dying, the animals have gone, and now the last few things I thought I knew are crumbling into the dust around me.

A tattooed man in a tie, living alone with a lizard on a faraway island, is the person Selwyn Stone hates the most?

I should feel relieved that he's not going to attack us but the truth is I feel kind of jealous. What makes him so special?

He smiles at the confusion on my face. In that moment, I realize I have seen a smile like that before. A smile like that, but not the same. Aida voices the question hovering in my mind.

'Who is you then?'

'You can call me Eck,' he says. 'Don't move.'

With that, he turns on his heel and disappears into the nearest bamboo hut.

So are you guys here on vacation? the lizard asks Dagger.

No, replies the dog. *We are on a mission to save all living creatures from the fate that awaits this planet.*

Cool, says the lizard, stretching out in the heat of the midday rays. *Well, good luck with that. Wake me up if you, like, need any assistance, amigos.*

Eck reappears from the hut dragging a large cylinder on a trolley, attached to a hose coiled over his arm. It could be from a hospital. As he attaches the rubber pipe to a nozzle, I have a sudden flashback to Mum, and for the first time I don't chase the memory away.

I think of her in bed, surrounded by oxygen tanks, nurses adjusting her dose. I never accepted that she wouldn't get better. I do now. I understand that sometimes people don't get better, that they do leave and don't come back.

At the same time, Mum hasn't gone away.

She's still here in my head, talking to me.

If I let her.

There isn't a chance to remember any more because I am blown off my feet by a jet of freezing water. As are the girls, and the animals. Only the toad is unfazed, like he can't get enough of it.

'Hey! What you do that for? I just got dry,' shouts Aida.

She's answered by another spray. Eck hoses us down again. The liquid smells chemical, but it doesn't hurt. Just

238

when I think it's going to take more than a lizard-length nap in the sun for us to dry off, the jet fizzles away.

'We're soaking,' says Polly.

'Yes, and decontaminated.' He gestures to the green hump rising behind him. 'You're not going there with any trace of virus or anything else you might have picked up on your travels.'

'How do you know we want to go there?' asks Polly.

'I don't. But you're never going to understand who I am and why I guard this island unless I show you. You'll get sprayed on the way out too, because we don't want you leaving with anything unwanted either.'

'Like what?'

'You'll see.'

With that, he wheels the cylinder back into the hut and remerges minutes later, setting off towards the greenery ahead without so much as a backward glance.

I start after him.

Polly grabs my arm. 'We don't even know who he really is or what he wants us to do. A moment ago he wanted to kill us.'

'For real,' adds Aida, rubbing her neck.

Too bad. The whale sent us to Faraway. We have to find what the secret of the her song is before the fire in the sky comes. And right now, this strange man who tried to kill me a moment ago is our only hope of doing that.

I touch my watch face and hope they understand, before hurrying after our guide. With muttered threats

239

about what will happen to me if I'm wrong, my friends follow, the wolf loping alongside, Dagger at Aida's heels, the toad in Polly's arms.

We take a track between two bushes dripping with purple berries, the wolf sniffing the man's trail. As we disappear into the shade of the jungle, I hear a cry behind us.

No worries, guys, have a nice trip. I'll hang out here and keep an eye on this dust for you. Stay cool!

As he walks ahead of us, Eck takes great care to step over the roots snaking across the dusty track. He doesn't dislodge a single petal or leaf as he slips through the undergrowth. Occasionally he will stop, and with a small grunt bend over to scoop something off the ground.

'Here,' he says, opening his hand to show us a handful of seed capsules with dark brown caps and slender, sand-coloured shafts. 'You can touch them, if you want.'

They look delicate enough to crunch in your mouth, like a chocolate egg, but they turn out to be tough as rocks. Polly studies them all over, holding them up to the light and sniffing at them. Wolf tries to crack one open and almost loses a tooth.

'Hmm,' says Polly. 'It looks like a hazelnut crossed with a euphorbia seed, but it can't be both. I've never seen anything like it before.'

'You're correct,' our guide replies, sounding surprised and impressed. 'It looks like both those things, but you won't be able to identify it because those are the seeds for a completely new species. No one in your Island knows what this plant is, of course. I'm the first to discover it, right here.'

'New? What it do?' asks Aida.

'It doesn't *do* anything, it just is. It's beautiful – you should see it in flower. In the short walk from the camp, we've probably passed thirty new species of plant that no one else on earth has even heard of.' Eck brushes more of the green dust from his hands off on his shorts, leaving streaks of luminous pollen. He points up to the top of the hill, where the soft leaves fringing the path give way to a crown of jagged thorns, silhouetted against the deep blue sky. 'But that's nothing compared to what I want to show you. The reason I guard this island.'

He stares at me, as if he is trying to see deep inside, make out the thoughts slowly whirring into place in my head.

'And, I suspect, the reason you are all here.'

Now we step as carefully as our guide, trying not to tread on the spiked leaves that look like a giant toad's feet, or brush the upside-down yellow bells that could be another undiscovered plant. The path slopes upward, and the dense air begins to clear, but we are dripping with perspiration as we climb the steep track. The others are too tired to speak, the only sound coming from the wolf and Dagger as they pant their way to the top.

I haven't eaten since the seaweed on the boat, and can't tell if it is the disinfectant in my eyes or the after-effects of the jellyfish sting, but everything is beginning to swim again.

As we emerge from the crown of spiked leaves, blinking in the bright light, I stop and turn around. The jungle canopy stretches out behind us towards the shore, like a sloping pile of treasure. Glittering red jewel flowers, golden coin petals opening up to catch the sun, and a speckled lizard basking on a branch.

It's pretty cool, isn't it? We lizards love a good view.

How did you get here? I thought you were guarding the camp.

Sure I was, and now I'm here, no big deal. Just keeping an eye out for my new buddies.

The toad shoots him a beady glance. I'm not sure if toads and lizards make good buddies any more than cockroaches and rats do.

Beyond the dark edge of the forest, the island is surrounded by a fringe of crystal sand, white surf and the plain of the world's sea. There is no sign of anything that was once a boat, or our birds, or even a dolphin fin.

'No time for gawping,' says a voice behind us. 'You're dead on your feet. Time to eat.'

We turn and find Eck sitting under the shade of a tree, one of several in a small grove on top of the hump.

Polly gasps.

In fact, we all do. Because they are not like any trees I could imagine existing on this planet. They are like palm trees, but the trunks are shiny and black, the leaves bright blue.

'The bark looks like rubber,' says Polly, touching it. 'Ugh,' she says, pulling her hand away. I can see it's dripping with something sticky.

That's not all.

There are no coconuts hanging under this alien-looking palm, but large green fruit, like the ones we saw piled up in the camp. They are a cross between a melon and a giant gooseberry. The man grabs the handle of his machete and hits the palm nearest to us a couple of times. Two giant gooseberry-melons bounce on to the ground, narrowly missing the wolf's head.

Eck slices one open, getting himself covered in the green pollen that seems to be everywhere.

'Oh my days,' says Aida, putting her hand to her nose.

Polly looks like she is going to be sick. The fruit smells like rotting rubbish mixed with vomit. It is my turn to gag when Eck hacks the strange grey-pink flesh into chunks, popping one into his mouth.

'Delicious,' he says between chews.

He offers me one.

I stare at the stinking, mouldy-looking fruit.

'It's not going to poison you, is it?' he says. 'I just ate a piece and I'm fine. Ignore the smell – that's to put people off eating it. Because this is the most delicious thing in the world.'

I sniff the gooseberry-melon and have to turn away, my eyes watering. It's the kind of smell that would send the General into ecstasies.

'Eat it!' Eck brandishes the machete at me.

I force the flesh into my mouth, my nostrils filling with the stench. Everyone is looking at me while I chew, waiting for me to spit it out.

But I don't.

Because, once you get beyond the stink, he's right. It is the most delicious thing in the world. (Perhaps the only delicious thing in the world left.) It doesn't taste of prawn-cocktail crisps, for starters. It tastes of . . . everything. Sweet and salt come together at the same time; in fact every flavour comes through at the same time. Tangy, fatty, chewy, soft, hard, crispy, filling, light, creamy – everything!

I hold my hand out for more. I am more hungry and tired than I have ever been, but even if I wasn't, I would want more. Eck smiles and gives me another piece. Then to Polly and Aida. Then to Wolf and Dagger. All of them sniffing it at first, then chewing, and taking more.

'This *is* delicious,' says Polly between mouthfuls. 'What's it called?'

'An omnium fruit.'

'What is it?'

Eck stands up, grabs his machete and holds it level with his eye. He flicks his wrist back – making us flinch – and flings the knife through the air. It sparkles in the sun before catching an omnium dangling above us, slicing it clean in half. He picks one side up off the floor and hands it to us. We can see the clear juice running between his fingers, the rough fibres of the fruit.

'You wanted to know why Selwyn Stone hated me more than anyone else on this planet,' he says, with a flash of that smile again. A smile that in the shadows of the blue palm grove, I now realize I *have* seen before.

On a face grinning in the shade of a creepy library far across the sea. A photo of a face striped with shadows in the Doctor's room at Spectrum Hall. And that same grin, moonlit in a leafy garden, just like now. A face I last saw on an ultrascreen introducing a new planet.

Eck must see the recognition in my eyes, as he takes another fleshy bite. 'This is the reason,' he says, holding up the fruit. 'This is why my brother wants to kill me.'

It is us who should be frozen with shock, but it is the man I now know as Eck Stone who freezes, his muscles taut, his bright eyes darting in the dusk, a twist of light from the machete.

'Wait!' he hisses. 'What was that?'

'What was *what*?' says Polly, her mouth still half full.

Eck Stone turns the knife towards each of us in turn. 'I heard something. You don't live alone on an island for seven years without getting good at hearing somethings. Do you swear you came on your own?'

'I didn't hear nothing,' says Aida.

All I can hear is the ticking of my heart, the rainforest around us that seems to breathe in and out like a giant outdoor lung, and a lizard muttering, *Alone? Gee, thanks a lot, big guy.*

Stone shushes the girls, still whispering. 'I heard something all right. It was very quiet, too quiet. Like

246

a noise that someone was trying to cover up. Wait here.'

He moves off towards the darkness, but Aida calls after him.

'No. We not waiting here.'

What is she doing? The man has a knife –

Eck pauses on the edge of the path, his back to us. Aida sails straight on, not caring what he or anyone else thinks.

'You just told us you the brother of our public enemy number one. You not going anywhere with your knife, leaving us in the dark to face who knows what, just cos you heard a "noise" none of us hear. Did you hear a noise, Kester?'

'No.'

'And Kester hears everything. That's why he's special. He can talk to animals, did you know that? You're not the only person at one with nature round here, mister.'

'I heard a—,' Eck starts to insist, but Aida is unstoppable.

'Then we stay together and face it together. We children, or did you forget? You can't just leave us in the middle of the jungle on our own. Or maybe you more like your brother than you pretends to be.'

'No!' Eck is back in front of us so fast we jump.

He moves like a hunter, says the wolf.

Eck hurls his knife into the ground, where it sticks deep, quivering. He quivers too, with a rage that pulses

247

off him through the sticky heat in waves. 'Don't you dare say I am like my brother, and don't any of you ever suggest that I could forget you are children.'

He collapses in a heap on the ground, his face flushed, covering it with his hands. 'Because children is where this story began. Where everything begins.'

'Tell us,' says Aida. 'We come a real long way. We survived killer jellyfish and a super-storm, and we not doing any more running or hiding until you tell us why you here.'

'Then you can help us find out why a whale sent us,' says Polly.

'Yes,' I add in my most definite voice.

Eck looks surprised at this. 'I don't know anything about a whale, I'm afraid. All I can tell you is my story.'

We sit back down around him in a semicircle in the shade of the omnium palms, and as the sun slides towards the sea behind the hump-hill, Eck Stone begins his tale.

'When I was a child there were three of us. Selwyn, the oldest, then me, and our younger brother . . . Lucien. We were lucky, growing up in a different world to you, that hadn't flooded, with plenty of animals. We lived in the countryside, at our parents' house. They encouraged us to make the most of everything. Swimming in their lake, climbing trees . . . in the long summer holidays day after day stretching into one another. We were inseparable as children, you see; we did everything together.'

Eck's face, burning gold and red in the light of the setting sun, breaks into a smile at the memory.

Aida's face sinks into her palm. 'Is this a history lesson? I hope not. I don't need no lesson on your brother. He a monster, you understand?'

Any trace of a smile disappears. 'No doubt. But don't you want to know why?'

She shrugs. He continues with his story.

'I was always the adventurous one, leading us on. Climb higher! Dive deeper! I dare you to jump! Selwyn was more cautious, never wanting to get into trouble. He was curious though. He liked to pick up rocks to see what lived underneath. Wherever we went exploring, he was never without a net to collect tiny bugs for analysis.'

'Huh! Sound like you,' says Aida, nudging Polly in the ribs.

'I am *not* like Selwyn Stone,' she says sharply.

'No, you are not,' says Eck.

'And Lucien?' says Polly, sounding keen to change the subject. 'What was he like?'

Our host gazes out across the sea, which looks awash with gleaming copper and scarlet petals, shifting colour as the sun sinks beneath the water.

'Lucien,' he says, 'was . . . something else. He was a true free spirit. It was impossible not to giggle when he appeared, dancing like a sprite. Selwyn was so serious. Lucien was the only person who could ever make him laugh, always teasing him. He had a quiff of blond hair and a habit of popping up when least expected: behind the sofa or through the gap in a tree. But he was also the most fragile. His skin was pale, his bones were thin and his chest was so weak that even a slight cold left him wheezing for days.'

'Something bad gonna happen,' says Aida, her eyes wide. 'Don't keep us waiting. Tell. I know something real bad gonna happen.'

I expect Eck to get cross, but he just gets quieter and sadder.

'Yes,' he says slowly, 'something bad is going to happen. A *lot* of bad things were going to happen.'

PART 5:
SOMETHING
BAD

As we sit around in the dusky shade of the omnium grove, on top of the Faraway hill, Eck continues with his tale.

'It all began one summer afternoon when Lucien suggested we go exploring by some holes in a hill that overlooked our house. Rain had worn away the limestone to create tunnels and caverns underneath. The afternoon felt like one we would never forget. The three of us hiking through the long grass, Lucien leaping ahead, while Selwyn poked at everything we passed, muttering to himself. I was enjoying the sun, racing to reach the caves first. We sat around eating sandwiches and drinking lemonade from a flask. Then we roared about in the old tunnels, shouting challenges to monsters who never appeared and making our voices echo.

'Lucien suggested Dares, an old game of ours. We each

had to choose a dare for one another, and anyone who failed would take it in turns to carry the others down to the house on their back. Selwyn said he wasn't in the mood. He never liked situations where he didn't have complete control. But, with Lucien, I persuaded him. So I suppose, in the end, it was my fault as well. I live with that every day. The first two dares were for Selwyn, and then me. He had to go as far as he could into the caves, until either the tunnel ran out or the gaps were too narrow to squeeze through.'

I shudder, thinking of my time trapped in the Underearth. Dagger eyes me from the other side of the circle, where he lies with his head on Aida's lap.

'So he disappeared into the caves for over an hour, not reappearing until dusk, his glasses smeared with dust, grinning as if he'd enjoyed himself down there. Then it was my go. In the main cave there was a small underground lake. The water was pitch black. None of us had ever dared go in. But Selwyn picked up our empty lemonade flask and chucked it into the far end, daring me to go fetch. So I did. The lake was too murky to see anything at first, although that didn't stop me imagining glowing eyes or jaws at every stroke, until at last I saw something glinting at the bottom. Feeling my way in the gloom towards the flash of steel, I discovered that the thermos had fallen between two rocks. A few minutes later I emerged gasping from the lake with the flask, covered in mud and weeds. I remember Lucien saying, "The swamp monster lives!" and pretending to be frightened. Then he plucked a strand of slimy weed from my hair and began weaving it into a crown. Finally it was time for his dare. He wanted Selwyn to choose it. Selwyn thought for a moment. His eyes darted around the mouth of the cave and then lit upon something. He scrabbled over the ground towards a bush near the entrance, which I hadn't noticed before. We watched him as he ducked back clutching a branch in his hand. The leaves were green and pointed, with bright red berries, not that different in colour to the sun behind you now.'

Just the mention of red berries makes my stomach leap.

We turn and watch the last of the sun, glowing as it melts into the water. Once it has gone, and the night is dark and warm around us, Eck continues his story.

'Selwyn told Lucien that he looked like a fairy king in his seaweed crown, and held out the berries to him, which looked like jewels in his hand. Fairy's rubies was their name. And his dare to Lucien was simple. He just had to eat one.'

Eck hangs his head.

'You will not believe how many times I have revisited this moment in my mind. I wish I'd intervened, or dashed the fruit out of Selwyn's hands. But the fact is I didn't, so I am as much to blame as him for what happened. Lucien looked at Selwyn, his face impish with glee, and scooped the berries up into his mouth. He began to chew and swallow, and then . . .'

255

Eck has to break off from telling us his story and looks away.

'What did happen, Mr Stone?' asks Polly, cradling the toad in her lap, his eyes wide with fear. 'Kester ate briar berries, but they just gave him a fever, which I cured . . .'

'It wasn't the fairy's rubies. They were harmless. He could have eaten fistfuls if he'd wanted. It was the thing hiding in them. Unbeknownst to us, there was a wasp crawling over the bunch, that Lucien swallowed in a single gulp. In a panic, it stung him. His tongue swelled up, his throat too. We rushed him back to the house, Selwyn and I carrying him, like we had both lost the dare . . . but we were too late. Our little brother.' He is almost unable to speak for a moment, as if his own throat has swollen up. 'Nature had taken Lucien from us, and there was absolutely nothing Selwyn or I could do about it.'

At first, no one says a word. Then Aida lets out a long low whistle.

'See! Told you something bad was going to happen.'

The big shadow of Eck's head shakes. 'No. That was the sad thing. The bad thing was what happened next.' He jumps up. 'Come on. It's dark. Let's go back to the camp and I'll tell you the rest there.'

Using the stars in the sky as his guiding light back to the huts, Eck shows us into his home. I see now that the huts are made not from bamboo but from sun-bleached branches of omnium palm. He thumps the wall of the singled domed room as we enter and it doesn't even shudder. 'Strong stuff this, as it happens. Knits together ... incredibly well.'

There is rustling, the noise of what sounds like a match, and a flickering flame appears, a wick in a pool of oil held by a massive version of the seed caps we saw on the path. In Eck's other hand he holds a smouldering flint stone.

The roof appears to be made from the fibrous blue leaves woven together. I look again at the flickering flame, already smoking against the low ceiling. Eck must notice my face.

'Don't worry. Just one of many uses I've found for these fruit. The sap burns like oil, but the outer fibres are themselves flame resistant.'

He hands the seed-cap lamp to Polly, who cups it in her hands. 'I want to know more about these plants,' she says, her eyes hollow in the glowing light. 'A lot more.'

'I bet you do,' Eck snaps, snatching the lamp back. 'We'll see about that.'

Startled, we sit down. There is not much else in the room. A small heap of omnium fruit piled next to a makeshift bed. On the wall the remains of a ripped and scorched business suit hang on a coat hanger, above a battered briefcase. Next to that is the decontamination kit, beside piles of big, broad leaves.

257

Polly picks one up. They are covered in writing and drawings, scribbled in a kind of smeared and blotchy red ink, like something squeezed out of a fruit. I catch a glimpse of a plant sketch, just like the ones in Polly's notebook, before Eck snatches that out of her hands too.

'Hey!' says Aida. 'Mr Snapping and Snatching. We your guests, remember. And you *were* telling us a story, about your brother. Sad things we got. You promised bad things.'

'Oh yes. So I did.' It might be my imagination, but in the cramped lamp-lit darkness of the hut, his eyes remind me of a wolf's. I reach out and stroke mine, who is curled up behind us, nuzzling next to Dagger. The toad sinks as much of himself as he can into a small puddle of decontaminant leaking from the cylinder.

With a sigh, Eck continues his story. 'Selwyn blamed himself for what had happened to our brother. He blamed me too, of course, for encouraging them – but could never forget that the berries had been his idea. He never forgave the fruit either. Two weeks after Lucien's funeral, I went for a walk by myself up the hill behind the house. This in itself wasn't unusual. We never played together any more, it was too painful without . . . the three of us. What was unusual was the mouth of the cave. There wasn't a berry to be seen. Not a single one, and not a trace of the bush. All that remained was a patch of blackened soil giving off a strange chemical odour. My brother had not only

258

uprooted the entire plant, but also scorched the ground where it grew, before coating the earth in black creosote so nothing could ever grow there again. Then it wasn't just those plants, but any with fruit that got destroyed. Next he started on the wasps. He set traps in jam jars, smoked out nests, sprayed flowers – decimating half our garden. At first my parents indulged him, then they ignored him, then they despaired over him. Wasps, then bees – he began not to care. His room, which had once been a lab for experiments, a place of curiosity and knowledge, became a slaughterhouse. Beetles, spiders, cockroaches, butterflies – each one pinned and labelled in glass-covered drawers. There was even the odd little mouse or bird.'

I shiver, remembering Selwyn's spooky collection of stuffed animals. Creatures much bigger than spiders. For the first time on this journey I am glad some of my wild are not with us.

'You mean he blamed them for what had happened to Lucien?' asks Polly from the shadows.

'Exactly,' says Eck. 'He hated nature for what it had taken away from us. Wild animals, plants – in his eyes they were unpredictable and unreliable. He couldn't communicate with them, he couldn't reason with them, so he had to contain and dominate them. He became obsessive over food too, controlling and checking everything he ate. And in the end, as you know, it wasn't just nature and food he wanted to dominate . . . but everything.'

'But it was an accident,' says Polly. 'It wasn't anyone's fault. I'm sure even the wasp didn't mean to hurt him.'

'It was an accident, you're right,' says Eck. 'One that cost me a brother and changed the other for life. There was no stopping Selwyn. So that was why, later on, I suggested we found Facto together.'

'What, so he could make money from being a sicko?' says Aida.

Eck grabs an omnium from the corner and whacks his machete into it with fury. 'No! Because I assumed we could harness his obsession and put it to good use. We would make the world's safest and healthiest food company. Factorium. I thought the ancient word for factory sounded old-fashioned and classic. A name to trust. Global food supplies were dwindling, you see. I believed we could,

261

over time, move mankind away from our dependence on animal-based products. Selwyn liked this idea too, but for different reasons to me perhaps.

'And for a while, it was perfect. We played to our strengths. While humans still ate normal food, I was the traveller, sourcing top ingredients and suppliers. Meanwhile, my brother was the scientist, testing every product in our labs – and trying to create new ones, of course. Together we ended up processing and selling most of the good food in the world. We were efficient, reliable and cheap. Facto grew and grew. But the world changed quicker than we had imagined, with the big heat. It became harder and harder to find food that met our standards. So Selwyn began to experiment. He accelerated his lifetime ambition of developing a universal foodstuff, one which didn't need him to go near animals or plants at all and which would provide for all our nutritional needs. I told him he was going too fast, that people would never eat an entirely artificial food. He swore that he would make them, whether they liked it or not.'

Even if that meant culling loads of healthy animals so we had no choice.

'In the meantime, I kept travelling the world. And that was how I discovered the omnium fruit. I came to this island after I spotted it by chance from a Facto helicopter, when the clouds parted for a moment. It was such an extraordinary shape – I knew I had to explore it.'

The island with a strange hump-like hill.

'We haven't seen it from the air, only from waking up on a beach,' says Polly. 'What is the shape?'

'The swollen hump over there, it bursts out of thick cylinders of land that cross and twist over each other like tubes and pipes. It doesn't look like an island at all. It looks like a heart.'

Slumped against the sticky rubber of an omnium palm wall, I sit bolt upright. Eck's last words struck me like a blow in the windpipe, leaving me dizzy and short of air.

The island looks like a heart.

And I know just what kind of heart. The diagram Polly drew in the beach by the Ams. The diagram of a stolen whale's heart. The heart with the secret to save the world, sang the whale, the heart of a giant prehistoric creature – one of the first ever living things on the planet.

Polly sneaks me a knowing glance, but if Eck has noticed our reaction he doesn't show it.

'It was an untouched paradise. Full of the most extraordinary creations yet to be discovered. Until the red-eye came.'

Hey, no big deal, but he always forgets the lizards, says the lizard. *Sure, there used to be birds with purple beaks and six feet, snakes with feathers, and beetles that could make themselves invisible – sure, they used to be here. But what about the lizards? We were here first and we're still here. I mean, you don't get cooler than that, right?*

'The most amazing thing though,' continues Eck, 'was the plant life. I have never seen any flora so lush, so beautiful, spilling out of the ground without end. A different species every few yards – to categorize every one would be a lifetime's work in itself. I was looking for food sources, of course – and preferably not animal. I ate many disgusting things, and some delicious ones: bitter roots, sharp fruit, even sweet flowers, which sent me to sleep. In short though, you would never starve if you got shipwrecked here. While I researched, I built this small camp we're sitting in now. Then I worked my way through the jungle and up the hill, testing and eating as I went. Until I arrived at the top, among a grove of palm trees unlike any I had ever seen anywhere else in the world. The secret of this island's riches – these amazing fruit.'

There's the familiar squelch and thud as he cuts another one open, the rotten stench filling the night air. Even in the dark the pale flesh seems to glow.

'What did this taste of to you?' he asks us. 'Fruit?'

'Yes . . . ,' I say, hesitant.

'It smelt rank, that for sure,' says Aida.

'I don't know,' says Polly. 'A bit of everything.'

'That's just it!' cries Eck. He isn't sitting down now, but dancing around the tiny room, a giant slice of omnium balanced on the edge of his knife. It will be a miracle if he doesn't trip over one of us. 'I thought the same thing the first time I tasted some. It tastes of everything. That's why I called it the omnium fruit.

'It's the food we need to grow, for energy and to keep us healthy. Omnium has vitamins and nutrients for our eyes, brains, skin, hair, muscles and every organ. It's even got fat, but the right kind and not too much of that either. Sugar, an ideal dose. It's perfect. You could live on this forever and maybe even live forever.'

'Wouldn't it get . . . boring?' says Polly.

'What?' says Eck. 'More boring than prawn-cocktail crisps? A pink sludge tasting only of one thing? These omnium taste of everything already, and you're eating it raw. But it can also be fried, toasted and roasted, boiled or mashed, turned into jelly and frozen solid. Ground, spiced, stuffed and fricasseed – you name it, you can cook it! Not only that, but I took a bunch of cuttings back to a research lab and conducted some tests. Although currently it only grows here on this hill, I discovered it will grow anywhere, in any condition, in the rain, in the heat. It won't carry the red-eye or any disease, and other animals don't mind eating it.'

The wolf next to me sniffs the slices of fruit. He takes one bite, and then another, and before long he has eaten the whole thing.

Be careful, you might make yourself sick.

I don't care, Wildness. I am so hungry I could eat a tree. And besides, I am the best at being sick so you will all be amazed when I am.

'If this fruit is so perfect, why don't we all know about it?' says Polly, sounding puzzled.

'Why do you think?' says Eck. 'I took my research to Selwyn, I gave him the fruit to eat, I showed him how it could take seed anywhere. In fact it grows so fast and so quick, it needs a lot of work.' He brandishes his knife, stained green with omnium juice. 'This gets a lot of use just keeping the things under control. They'd be all over the island otherwise.'

To demonstrate, he takes the machete and hacks at a palm branch lying on the floor, swiping and slashing until it is nothing more than a shorn and naked stump.

'The contamination spray – it's not just to stop viruses getting in, it's to control these brutes and stop them taking over the whole island. Look.' He points to the ragged stump, where already a fresh green shoot is beginning to emerge.

'No plant grows that quick,' murmurs Polly, touching the tiny tip with her hand.

'Indeed. They help other plants grow as well – you've seen those extraordinary flowers in the jungle. I discovered . . . other properties too. Highly unusual ones. But when I reported them to Selwyn, he told me to destroy it.'

'What? Why?'

'He said that it would destroy us. How could Facto make money out of a fruit that fulfilled every nutritional requirement, that anyone could grow anywhere? There would be no control, no production required, and no profit for us. I disagreed of course, arguing that not everyone would want to grow their own, but Selwyn dismissed my every argument. He said he was developing another plan, one that meant the whole world would be reliant on Facto for eternity. A plan that was the ultimate result of his hatred for nature that began with Lucien's death. It was . . .'

He stops, staring at the palm-strewn ground between his feet. For the first time since Eck began talking, he seems lost for words. He closes his eyes for a moment, like he is trying to calm himself.

After what feels like forever, he speaks again.

'His plans for humans, for earth, was . . . horrific. Indescribable. And it began with something called Formul-A. But his dream was my nightmare. He had to be stopped. We argued, we fought, and in the end, he attacked me. My own brother, beating me with his bare hands. He tried to destroy the omnium samples I had brought him, demanding I reveal where this island was. I refused and, fearing for my life, made a break for here.' Our host points to the ragged and faded tie dangling around his neck. 'I fled in my suit. I keep this on to remind me of how close I came that day to failing these unique plants. I swore to guard the omnium with my life from then on. Because I knew one day we would need it.'

Eck sighs. His story has taken most of the short night and now day is here again. He stands in the narrow doorway of the hut, gazing out, his hands braced against the palm frame, for a moment looking like a paper cut-out against the lilac sky.

'Which is why you have come, haven't you?'

'No,' I say, also standing up and stretching my arms and legs, which are stiff after sitting for so long.

'No,' says Polly, 'I told you. We came because of a whale.' The toad sits on her shoulder, puffed up with pride.

'We saving our home and the world,' adds Aida, as they both stand too. Dagger goes to her side, and the wolf to mine. 'That's why your brother hates us. We on the same side as you. Kester talks to animals. Polly knows everything about plants. And don't talk to me about rich people trying to take over the world.'

In the early light of morning, Eck looks very tired, deep bags under his eyes. No wonder – he has been talking all night long. But it seems he is tired of listening too, because –

'Don't lie,' he snarls, whipping round in the doorway. 'You came for the fruit. For the island.'

'We never heard of it till now!' protests Aida. 'But so what if we did?'

'You can't have them. I decided that long ago. Even if my brother does despise you all just as much as me. It makes not a shred of difference. No other people allowed anywhere near this island or this fruit.'

'Why on earth not?' asks Polly.

He grabs his machete off the floor, and points it at us. 'Because no matter how noble your intentions, you are still human beings – and like everything else on this planet, you will only destroy them.'

With that, Eck makes it clear that the time for stories and talking is over. He turns away from us and curls up on his bed. Even though it is early morning, we are tired too, and do the same – on the floor of his hut.

But later that morning, after a few hours of fitful sleep, he wakes us with slices of toasted omnium, grilled over a seed-cap lamp. Our host is all smiles again, as if nothing had been said. In fact, he is full of questions, quizzing us the whole morning long, about our Island, Facto, the red-eye, the dark wild . . . everything. Almost like he is glad to have visitors to talk to.

We have told our story so many times now I thought we might be bored with it, but when Eck's eyes light up at the news of Dad's cure or the new wild covering the Four Towers, I flush with pride.

Then as soon as we have finished our tale, I feel flat and low. We did so much. Now we are stuck out here with this strange man who doesn't want or trust us, but gives no sign of helping us leave.

In fact, he sets us to work. 'Well, seeing as you're here . . .' He grins, gripping the machete handle. He gets us sorting and peeling the pile of omnium fruit I saw when we arrived.

We toil in the afternoon sun for hours, while the animals pace in the shade. Eck never lets us out of his sight. He is still freaked by the noise he's sure he heard in the grove last night, and keeps whipping around with his knife at the smallest rustle in the trees.

'Kester!' hisses Polly, as she peels an omnium fruit the size of her head with a sharpened stone, making a much better job of it than me. 'Do you think Mr Stone is why the whale sent us here?'

'No.' My head lowered, I keep peeling, so Eck doesn't get curious over our conversation. Not that it's anything to do with him. Because whatever the whale wanted us to find on Faraway, I know he isn't it.

These stories he has told of his brothers, of Facto. They explain so much, but I can't believe they are why we are here. I don't want to be a part of Eck's story. I can't see how one terrible thing will stop another.

An accident turned into revenge and destruction.

A tale where by the end no one believes in anything any more, apart from their own story. There's no secret

271

in that, not one that could save the world, that's for sure. And we're still no nearer to discovering how this island could stop a fire in the sky or help us when we find the mouse and the Iris.

'Then what?' says Aida, echoing my thoughts. 'We better be here for a reason other than to peel watermelons stinking of sick.'

Both of them watch me, waiting for an answer. Unsure how to respond, I turn to the animals lolling under the trees.

I don't know Wildness, except that I want more fruit, says the wolf, licking his chops.

Dagger is more helpful. Kind of. *I am not apprized of the solution to the whale's question any more than you, boy, but based on your previous record it's bound to be right under your nose.*

'Well?' demands Aida.

I don't know. But I am sure that if the hill rising up behind us is what remains of the great whale's heart, then the secret of her song must lie there. We have to get back to the grove when Eck isn't watching. I lay my peeling stone on the ground and spin it slowly towards the start of the path up through the jungle.

Polly nods and, without looking up from her chore, says softly, 'We go back tonight then. I'll wake you when he is fast asleep.'

I nod and we keep on working, while a speckled green lizard frisks on the white dust in front of us, until the sun sinks beneath the whale hump and we finish for the day.

But it's not Polly who wakes me later. It is a wet nose and tongue, licking my face, a voice insistent in my head, claws ragging my arm.

I am groggy, unable make out his words at first.

Then they strike me, making me sit upright on the floor of the palm hut.

Danger! my wolf is saying. *There is badness coming.*

I look around. Everyone else is still asleep. The bulky lump of Eck, curled up on his omnium matting and wooden bed, hands clutched tight about his knife. Aida and Polly snuggled up close together to stay warm – it gets cold here at night. In a wash of moonlight, I catch a glimpse of their watch straps, dangling from their necks. Trying not to wake them, I step across to peer out of the doorway, but can see nothing apart from darkness.

An empty clearing.

I said danger is coming, repeats the wolf, tail high, sniffing the air outside. *It is not here yet, but I have the scent and sound of it.*

As quietly as I can, I wake the others. Dagger is already prowling, his ears pricked and alert. The toad is cowering by the disinfectant, bounding into Polly's arms as soon as she sits up.

'What going on?' says Aida, looking around.

Eck is awake in seconds, leaping straight to a

273

standing position, machete at the ready, an uncoiled spring. As if he wasn't even asleep to begin with. 'What's happening?'

Before I can reply, we hear a noise from the clearing. I peer out again.

The camp is no longer deserted.

It is full of men in black, shining torch beams, with their familiar boots and coils of rope, toppling and smashing the piles of omnium with their dart guns, as if they are looking for something.

'Cullers,' whispers Polly behind my ear. 'How did they even find us? Eck said no one knows where we are.'

'They followed us,' says Aida into my other ear.

I twist to stare at her. How?

In her eyes I see the answer as clear as it comes to me. I wasn't imagining the boat behind us on the Ams, the buzzing over the world's sea, the noise Eck heard in the grove and, most of all –

'Who opened the Amsguard?' she asks.

Eck wasn't being paranoid. We have led his enemies right here. Fenella must have alerted them in time to follow us. What have we done?

He pushes past, undressed, machete spinning in the starlight, roaring at the invaders. 'Leave that fruit alone, you monsters –'

They glance at him and return to smashing the fruit.

Then something smashes into Eck's head, making the same noise as if it too was just a fruit.

The tip of a metal crutch, wielded from the shadows by the hut.

Selwyn Stone's brother jerks like a puppet, and then crumples to the ground without another word.

'No!' cries Polly, rushing out to him and cradling his head in her lap. Eck's chest still rises and falls, but he gives a low, long groan. Her toad croaks in a mournful echo.

'Hello, childrens,' says a voice emerging from the shadows. 'What's this weepings and wailings? This here Mr Stone is a baddy, an island loony.'

I don't care how many crutches Captain Skuldiss has, or what they can do. Behind those long metal poles, their buttons and secret cavities and spring-loaders, the white face, the long black coat – he is still just a man.

I throw myself at him, arms wheeling, lashing out, none of it making any difference, and all the while he keeps laughing.

He doesn't even push me away.

It's the girls who pull me off him. Together forever, their watch straps rubbing against the back of my neck.

There is no stag here to save us now, but there is a wolf, who more than owes Captain Skuldiss one. *I shall tear out his legs!* he roars, leaping for the Captain's crutches, before being flung aside with a howl into the bushes at the edge of the clearing.

Dagger fastens his jaws around a metal leg with a sickening crunch, and staggers back, shattered crystal crumbling from his mouth.

Mrs Clancy-Clay's glass dentures are not so strong after all.

While Aida restrains me, as I kick and bite, it's Polly who speaks. This is not the girl who cowered from Skuldiss before. She is no longer afraid.

'Why?' she asks, her face a mess of tears and dust. 'Why did you hit him? He looks after this island. Eck doesn't even tread on twigs he's so careful. He's found this fruit you're destroying. It could feed everyone.'

'A dangerous little story-tale,' says the Captain, touching his finger to a scratch I've drawn on his neck, glancing at the blood. 'Not one my employer-man agrees with, alas.'

He slams a crutch tip into the nearest fruit, spattering the precious flesh everywhere.

'But why did you have to hurt him?' repeats Polly. 'Why do you always destroy everything good?'

Skuldiss flicks her in the head with his metal stick, and she staggers back, clutching her temple.

'Because, my little Girl Fridays, Mr Stone is trying to save us all. Not only one naughty younger brother on a desert island. Not only three runaway kid-nonks.' He rakes through the remains of the pale flesh with his crutch tip, his nose wrinkled in disgust. 'No vegetable matter can be allowed to stand in the way of mine employer-man. He has a much more cleverer and better solution to our woes than this old stink-fruit.'

'Which is?' demands Polly, still holding her bruised forehead.

'If you stop your poutings, and come with me, I will explain.'

'Never. We're not going anywhere without Eck.'

'Leave him to the fire,' says Skuldiss, and hops away from us back towards the jungle.

'What fire?' asks Polly, but the words die in her throat as one of the cullers takes a small bottle out of his bag and squirts a clear liquid over Eck's camp. Petrol fumes fill my nose and mouth. The fuel puddle trickles to the man's boots, and at the flick of a lighter, a line of blue flame shoots towards the first hut.

We recoil from the heat, black smoke curling into the air. One by one, the cullers surround us in a semicircle, sweaty stripes of camouflage paint over their faces.

'I ain't going nowhere,' declares Aida, yelling over the crackle of the burning. 'You gonna whack me with your crutch too?'

They don't reply, but the noise of rifles being cocked is enough.

'Together,' murmurs Polly under her breath.

'Yes,' I say, standing with them in the clearing. A camp that was so peaceful. Now it just stinks of horrid things: sweat, scorched fruit and fear.

I take one last look at the prone figure of Eck on the ground, before a gun butt in my back sends me sprawling forward. Picking myself up, in single file we follow the path the hobbling Captain has taken, back into the dark of the jungle, his guards marching behind us.

I try to close my ears to the sound I feared, of a fire feeding and spreading on to a whale hilltop, the whoosh of flame. Heat on our backs, black smoke in the air.

All would be lost were it not for a small speckled lizard on my shoulder, his tongue flicking in my ear. *Don't worry, amigo. Something cool's gonna happen, I totally know it.*

I totally hope he's right.

We follow the Captain through the jungle and away from the burning camp. The reek of scorched omnium is so overpowering I have to press the remains of my sleeve to my nose.

Walking all night through to dawn, we somehow summon enough energy to keep putting one foot in front of another as we trudge along a path hacked through the undergrowth by the cullers. They trample over matted rare leaves and snap off delicate branches, stripped raw like kindling. Only by holding hands as we walk are we able to stop ourselves from collapsing. If we pause to catch our breath, or wipe the sweat from our brows, a culler jabs the butt of a dart gun into our ribs.

Wolf is exhausted and overheated, padding alongside us more slowly than I've ever seen him go. Dagger traipses behind, the shattered remains of his glass jaws hanging wide open. The lizard alone doesn't mind the heat, skipping from bush to bush, urging us to *Stay cool*.

I wish we could.

The fire smoking into the air behind us isn't just swallowing up the remains of a good man and his dream. It isn't just frazzling a wonder-food into cinders, twisting a paradise of undiscovered riches into blackened roots. The flames licking at our heels are devouring something inside us as well.

My face hardens, but behind the mask I am fading fast, my mind clouded with confusion. How did these monsters get here? How are we going to escape? If I can't stop them destroying a good person and such a beautiful place, how can I ever hope to save the world?

If the whale sent us here to make a point about how horrible humans can be, she's succeeded.

Skuldiss, cackling to himself, leads us out of the jungle shade into the blank light of the midday sun, along one of the tubes Eck described. A twisting, giant pipe, jutting out of the burning hump, scattered with a fringe of straggling plants along the top. Down each smooth side there is a sheer drop into an oozing swamp.

'Watch your step!' sings out Skuldiss as he pegs ahead.

We exchange glances, eyeing the neck-breaking fall into the mud, measuring our steps with extra care.

The lizard skitters along the pipe at breakneck speed, apparently oblivious to the danger. *Stay cool, stay real cool. No sweat . . . hang loose, guys.*

But the poor toad is beginning to shrivel in the blistering sunlight. Polly tries to keep him in her shadow while I concentrate on not falling over the sides, holding my arms out for balance.

One step at a time.

With a smouldering crash, a burning tree from the jungle lands smack on top of the pipe. The whole structure shudders. Polly screams as the culler behind her stumbles and slips. With half a shout, he disappears over the side of the tube and into the swamp.

It swallows him up, and his helmet bubbles to the top before being sucked deep in again.

'Ah well,' says Captain Skuldiss, stopping to peer into the bog for a moment. 'These things happen. Very sad. Quick march!'

I hate him. I hate him. I HATE HIM.

'Really hope it you next time,' mutters Aida under her breath.

'I heard that, girlie!' he says, without turning round.

But there won't be a next time, as we make it to the end of the pipe at last, helping each other to swing off the hollow rim, clutching at creepers. Skuldiss jumps, using his flexible crutches as suspension springs to break his fall.

He gathers himself together, smoothing his hair, waiting for us. He is filthier than I have ever seen him, his white face smeared with soot and blood.

'Wow,' says Polly.

It's not at the Captain's blackened face though. It's at what we can spy ahead of us, following the crooked creek that burbles out from the pipe behind us. The stream flowing down from the burning hill that, despite the fire and smoke, is sparkling clear. Immediately the toad leaps straight in from Polly's arms, giving a sigh of relief as he soaks himself.

The brook threads a glittering line through dry scrub and thorny bushes towards a lagoon. A pool of a thousand different blues, mauves and greens, stretching out in a sandy shallow. It is separated from the sea beyond by a ramp of what looks like honeycomb, bleached skeleton white. The ocean floods in through the far end, between the honeycomb and a knot of trees, their roots tangling in the water.

But that's not the Wow thing.

The Wow thing is floating on top of the lagoon.

A seaplane.

Painted propeller to tail in Facto purple, balancing on two curved floats. Waffles of heat rise off the engine, sun flaring on the windscreen.

'So that how they got here,' says Aida, shielding her face from the glare.

'Yes, indeedy, Miss Clever-Clogs,' says the Captain, turning to face us, his plane wobbling behind him. 'You really did for poor Councillor Clancy-Clay. Luckily she managed to tell us your plans before she went quite doolally. That toxin was most effective. Almost like you gave her a taste of her own medicine.' He glowers at the toad, who glowers right back. 'And then, what a job you made for us! I mean, opening the Amsguard was no problemo, but that storm was something else.'

The air is thick with floating sparks and ash as Faraway burns all around.

'Praise the skies for sophisticated navigational technopokery, says I.' He points a crutch at us. 'Now, chaps, tie these childrens and their menagerie together for me, pretty please.'

Before we can resist, the men uncoil the ropes from their belts and wind them tight around us. Everything moves more slowly in the open sun. We're swaying, drowsy with heat. The wolf is panting, fit to explode. Both he and Dagger look confused, no match for the thugs lashing them to us.

The only animal they don't spot is the lizard, darting into the swampy shade of the giant pipe. *Stay cool,* he calls from its shadows.

If anything I am burning up, my skin flushing red, my scalp crawling.

'Well, if we weren't together forever before, we sure are now,' says Aida, struggling at her bonds.

'That's not funny,' says Polly in a faint voice. 'Aren't you going to take us with you, Captain Skuldiss?'

'Regret to say, Miss Pollypops, no. As you can see, this here sky-boat behind me has space for one captain and his six cullers. And that a blooming squeeze, I can tell you!'

Even from here it's obvious he is telling the truth. There are just three porthole windows, and the cabin can't be more than two seats wide. Skuldiss gives a short barking laugh, mopping at his bloody brow with a handkerchief.

'Sorry. Your exciting escapade ends here. And I mean End, with a big capital E.'

He nods at a culler, who empties the last of the fuel canisters over us, shaking it until every drop has gone. It's cold and stings, choking us with petrol fumes. Wolf tries to shake himself clean but to no effect.

I know what happens now.

I saw it at the camp, what happened to the omnium fruit, to Eck, to this whole paradise. With my throat tightening, a dullness settling behind my eyes, I realize this really is the End with a capital E.

No one knows where we are, or can help us now.

My short life flashes through my mind. Imprisonment, rescue, mission and cure. My wild restored. A dark wild vanquished. It felt like we had achieved so much. But we had so much more left to do. We answered the whale's song to save the world, but this is how we end.

A tropical bonfire.

'Don't worry,' says Polly, her voice choking. 'It isn't your fault, Kidnapper.'

284

'No,' says Aida. 'It not your fault.'

I don't believe either of them.

'No. Yes,' I say. They are wrong. It is entirely my fault we are on a burning island in the middle of the world's sea, about to be incinerated by a psychopath.

I have a confession to make to you, Wildness, says the wolf, his eyes rolling at the flaming crutch. *I am the worst ever in my pack at being burned by fire and would like to be excused this game.*

I can't bring myself to reply. I can't even reach out to stroke him.

The cullers retreat into the scrubland, leaving us exposed on a small patch of cracked earth.

Skuldiss steps forward, extending his crutch one more time.

A blue gas flame flickers from the tip.

Stay cool, says the lizard from the cave behind us. Simultaneously I'm aware of another voice in my head, a deeper voice. Dagger? But he's weak with heat exhaustion, trying to nip his own tail.

'I'm sorry you can't come with us, I truly am,' says the Captain. 'But Mr Stone was most particular, he was. You finish here, otherwise you might try to stop the whole experiment.'

I blink the sweat away. WAIT.

'Experiment?' repeats Polly, understanding creeping into her eyes.

An experiment that, even as we stand here on this

shore, a mouse and a cockroach, thousands of miles away, might already have been subjected to.

'Yes, experiment – don't look so surprised. A new planet! That's where the ARC is headed. But it won't just be the planet that's new. Mr Stone has a vision for a whole new world. He has your precious Iris, thanks to that sneaky rodent, and he has the technology.'

The deep voice calls in my head again. My imagination, torturing me before death.

Aida grunts with laughter. 'So this the bit where you tell us Stone's plan just before you kill us?'

The sun is dazzling my eyes, making spots appear.

Black spots, moving in the bushes.

'No, my dear,' says Captain Skuldiss, the man who kills animals and people for a job.

He smiles his biggest smile, and I realize for the first time, he doesn't do this because he's ordered to, or because he believes in anything. He just enjoys it.

'This is the bit, the long-awaited bit, where I fry you to a crisp.'

No more waiting. He jabs forward with the flaming crutch.

We rear back –

Shuffling, shrinking, Skuldiss jabbing, cullers laughing. So near, next time, the flame will catch –

Black spots in the bushes again.

The deep voice in my head, hissing and rumbling.

I wonder if that is Death I now see and hear. Death

in the bushes, waiting for us. And I stop stumbling back. If Death is what waits for us in the bushes, we are not facing it alone. The Captain comes too. So I tug forwards, towards the flames.

'You crazy?' yells Aida. She has to trust me.

'Stay still, damn you!' hisses Skuldiss, waving the crutch in shock, as I lunge at him.

Death in the Bushes hisses back.

One more step.

I thrust at Skuldiss, who turns, to see Death in the Bushes stomp out from behind the thorns. Two Deaths in the Bushes.

Each Death has a flickering tongue, tree-trunk legs and a sweeping tail. Each Death grabs a metal pole between dripping jaws –

Captain Skuldiss screams. He tries to pull away.

Two Deaths pull harder. It's like ripping a twig in half.

And the Captain falls over in opposite directions at once, the flaming crutch left smouldering on the ground. He looks at me one last time, an eye rolling up, and says the strangest thing.

'Not again.'

With that, the two halves of Captain Skuldiss are dragged into the bushes. There are roars and screams. There are crunches and rips.

Even the cullers don't know where to look.

Just as we think it can't go on any longer, there is finally stillness by the lagoon again.

I look again at the little lizard, with his hooded eyes and mottled colouring, a mix of luminous and dark greens. A dark green which could appear black in some lights.

Are you actually a lizard? I ask him.

Sure. I just grow into a much bigger one.

'Whoa. Dragons!' says Aida.

That is, it has to be said, pretty cool. *There's only a couple of things that aren't very cool,* I say to our friend.

What's that?

The men with guns heading in our direction right now. And the flaming crutch still on the ground.

Oh, says the lizard-dragon. *That isn't cool.*

The men surrounding us have overcome whatever shock they felt at their boss's sudden end. They move in through the undergrowth, a tightening noose of helmets, boots and guns.

Aida and Polly drag us back towards one of the thorny bushes, a shuffling sheaf of feet, and start rubbing the rope against the spikes.

Out of the corner of my eye, I see the flaming crutch set fire to the dry grass it fell in. A line of fire rips up and zips towards us.

'Kidnapper!' says Polly. 'Now might be a really good time for you to call for help.'

The lizard dives for cover as a culler shoots a dart towards him.

I'm not sure what's approaching more quickly, the men or the flame.

Polly is frantic. 'I don't mean to pressurize you, but there aren't any other people here for us to ask. There are only animals. Aida and I have nearly undone the rope, but you have to do something!'

'Hurry!' grunts Aida.

There is only one word I can think of in situations like these.

HELP! I scream as loud as possible.

The two dragons of death reappear from the bushes, their saliva dripping red, tongues darting in the air. Their gaze flickers over us as they lick their lips.

I hope it's not all humans they tear in two.

Dad! That was, like, totally AWESOME! squeaks their son behind me.

You too, junior, says the dragon of death on the left. Then he twitches towards me. *It was pretty cool, wasn't it, fella?*

Yes, I say, trying to stay calm. *But what about the FIRE?*

No sweat, says the lizard's dragon of death mother. She moves fast for something the size of a sofa. Her feet are covered in scales, with finger-like talons. She stamps on the fire, puffs of dust rising up as she puts it out.

For a moment, as the last tongue of flame flares and falls, it looks as if she herself is breathing fire.

I can do that! says the wolf, and promptly sets his tail alight. He chases it to try and put it out, without any success.

The cullers' darts rain down on the lizard's hides but bounce off. Now the men are drawing knives, and the dragons are hissing and opening their mouths, all pink gums and bloodied teeth, but the animal killers aren't scared. They jab the butts of their guns at the lizards, pushing them back.

Which is a perfect time for an eagle and a flock of pigeons to descend from the sky, calling out, *Kester Jaynes! We couldn't find you, we were so worried.*

A white bird lands on my head, saying, *I was worried we were going to find you.*

Then the men don't know where to aim their guns: Us, or the dragons snapping at their boots, or the screeching golden eagle pecking at their eyes, tearing their skin . . .

They turn and run, back towards the jungle.

The jungle that is on fire.

Polly looks after them. 'But . . . they'll burn to death in there.'

'Can't they swim?' says Aida. 'They can jump in the sea.' Then with a triumphant flick, she severs the rope on the thorns.

We're still both staring at her.

'Why you giving me that look! I said they can jump in the sea. The fire won't go there. Besides, they started it. Now, are you just going to stand there, or do you want to burn to death as well?'

The fire engulfing the island now crashes down the hillside towards us, roaring louder than any dragon, obliterating all in its path. A demon erupting from the ground, ripping up the green to reveal the molten lava deep underneath.

There isn't time to stand and gawp.

We stampede through the thorny bushes towards the lagoon, not caring if we get ripped and torn, the animals flinging themselves into the water to cool off, the wolf's smouldering tail hissing as he splashes in. The toad has never looked more relieved.

Then something makes me stop and stand at the edge.

The two dragons and their lizard son are watching us, a hazy wall of orange and black crackling behind them.

What are you waiting for? I call. *We can fit you in the plane, come on!*

But they don't budge.

Behind me I can hear Polly and Aida opening the doors, splashing and scrabbling as they haul the animals in.

The lizards stare at me. I wave my hands at them.

Hurry!

The dragon father flicks his tongue. *This island is our home. We have lived here all our life. As did our ancestors. We do not want to move anywhere else.*

But it's burning . . . You will have nowhere to go.

We have burrows, says the mother. *This is our home.*

A hole in the ground won't be much defence against this inferno.

Not even your son? I could rescue him, I could . . .

The words die in my head before they are out.

That wouldn't be cool, says the little lizard. *I'm staying with Mom and Dad.*

It is getting hard to see them now, trails of smoke wafting over their crested heads. Someone has found a key and started an engine, a propeller whipping up waves on the lagoon.

'We not gonna wait for you!' calls Aida, hanging out of the cockpit.

Goodbye then, I say to the dragon family. *Thank you.*

It's cool, no sweat, says the little lizard.

I'm about to turn away when one last thought occurs to me.

There was a great-fish that used to swim in the wet around here. She sang a song.

We know of her, says the father dragon.

She's the one that sent us here. She said we would save the world with what we discovered on this island, but whatever she meant, I don't think we found it.

Oh, I think you did. I think you very much did, the giant lizard replies. And with his son on his back he turns his lumbering body away from us, making for the one patch of scrubland not yet ablaze.

The little lizard waves to me as they stomp off into the thorns. *And remember, stay cool!* he squeaks.

Then, with a last swish of a tail in the dust, they are gone. In their place are clouds of black smoke. Clouds that are getting closer and closer.

'Come *on!*' calls Polly from the seaplane.

I turn and run towards the lagoon, feeling the heat of the flames on my back, plastering the remains of my shirt against my skin, hot and sticky. It is so powerful it feels like the island is one large rocket engine, firing on all thrusters directly at us.

The warm water is a relief. It is crystal clear and totally empty. You would find more wildlife in a public swimming pool than in here. I twist and scrub, washing the fuel, grime and sweat away. It still has the rotten-smelling, acidic fizziness of the world's sea, like diving into a soda can.

Holding my breath, I swim across to the plane, grab the nearest float and haul myself up the cross-struts into the cabin, my friends dragging me in.

The Captain was right about one thing. It really is cramped in here. It's a tiny cockpit smelling of sun-baked leather and wet dog/wolf.

The pigeons gather on the wings and the front of the plane.

Birds, can you guide us home?

They nod and begin sweeping off into the sky.

Wait! We need to learn how to fly this thing.

Yes, wait. This thing needs to learn how to fly, says the white pigeon, tumbling off the wing into the water with a splash.

'Right,' says Polly. 'Who knows how to fly a sea-plane?'

All three of us examine the controls. There are a million dials, switches and gauges, none of which make any sense. In the middle, a large joystick.

The spinning propeller at the front of the plane is making so much noise it's hard to think straight. With a whoosh, the last dry scrub round the edge of the lagoon goes up in flames. Sparks land like fiery rain on the water and hiss.

'We need to go,' says Aida. 'Now. Before we go up like the jungle.'

I don't understand. We're surrounded by water.

'Fuel, dummy,' says Aida. 'Why those men had petrol cans. For the tank beneath us. Just one stray spark and . . .'

Can't you just tell this giant metal bird to start flapping its wings, Wildness? says the wolf, sprawled over the passenger seats.

It's not that simple.

Panicking, Aida grabs the joystick and jerks it towards her.

Immediately the plane tips back and begins speeding towards the end of the lagoon, water foaming up from the raised floats.

'Now what?' she says, looking not wholly in control of the situation.

'Maybe relax it a little?' says Polly.

Aida releases her grip on the stick. The nose of the plane now drops back towards the water, and we start to spin around, so we are facing the burning forest. On Polly's shoulder the toad gulps with alarm.

'OK, bad idea,' says Polly.

We are just drifting now.

Aida is frantic. 'I don't know how to turn it around again.'

Something bumps the bottom of the plane. I press my face against the window and catch a flash of grey dorsal fin leaping in and out of the lagoon.

I would advise your friends, says Alpha, *that to get maximum airflow over the wings and therefore achieve the lift required for take-off, the throttle must be fully extended.*

What does that even mean? Where is the throttle?

The throttle is operated via a foot pedal beneath the control yoke, says Beta.

I point to it, and Polly slams her foot down. The plane begins to really accelerate now, only heading straight for the coral wall.

But maybe you should be facing in the right direction first? suggests Alpha. Then they are at the rear of the plane, nosing the pontoons as we bump along until we are once again facing the gap between the trees and the reef.

A gap big enough for the plane's nose but not the wings.

Keep pulling the stick and pressing the pedal! urge the dolphins.

Gamma makes the noise of an aeroplane seat-belt sign.

Then Aida is pulling the yoke and Polly is pressing on the pedal with both feet, and I'm calling to the dolphins –

The watery spray flies off as the plane lifts into the air, the blue of the lagoon falling away behind us.

I watch out of the window as the propellers whine, the lagoon dwindling into a pond and then a puddle. There are three small snouts just visible in the water below. The rest of the island is covered in burning trees, small explosions and plumes of smoke. On the other side, six tiny black figures run down a beach towards the shoreline. There is no sign of the lizards, any omnium fruit or Eck.

There is only the smouldering outline of a giant whale's heart, which crumbles into the ocean as we set our course for home.

Except that isn't quite all.

For as I stare out of the window, watching the paradise of the giant whale's heart burn black clouds in the middle of the sea, something else happens.

Something unexpected.

First, the sea around the island begins to bubble. And I mean really bubble. The little plops and belches we saw as we travelled across the ocean, the fizzing soda water I found myself swimming in at the seaweed forest and in the lagoon, starts to froth.

It foams and erupts in white fountains, like someone is pointing a hose up from the bottom of the ocean. The gaseous fountains start to leap up in the air, spitting out balls of grey cloud. The clouds shoot into the sky, and then –

Something *terrible*, something I never thought possible.

This is what the whale must have seen, the thing that will consume us all.

A thing that burned and dazzled in the sky like the surface of the sun itself . . . and scared me more than anything I have ever seen.

It also scares me more than anything.

The sea is catching fire.

The water full of gas bubbles, expelling grey clouds into the air – catches a spark from the burning jungle, and what was one island inferno turns – with a mighty, apocalyptic whoosh – into the whole ocean on fire, flames ripping across the sky and sea in all directions.

A sky of flames.

The white pigeon wasn't delusional. He did see clouds of fire.

Clouds of fire that flash, lighting up the inside of the plane and making it rock. And with it my heart, as we lurch to one side. The gas may have come up from the sea, but the fire was started by Skuldiss. Without us, he would never even have been on the island. We led him there.

I started the terrible thing. It's my fault. And I still have no idea how to stop it.

'Whatever makes this plane go faster, we need to press it,' says Polly.

Aida puts her foot down. For a while no one speaks, as we listen to the screeching whine of the propeller. The golden, electric light of the fire-clouds floods the cabin as they chase after us, their bangs and cracks filling the sky.

With one last surge of acceleration, the plane jerks ahead and the fire-clouds recede behind us.

But they will spread.

Where there is sea, there is gas. And the sea is everywhere.

The fire in the sky is coming. We have outrun it for now, but how can we stop it?

Aida has the stick, moving it when the birds call out to me or head off in a different direction. Polly studies the various dials and controls, trying to work out their purpose.

Altitude – we are very high.

Fuel – some, but running out fast.

Temperature – too hot, but what can we do?

'You see this one here with the flat line?'

'Yes.'

'It tilts if Aida moves the plane. I think it's important to keep it as level as you can.'

Aida nods but her eyes never leave the sky ahead. I am just glad to be up here, flying above pillows of white clouds, rather than swallowed up by black ones, or surfing the peaks and troughs of the world's sea. If I press my face against the window, I can see the water below. Here and there a giant bloated shadow hovers below the surface, a bloom of seaweed like an ink stain spreading across the world. Occasionally I glimpse a flash of light, which could be nothing, or a giant jellyfish, or another cloud of gas exploding.

I shiver and gingerly touch the skin around my eyes, which is still swollen and sore. The faint reflection in the plane porthole does not bode well. I look half asleep because my eyelids are so inflamed. I glance at the tattered and singed ribbons of my clothes, my bruised and scratched legs.

The girls are in a similar state, minus the puffy eyes.

Either way, we don't look like the world's best rescue party. Or the world's only rescue party, as far as I'm aware. As we power through sky and over sea, I try to make sense of things.

A whale told me the end of the world was coming, that we had to find an island called Faraway to stop it.

I listened to her, and did what she said.

Selwyn Stone thinks the world is ending but wants to create a creepy new world in space instead, and sent people to kill us. Dad didn't want me to leave again. Polly's parents didn't want her to go. Even the stag wasn't sure.

But we went regardless, Polly, Aida and me. And our animal friends. We survived a giant jellyfish attack, escaped a seaweed forest and almost drowned in a storm.

We found Faraway, met Eck and tasted his omnium fruit. We discovered the true story of Facto. With the help of a dragon family we managed to escape with our lives.

What have we got to show for it? I scan the tiny cabin

that vibrates with engine noise, now and then making a sickening bump as we hit rough air.

'Just hold it steady!' says Polly.

'I'm trying!' snaps Aida.

We still have to find the mouse and the Iris, and now I'm not sure what, if anything, we have brought back that can help. Nothing that could save the world, that's for sure.

A wolf with a singed tail. A mute poisonous toad. A dog whose glass jaws are smashed. One girl with a bruise on her forehead and another who appears to have at least picked up basic seaplane-flying skills.

And a trail of something leaking out of her pocket on to the floor.

I lean forward and touch it with my finger.

Dust. Luminous green dust.

Green omnium-palm pollen.

I put my hand inside Aida's pocket.

Which, it turns out, you should never do to someone flying a seaplane for the very first time.

Aida jerks and the plane banks hard to the left, sending us and the animals falling over one another, as if we've lost gravity. Wolf, wet and shaggy, presses me against the window; Polly grunts, winded against the side of the cockpit.

Pulling as if her life depends on it – *because* her life depends on it – Aida drags the plane back on course, the propeller and engine screaming at each other.

The horizon becomes level again.

We pick ourselves up off the floor.

Aida doesn't speak. Her jaw is still set, staring at the skyline, ignoring the sweat beading on her forehead, the whiteness of her knuckles as she grips the yoke.

Then she proper goes for it. (Which I know, because she isn't yelling. Yelling is what Aida does when she's in a good mood, what she does when she likes you.)

She's like a wolf, I say to the wolf.

How so, Wildness?

Because you growl when you're messing around. It's when a wolf goes silent that you need to be worried.

He growls in approval.

Aida is very quiet and level, like the plane. 'I reckon you trying to kill us.'

I raise my hand –

'Don't even begin to interrupt me. You drag us to this middle-of-nowhere island, nearly drowning us all on the way. When we arrive we get sprayed by a madman in war paint, then that crutch-man tries to burn us alive, now you send this plane into a nosedive. You don't want to save this world, you don't believe you can save this world. So you going to kill us way before the end gets here.'

I can see her looking at me in the reflection of the windshield.

'No.'

'You think we the same as you. We're not. I can be crazy, but that don't make me crazy. Look at this. Right now I'm flying a plane, which I never done before, and it scaring the world outta me. I'm thirteen. I want to be at home. So you had better have a good answer. Why did we do this? Why?'

I wish I knew.

'Tell me or I stop flying the plane. Right now.'

She begins to lift her hands from the stick, when Polly picks something off up the floor. The thing that fell out of Aida's pocket when the plane rolled.

Not the pile of loose change. Or the culler's dart pistol, the last remaining fronds of hulse or the gold bracelet. Aida keeps lots of things in her pockets, most of them not hers.

Including the thing Polly is holding.

Covered in luminous green dust, a twisting coil of black rubber, the size of Polly's palm. Tiny blue leaves sprout from one end.

'I have a feeling it was this,' she says.

A tiny twig from an omnium palm.

'You took a cutting from an unknown species in a foreign island. They might not let us back into the country.'

Aida nearly sends the plane into another nosedive. 'No! You right. Because otherwise they gonna love three kids and half a zoo in a stolen seaplane belonging to some dead cullers!'

Aida and Polly no longer get on as well as they used to.

'Don't give me no grief over stealing things. Everything

I steal help us. We steal the boat together. The umbrellas. The suncream.'

'Why do you always imagine I'm getting at you when I'm not?' says Polly. 'But you did take a cutting without asking Eck.'

'He dead!' says Aida. 'He not going to mind. The whole island is gone. At least I save something!'

Polly sighs. 'Which is what I was trying to say. I wonder if this is what we were meant to bring back from Faraway.'

'Why? What good a piece of fruit against a cloud of fire? But I know this much – everyone's gonna want to eat some of this. Even that little mouse when we find her. *Everyone.*'

'It has to have some other use though, don't you think? Why did you take it in the first place?'

Aida looks embarrassed. 'I can't help it. After everything he said I thought, I'm having me some of that. To eat. Or to ransom to Selwyn. Or maybe the Professor do something with it. Who knows why.'

'Yes,' I say. Not because I know why, not exactly. But I'm beginning to.

And I point to the rear of the cabin.

To the patch of damp on the floor between the passenger seats where the wolf was lying before I almost made Aida crash the plane. A patch of damp carpet, the size of a wolf, in the aisle of a seaplane.

The patch of damp which the green dust found.

Where several curls of black palm, identical to the one in Polly's hand, are beginning to open up and extend baby-blue leaves.

The omnium fruit is growing in the back of our plane.

'I can't look at no overgrown plant now. Don't blame me. I got a plane to fly!'

With that, Aida dismisses the jungle forming in the rear of the cabin, while Polly edges forward to inspect the shoots unfurling before our eyes. There are even root threads frayed out across the carpet, searching for something to bury themselves in. The toad licks one suspiciously.

They began growing before this machine had left the water, says Dagger.

Why didn't you say so?

Must I always point it out to you when nature is remarkable? You have eyes in your head, he replies.

Polly turns the tender blue leaves over, examining them. 'I've heard of bamboos that can grow super-quick, but never a palm. The omnium must have a similar structure. Look.'

Peering over her head, I can see that the rubbery stem is segmented. Like bamboo, a new cylinder is already pushing its way through the top section. The texture is tissue-thin, like a plastic sheet.

'Eck was right. It doesn't even need soil. Just moisture. I've never seen that. You can grow orchids in water, but they need rocks too.'

I rest my hand on her shoulder to get a closer look, and she grazes mine with hers. Automatically I snatch my hand away, hoping that neither she or Aida notices what colour I've gone.

They don't. Polly is transfixed by the writhing omnium, studying it from every angle, while Aida doesn't dare take her eyes off the horizon.

That leaves me with my thoughts, and the animals. For the next hour or so, I press my face against a porthole, staring at the clouds floating beneath us. It's impossible to know where we are or how far it is to the Island. We have to hope that the pigeons' instinct for finding home is as strong as it was. Even with clouds of fire following us.

I strain my head to see what lies behind the plane, and catch a faint golden glow.

The fire in the sky is coming.

I can smell it, says Dagger, breaking my daydream.

Smell what?

309

The terrible thing is coming. The end approaches.

The end of what?

The end of all things, says the wolf. *I can smell it too. The stag was right, Wildness. There will be no escape.*

But . . . we answered the whale's song. We found the omnium. Now it's growing in the back of our plane. Doesn't that count for anything? You said yourself, Dagger, that the secret she sent us to discover might be right under our nose.

It might be, he snorts. *That still does not change the fact. The end of all things is coming.*

Suddenly I don't want to listen to the animals any more. I don't want to be in this plane with them, or the freakish plant twining itself around my calf, or my friends squabbling over the controls. I just want to be anywhere else.

Even outside, perhaps, floating above the clouds with my birds . . .

Wait. Where are the birds?

The clouds have gone too, replaced by thick grey fog, streaming past the windows and enveloping the plane. In the few minutes I turned away from the window to talk to my beasts, the eagle, pigeons – and in fact the whole sky – seem to have disappeared.

'Hey! Where did everybody go?' says Aida, squinting through the darkening windscreen.

'There must be some lights somewhere,' says Polly,

flicking every switch on the flight deck until fierce red beacons flash from the wingtips and a powerful headlight beams from the nose of the plane.

But the fog is so dense even they keep vanishing.

The air is woolly and thick, drawing us in. Our plane begins to judder, then the judders become bumps, as if we're flying over potholes in the sky. The potholes turn into ditches and, despite Aida's best efforts, we begin to pitch through the clouds.

Something starts banging on the bottom of the plane.

'It only air,' says Aida.

Then why does that air sound as if it's trying to punch through the fuselage?

Wolf is cowering behind a seat with the toad. *Wildness, I am the best in my pack at floating in the wet and flying in the air, you must agree. But deep down I prefer the ground.*

Me too, I say as everything begins to shudder and bounce.

'I don't know where we're going!' yells Aida, over the noise of every rivet buzzing fit to pop right out of its socket.

Closing my eyes, fingers in my ears to try and shut the distractions out, I call for the birds. *Can you hear me? Where are you?*

There's a muffled reply.

I try again. *Speak louder! I can't hear you!*

I hear the muffled call again. It sounds like the eagle,

311

and I think he's saying, *Watch out. There's white rain ahead.*

There's a squeakier reply after him. *Watch out! There's no ahead.*

Before I can ask the white pigeon where they are, a splodge of white stuff hits the screen, like one of the birds decided to start a snowball fight. Then another, and another, till the whole windshield is frosted up.

Then the same happens to the wings, icy winds swirling over them, building up small drifts either side of us. Polly pushes every button she can find till wipers start dragging across the glass, but they can't cope, and anyhow, there is nothing to see but more whiteness.

Aida is trying to hold the plane steady, but it gets harder and harder.

Birds, I call, *you have to guide us.*

The eagle replies again, his voice fainter than before. All the same, I think he is calling from our left, so I tap Aida on her left shoulder and she tilts the controls accordingly.

I strain to hear what he says, but his words are jumbled and lost in the swirling winds of the snowstorm.

Boy, says Dagger, nipping with his jagged jaws at my ankle, *look at this.*

Not now, dog. I need to concentrate on the birds.

I know. But you must see this.

I shake him off, straining to see over Aida's head into the tunnel of white we are speeding through. A tunnel that seems to be getting narrower and darker as the pigeons' cries fade further away.

The dog is right, Wildness, says the wolf.

What?! I say, whipping round.

And then I see exactly why Dagger is right.

In the time it has taken us to fly into the heart of a storm, the palms have grown.

I don't just mean a bit. The small thin black stalks are now tall thick trunks, curving out of the cabin carpet. And the thread-like roots have transformed into tentacles, burrowing into the fabric. Black branches and blue leaves spread out, fanned against the low ceiling. Unbelievably, the first omnium is beginning to swell into being at the tip of the biggest one. The toad looks up in alarm at the fruit of Faraway dangling over his head.

'It's so alive,' says Polly.

'Yes,' I say. The whale's intention is becoming clearer to me by the second. The omnium isn't just alive. It is *life itself.* Nothing grows that fast, nothing can double in size in such a short time, but this plant has.

The secret of the whale's song . . . The secret of creation . . .

It's in the back of our plane.

Even if every last omnium palm in the world grew to the height of the Glass Towers, I still don't know how they would stop a sky of flames. But I realize we are doing the right thing. We need to get these plants back to Premium.

Although whether we will is another question. There

is only never-ending snow in the plane's headlights. What daylight there was is fading.

'So much for clouds of fire,' snorts Aida.

Somehow I don't think it works like that. The snowy weather must just be another example of how the planet is broken, exactly as the whale described. It can be boiling hot in one place and frozen over in another, all at the same time. Not even the weather makes sense any more.

The palms continue to expand behind us. They fill the whole rear of the plane, the branches pressing up against the windows, forcing Wolf, the toad and Dagger up to the front with the three of us.

'You know something?' says Aida, grimacing at the screen, hunched over the joystick, 'I don't care how alive these trees are. You need to stop them growing, or lose some, or we not gonna stay up in the air for very long.'

I shake my head. The omnium is unstoppable.

These plants are the true force of nature, boy, says Dagger. *Do you see their power?*

I do. All too well. Because the trees, swelling and extending before our very eyes, are unbalancing us.

The tail begins to dip.

'Try making it go faster,' suggests Polly.

We press our feet on the accelerator pedal, and the engine screams, but the plane is tipping vertically, nose rising, till we are all clinging on to Aida's seat. I grab Wolf by the scruff of the neck and Polly tries to hold

Dagger's massive weight, to stop them sliding back into the writhing mass of omnium.

'I don't know what to do!' shouts Aida.

Turns out she doesn't need to.

With a slow cracking hiss, an omnium branch punctures the rear window of the seaplane. Freezing air rushes into the cabin, jerking the plane down.

The pressure pulls the palm tight against the crack in the glass, trying to suck the whole plant out. Everything loose in the plane – bags, clothes, the remains of the cullers' kit – flies towards the hole.

The engine hums and splutters and stops. Aida waggles the joystick, slamming her feet on the pedal. 'It not doing anything. It stalled.'

Then, as if our strings had been cut –

Our seaplane starts to plummet. I mean straight down. You know that noise in films, that zooming drone noise?

That really happens.

We're no longer in control. Aida is unbuckling herself, and we're clinging together.

'I don't want to die, Kidnapper,' says Polly.

'No.' I don't either.

'We gonna die,' says Aida.

Together forever. Whatever the weather.

We're falling, spiralling –

Then the birds are calling, warning me about something else –

315

And I see, looming out of the swirling snow, capped in ice, the towers of the Amsguard.

Home. Just not quite the way I expected.

There is so much I want to say to everyone in this plane. I wish I could. The words bubble in my throat. I try to let them fizz from my fingers –

The River Ams racing up towards us in the moonlight.

'Lucky this a seaplane,' says Aida.

Except this river is very still, very flat – and very frozen.

I close my eyes. I've read about what happens when planes crash-land. I learnt about gravity, speed and mass. We brace ourselves, as with a roar, a crash and a jolt –

The omnium branches explode out of the back windows, creating a twisting, giant canopy of leaves, interlocking together.

A palm parachute.

We slow down. Not much. But enough. The pontoons hit the ice with a smash and shear off, bouncing to the sides.

On its belly, screeching against the solid mirror of frozen water, glass-like fragments churning into the air, the plane slides along the river. We glide past the docks, the Glass Towers, the *Glasscutter* and towards the remains of the bridge, the palm canopy ballooning behind us.

The plane passes under the bridge –

The wings snap off –

Everyone yells –

Finally, spinning like a needle in a compass, we slither and scrape to a halt. Sparks fly from exposed wiring, and every metal joint in the plane is screaming at once. And in the middle of a wintry night, the whole cockpit is infused with light. Golden light, radiating down on us, blinding and warming us.

At first, I worry the terrible clouds of fire have got here first, but in fact the light is from a thousand small porthole windows, set in a steel-domed space rocket, which has now extended its full height from between the four towers, the tallest structure in the city.

The light of a humming, gleaming Advanced Relocation Craft.

PART 6:
THE
WILD
BEYOND

In the crushed cabin of the Facto seaplane, leaves and branches of the omnium are spreading over us, filtering the light through a canopy of blue. We are a ball of people coiled up tight, protected by a wolf and a dog either side. A toad hops on top of us, his tongue shooting out and licking the underside of a palm.

'Kidnapper, are we home yet?' murmurs Polly, pushing a branch of omnium off her face.

Home.

We have been away so long – I can't count how many days and nights; I lost track at sea. Who knows whether 'home' is even what we can still call this place, and how much longer it will be here?

Aida stirs, picking flakes of snow and glass from her hair. There is blood trickling down her face, which I wipe gently with the half a sleeve I have left.

'Don't touch me,' she murmurs. Then – 'You good?'

I just manage a 'Yes,' although good isn't quite the word I'd choose.

'I'm not,' says Aida. She shows us her left arm, the one that was gripping the controls. Stained with blood, it is not pointing in the direction it should. 'Real sore,' she says. 'My chest hurts too. Everything hurts so bad.'

Aida.

I can't believe it for a moment. I mean, I can see her wounds, the fear in her eyes, her dark skin waxing pale in the glow of the ARC. But Aida doesn't get hurt, she's the tough one, the brave one, who always knows how to fix stuff.

I don't know if she can fix this.

'If you can walk, we need to get going,' says Polly. 'Fast.'

She points to the sparks showering from the smashed control deck and exposed wiring sagging from the ripped seams of the plane's gutted interior. 'Those and the rest of our fuel are not a good combo.'

I give the door a heavy kick. It's jammed. I try again. At my command Dagger throws his weight at it, followed by my wolf. Together we bust it open, sprawling on to the iced-over river. Fighting my way back in through the ever-spreading palm jungle, Polly and I help Aida up and drag her free of the wreckage.

The toad is the last to follow, bounding out of the crumpled cabin in a single hop. He skids on the ice towards where we lie heaped up in the shadow of the riverbank.

He is just in time, as, with a guttural roar, the plane explodes in a tower of fire, flames leaping up as if they want to touch the moon. The bonfire of metal and leather and fuel and palm spits dark red cinders at us for a few moments, before, with an almighty crack, the ice splits apart. The molten ball of struts and panels – which was speeding through the sky only minutes ago – sinks into the jagged hole of black water, the fiery jets hissing into clouds of steam.

Aida lies slumped between us, shivering, in the glow of the dying inferno. Just looking at her mangled arm makes me nauseous. She murmurs something.

'What's that?' says Polly, mesmerized by the collapsing fire.

'Palm,' says Aida, louder this time.

The omnium! I start forward, but Polly grabs me. 'It's too late, you'll freeze to death in there.'

We brought a precious cargo all this way, only for it to be incinerated on arrival.

My head is in my hands. I want to cry.

Why do you not trust in nature? says Dagger next to me.

Because we will always be one step ahead, I say. *Even when we don't mean to, we destroy everything.*

323

Eck was right.

The blackness is coming, my wolf says, staring across the mirrored plain.

He's right. The final dream of the animals is playing out before our very eyes.

Watch, says the dog.

At first, there's nothing to see. A scorched hole in the ice, the rim fractured with zigzag cracks, radiating out like a spider's web. Mists of steam rise from within, obscuring our view.

Then – it's impossible, it cannot be.

'Oh, goodness,' breathes Polly.

As the steam drifts into the air, the last few oily jets of flame dying away, something emerges from the water.

A single long and rubbery shoot.

Blackened and burnt, but still living.

A tendril of palm that clamps on to the side of the ice and inches across it.

I could stay and watch this for the rest of eternity. A plant hauling itself out of a sunken, burning plane wreck through a hole in a frozen-over river. I have never seen anything more determined to live.

'Kidnapper – we need to go. Now.'

Polly points. Cullers are clattering down the other bank, tramping across the ice, flashing their torches and calling into radios.

Aida doesn't moan or complain as we hoist her upright again and move up the bank, the toad hopping and slithering after us. From the shouts on the river, I can tell we've been spotted.

Boy, says Dagger, not following, *you take the girl. Wolf and I will despatch these murderers.*

We will? says the wolf, with a catch to his voice.

Are you a brave full-grown wolf or not? demands the dog.

Yes, but the blackness is coming. What can we do?

We can do everything within our power to resist until the final moment. Right?

Right, says the wolf, and I have never believed him less in my life. I pause and turn back to them. His amber eyes have gone glassy in the glare of the light from the ARC. He flattens his ears and drops his tail.

Don't do anything stupid now, will you? I say to my old friend. *Hold them off, scare them, but don't get shot . . .*

I'll try not to, he mumbles.

I stretch my hand out to him across the rocky slope –

He sniffs it in the air, and then turns, bounding after Dagger, howling and roaring at the cullers careering over the ice.

I don't want to watch. I can't bear to.

Everything good seems to be ENDING and I hate it.

Polly and I concentrate on guiding Aida along the bank, her injured arm hanging at a strange angle. Blood drips from the end of her sleeve like a leaking pipe. She is passing in and out of consciousness, her head lolling on her chest. We try to ignore the shouts and growls from below as we squeeze through the gaps in the railings at the top on to a road.

'Look,' says Polly.

Except it's not what we can see. It's what we can't see.

Something in Premium has changed. The snow that fell before we left is still here, piled in drifts, blurring the line between tarmac and kerb, fringing the tops of towers.

But nothing else is. Or rather, no one else is.

There are no people. The world's most crowded city has become the world's emptiest one. There are footsteps and tyre tracks in the snow, half covered by a recent fall, like a ghost trail. Snow makes everything quieter . . . in this case, dead quiet.

'Hello?' calls out Polly, and the only reply is a pile of snow slumping off the end of a gutter to the ground. There are no people in the streets, no lights in the houses, no cars or trucks on the roads.

Hello? I call in my animal voice, but I see no sign of the wild we left behind either. All we can hear are the faint sounds of an eagle's cry and a wolf's howl from the river.

The toad sits shivering between Polly's feet. He gives a forlorn croak to the empty street. Aida sags deeper between us.

'Hold her,' says Polly. I do my best, my own injured arm still stiff and sore. She kneels on the pavement and with her bare hands chips away at a frozen puddle. As the ice splinters, she gathers up the shards and rips another shred off her tattered top.

She'll freeze.

'It doesn't matter,' she mutters, as if she can hear me. Placing the ice fragments in the fabric, she wraps it into a tight bundle and presses it against Aida's arm. She watches her for a moment, holding the ice pack in place.

'It might soothe the swelling, but we need to get her proper help.'

I nod.

'You know where?'

'Yes.'

The only possible place where all the people could have gone. The colossal spacecraft I was hoping to stop people going anywhere near. It rises above the flats and towers like a god, beaming out golden light from a million windows.

Polly grimaces as I point.

She must know we have no choice. We look back across the river, to the unlit Glass Towers. Even the top of the Waste Mountain is just visible above the buildings on the other side. All of them lightless and lifeless. The city I was born in is white and dead. Aida grows heavier and heavier between us, and the night gets colder.

I look at the dazzling rays of the ARC ahead. What choice awaits us there? If we stay in Premium, the fire in the sky will come. If we board the rocket and take off for Nova, we become part of Stone's shadowy experiment.

A chill wind slices my ears, blowing splinters of snow into my eyes as we stumble together along the road. But it doesn't stop me from thinking straight.

I know this city isn't much. In fact, it's a mess.

Glass towers, ordinary homes, a broken bridge, a giant rubbish pile overlooking the lot. At the best of times it's crowded, stinking and chaotic. The storms did masses of damage. There are still piles of debris everywhere, buildings with their fronts ripped off, collapsed roofs and frozen floodwaters piercing the gloom, mirror shards in the moonlight.

But it is also my home. For six years Facto locked me away in Spectrum Hall, as a hostage for Dad, to stop him secretly developing a cure for the virus. All that time, I dreamed of coming back here. We fought so we could stay here without fear of a deadly disease. We battled a dark wild so humans and animals could live together in peace again.

This is where I grew up, where my mum lived and died.

This is where I belong – not on a tropical island or a distant planet.

And, gazing out over the deserted blue scene, a skyline of snow and ice that could melt away any moment, I realize I've seen this view before.

In my animal dream.

I stride harder and faster into the snow, which grows deeper and deeper, coming up to my knees. The toad explodes out of holes at intervals, like a mine. Aida's head lolls against my chest. She is so cold.

'Wait for me,' says Polly. 'I can't keep up.'

I don't stop. We have to hurry.

I know it's not perfect. I know we need to change things. But there's one thing we don't need to change.

Where this city is. Our world may be broken, battered and flooded, but it's still our world.

Our home. And I don't want to be left here alone.

The road leads along the river to the front of the Four Towers. What was the car park for Facto delivery vans is now one giant refugee camp. The floodlights no longer illuminate shiny bonnets and windscreens, but makeshift tents, campfires and a lot of people.

By a lot, I mean *a lot*.

The whole world is squashed in between four wire walls.

Men, women and children by the thousand, shivering and packed together, bags and bundles of clothes at their feet. We desperately scan the crowd for the faces we want to see so much. Dad. Mr and Mrs Goodacre. My Wild. But there is no sign. Instead we spy the Glass Towers citizens I saw in Fenella's lair, looking even more worn and bedraggled than before. Outsiders wrapped up in their threadbare farm clothes, and Spectrum Hall kids sheltering under a tarpaulin canopy.

Perhaps at least some of my old friends might be there, lost in the crowd. Like Big Brenda or Justine.

They must be.

Because it seems like the whole Island is here.

Cullers push their way between the throng, barking orders on megaphones. Some of them sit on high mounted chairs, like they're lifeguards, surveying the scene. Occasionally a shot is fired into the air when a fight breaks out, which seems to happen when people collect their formula rations from the back of a culler truck.

'They get such a small cup,' says Polly. 'The supplies must be really running low now.'

Perhaps there will be more food on Nova. But we have the omnium now. We need to tell people. We need to warn them that Stone has a secret experiment that Skuldiss boasted about before he died. That the ARC is not just designed to transport them to a new planet, but for something else.

Something bad. I know it.

At the front of the camp, the gates are heavily guarded, with a queue of stragglers stretching down the street, past the Maydoor Estate, waiting to get in. The reason there are so many people gathered here, waiting their turn, is plain to see. Raised above the gates, mounted on platforms throughout the crowd, hung from every fence, are ultrascreens. They show the same pictures, over and over again.

Satellite pictures of the firestorm from Faraway. Super-powerful cameras zooming in on the flames, and digital maps plotting their path towards this Island. There are close-up pictures of the burning inferno Skuldiss and his men began.

Everyone is here for one reason only. Fear.

And that's why, when a number or a name is called out by culler guards, small knots of people willingly break away from the crowd and up a ramp that leads straight into the ARC.

By the sodium glare of the floodlights, I can see them getting medical and dental checks, poked and prodded before they board. They pass through metal detectors and their luggage is X-rayed before chugging off deep on a conveyor belt into the belly of the ship.

Positioned above the entrance is a gigantic digital timer counting down, in flashing purple numbers.

$$1{:}00{:}59$$
$$1{:}00{:}58$$
$$1{:}00{:}57$$

The flashing numbers are accompanied by a smooth voice, intoning.

'T-minus one hour until launch. This is your final call to board the ARC.'

A voice I recognize from the ultrascreen in the Culdee Sack. The silky tones of Coby Cott, Facto's chief newsreader, making his final public announcement on this earth. A countdown to the ARC's ramp closing for good, and the fiery skies devouring those left behind.

We scan the crowd, desperately looking for a single animal face or tail, but I can't see so much as a whisker. I grab the fence with my free hand and rattle it, but a child with a dirty face on the other side just picks up a stone and throws it at us.

Aida is muttering and moaning. Polly feels her brow.

'Come on. There must be a doctor somewhere.'

We hobble round to the main gate, where there is a mob, pushing and screaming to get in. Passports are waved in the air, frail grannies are shoved forward looking bewildered on their sticks, tiny babies are thrust up in swaddling clothes to unfeeling cullers, anything to try and swing entry to the ARC.

'I keep telling you, we're full,' shouts the Facto official standing at the gates.

'There must be room!' yells a woman clutching her frightened child's hand. 'We'll burn to death out here.'

It seems the ARC isn't quite the perfect solution we were promised.

'I can't help you,' says the official. 'Now beat it, before I call the cullers over.'

'Excuse me, please let us through,' says Polly. 'Our friend is badly hurt – she needs medical attention.'

'Does she indeed? What about my old mum? She can barely walk!' says a large man holding an ancient crone by the crook of her arm.

'And my daughter – she's not eaten for days. Why should you go in front of her?' shrieks the woman with the child.

Then she stops and stares at Polly, peering into her eyes as if she can see something. She stands back, pressing the baby to her chest, taking us all in.

'Look,' she says, a sly smile creeping over her face. 'It's them.'

'Whaddya mean, *them*?' says the large man, looking at us properly for the first time. The realization dawns in his eyes too. 'Oh, *them*.'

'Off the ultrascreen!' cackles the crone with her hand hooked round his elbow. 'The little ones who promised us paradise!'

The woman thrusts the tiny frightened baby in our faces. 'Get *her* in then. You promised a new world for everyone.'

'But we didn't . . . I mean, we were forced to,' says Polly, taking a step back. 'We need to help our friend. She's hurt.'

'Get us in,' says the large man, pushing past the woman.

'Get us in!' shouts someone else behind him. And

then they're all shouting at us, heads inside the fenced enclosure turning to look at us too. The shouts multiply. 'In! In! Get us in!'

Aida murmurs something. I can't hear, and I hold her tight.

The crone is jabbing me in the shoulder. 'Help us, young man, help us!'

That's what I'm trying to do, just not like this –

Then the crowd is swelling round us, shoving and shouting, the official shaking his head, retreating to safety behind the closed gates. Meanwhile, we are encircled by a cold, hungry, angry, frightened mob, pushing us back, and we stumble into the darkness against the fence.

'There must be another way in,' says Polly fiercely. I wish I could believe her. Aida leans against me. She is no longer muttering, but keeps convulsing.

'No. No.' I turn her face towards me. Her eyes won't open. 'No!'

A throaty roar drowns out my thoughts.

'Hey! What you doing with her?'

The voice comes from behind the crowd. From a circle of children on electric bikes, roaring round us in front of the Four Towers' gates, spraying snow in the air, caught by their criss-crossing headlights. Electric cattle prods flash blue in the night, and the mob scatters.

'Mind yourself,' snaps the large man. 'We only want the same as everyone else.'

'Join the queue then, mate,' says the boy on the bike

335

at the front, giving him a jab with the prod, so the man jumps and yelps all at the same time.

If I wasn't so frozen and tired and worried, I would laugh.

The boy with his name on his sweatshirt. 123. Who now also has a woollen muffler wrapped around his face, so only his eyes are visible, glaring at us.

'Thanks,' mumbles Polly.

'Thanks for nothing! I warned yer, didn't I? If you didn't help 'em, I warned yer what would happen . . .'

'We've been trying to help them,' says Polly quietly.

'Yes,' I say, my teeth chattering.

'Funny way of going about it,' he says through the scarf. 'I saw you on the screens too. You mental or what?'

'It doesn't matter now, all right!' Polly is losing patience fast. 'Aida's injured – we crashed a plane. We need to get her help. Fast.'

'A plane?' says 123, incredulous.

'There isn't time to explain. Can you get us into the ARC?'

'Are you mad? Go into space with that loony and our old boss? No, thanks – we'll take our chances in Waste Mountain. And anyway, it's too late for the likes of us now. You saw what they're like.'

'But what about the clouds of fire?'

A different cloud passes over 123's face. 'Don't matter. We'll stick it out.' He revs his engine noisily but it doesn't make me believe him any more. 'Give her here.'

I clutch Aida to my chest. She's too warm. She needs a doctor. 'No.'

'She belongs with us. Not you. This is all your fault!'

I know.

'But how can you help her?' asks Polly.

He brushes some snow off the handlebars. 'We have stuff. We nicked it. Bandages, pills, drugs. She's ours. We'll take care of her.' Straddling the bike, he stretches his arms out to catch her.

The night wind whips around us.

'Are you sure you don't want to help us get on-board the ARC?' says Polly, clutching her arms and stamping to stay warm.

123 doesn't even bother to answer that, but revs his bike one more time. 'Come on,' he says. 'She one of us.'

'But we made a promise,' says Polly. 'We would do everything together. Forever.'

'Nothing lasts forever,' says the boy with the Mohican. Leaping off his bike, he grabs Aida, helped by Eric, whose hair tumbles over his face from under a bobble hat dusted with snow.

I don't try and stop them. He's right. They can help Aida now more than we can. We watch as they guide her, stumbling, barely conscious, to 123's bike. He is gentle, as if he was handling a newborn baby, propping her on the seat and draping an old fleece jacket over her shoulders. He mounts the bike and she slumps against him. Eric manoeuvres his cycle alongside, a broad hand on Aida's back, to keep her upright. 123 turns to look at us, a sliver of eyes between wool.

Then they are off, spluttering away in a cloud of snow. We watch until they become dots at the end of the road, a jumbled silhouette of hats and handlebars, their headlights beaming into the empty sky.

We're one down.

Polly touches the watch strap round her neck. 'We broke our promise.'

'Yes.'

'It was probably for the best though, don't you think? They'll look after her.'

'Yes.'

'We're not going to break *our* promise though, are we?'

'No.'

Then Polly is hugging me, weeping and shaking. 'Why is everything so horrible? Why does it feel like everything is about to end? We don't know where anyone is who can help us. We can't find anything –' and she stops, suddenly.

Letting go of me, she kneels down on the ground, in the patch of road smeared and spun free of deep snow by the Waste Mountain bikers.

'I touched something. My foot touched something.'

Rubbing away more snow by her foot with frozen blue hands, not caring, rubbing and scraping until –

I see what.

The ridged dome of a manhole cover.

'T-minus fifty minutes and thirty-nine seconds until launch,' calls out Coby Cott's voice from the loudspeakers on the fence.

At first, as Polly digs away at the frosted snow around the edge of the manhole cover, I don't get it. My deep-frozen brain, starved of food and warmth, running empty on a lack of sleep, is struggling. The wires spark without making a connection.

'Don't you see?' she says. 'You of all people must remember.'

Then, my mind spinning, I am here again. When the snow was freshly laid, not muddy and smeared. These screens were full of an exciting new planet, not burning skies. The crowds gasped in wonder around braziers, not penned in by wire fences. My wild sat in a semicircle in front of a glowing screen and tried to understand our human plans. An ultrascreen we spotted a mouse on, whom I sent a rat and a cockroach to rescue.

This is the hole the rat came out of, filthy and broken but alive.

I crouch to help Polly, scraping and pulling till our numb fingers bleed, the wind lashing our faces, until at last the heavy iron cover starts to budge.

We prise the lid off, and it falls into the snowy street with a dull thud.

I stare into the black hole, which looks like a mouth has appeared in the snow. Polly feels around and picks up a small stone, which she drops down the pipe.

We listen, and listen, but no sound comes back.

No splash or clunk. Nothing.

We glance at each other. Polly is shivering, her eyelashes fringed with a dusting of frost. The toad hops away from the edge, shaking his head.

'It's the only way in, Kidnapper,' she says, picking up her friend and keeping him warm in her arms.

I'm still not sure. We don't know what's lying in wait at the bottom.

The voice calls out again, and the giant speaking clock counts down fewer minutes and fewer seconds till the end of all things.

There is not one spot of light in the narrow cylinder. It really is rat-sized too. I'm not sure I'll fit.

You are joking, right? I say to the cockroach.

It's our only way out . . . We thought you were thinner.

A different tunnel, a long time ago. Now this one is the only way to rescue him, the mouse and possibly everyone else. I hope it is the last I go down for a while.

I help Polly slide in, holding her hand before getting one last glimpse of the world above. The waiting crowds and guards are too preoccupied with each other to notice two children slipping down a manhole in the shadows.

The pipe is as the rat described. Except that where he and the General could move with ease, we are a tight fit, our shoulders squashed against the walls. It is airless, reeking of metal and chemicals, mingled with an animal stink I don't want to think about.

My friend has her hands and feet braced against the sides like a rock climber, and I'm trying to do the same above her. It is pitch black, the only sound our panting breath, and a croak of fear from the toad perched on her head.

'You promise the rat said this was safe, Kidnapper?' Polly whispers. We don't know who or what can hear us.

I'm not sure safe was exactly the word he used, but . . . 'Yes.' My voice sounds hoarse and dry in the narrow pipe.

And with that, I feel the girl beneath me let go with a long scream, her hair and clothes and toad and hands disappearing, rocketing away into the unknown.

Then I let go, also screaming inside. Because we're moving super-fast, rattling down the metal cylinder like we're on a helter-skelter, only it's a slide that goes on for

341

miles and miles. The tunnel swerves and turns just like the rat described, each bend jolting electric currents of fear through my belly, as we career round them in a split second – with no idea of what lies ahead.

We're going at such speed I almost miss Polly telling me to mind myself as we curve round one last corner, and . . . with a thump, tumbling like bags of rubbish from a chute, we pile on top of one another, the toad narrowly leaping free before he gets squashed.

Untangling ourselves, I can see we're in some kind of air duct. A grey light slants between the bars of a grille, through which we can see the lab my rat described. The one we saw on the ultrascreens. It is quiet, no feet clodhopping on the shiny floor, just a dull emergency light glowing over the tables, and the squeak-squeak of a gyrating wheel.

Mouse! I call, my fingers gripping the grille. *Are you there?*

Polly watches me, searching for what's going on in my mind. I so want to talk to her like I can to mice and rats. Just for once. But we stay in silence, with the only sound she can hear coming from the squeaking wheel, a dripping tap and the hum of the air conditioner.

There is no way we can climb back up that pipe. I don't have a rat's claws. I think of the deserted city above, the frozen crowds, Coby Cott's countdown, the terrible fire thing drifting across the sea – we can't be trapped here. Not now.

I try one more time.

Mouse! We've come to rescue you!

I hang my head, waiting and trying to be patient, but I don't feel patient in any way. I call again and again, banging the bars. Then, as I am about to give up hope that any of us will get out of here alive, I hear something.

Not a voice. But movement.

Above the air-conditioned hum, a rustling sound. Something moving in straw, spinning faster and faster, louder and louder. The longest mouse dance ever, it rises and falls, unending. I know what it must be before I hear the words, faint but unmistakable.

A Dance of Never Giving Up, she says. *For that is what you must never do.*

She's right. I kick and kick at the metal slats between us for dear life, Polly joining in, until they land clattering on the lab floor. We crawl out, stretching our stiff arms and legs, the toad bounding over us as if this happened every day.

Where are you?

Over here, Wildness.

I scan the assorted cages, trying not to look. I don't want to see. But I can't help it. There are so few animals left in the world. This man finds the ones that are alive, and he does this. The cowering faces behind bars, the drips, the attached wires, the bodies suspended in fluid.

Polly nudges me. 'Kidnapper! There she is. And she's doing another dance.'

343

In a shaft of blue emergency lighting, in a tank on a worktop, just as the rat described, is our mouse. She had the future of the world in her cheeks; now they are sunken, her whiskers limp. The light seems to have gone out of her eyes and there are patches of fur missing all over her body. Still she twirls, her tail thumping the shavings on the floor of her cage. The bravest mouse in the world, no question.

What dance is that? I say.

A Dance of You Took Your Blooming Time!

I grin, but there is no sign of the insect I also hoped to find here. No glimpse of orange shell, no flicker of an antenna. I just have to hope the General is somewhere else, still safe. I unscrew the lid of the mouse's prison and scoop her out. She weighs so much less than she did, but at least her heart beats and her body is warm.

Don't look so gloomy, my dear. I'm grand – nothing a good bit of corn and a rest won't put right.

Cornfields seem very far away right now. I nod all the same.

What happened to you?

Her whiskers tremble and she looks away. *I'm so sorry, my dear. I failed you. After them fellers came for you in the night, and I ran . . . I thought I was running away, to keep your precious secret safe. I thought underground would be the best hiding place, no one would ever spot me there.' She blinks. 'I only ran straight in here, didn't

I? Us mice never have been great at avoiding the human's traps.'

It doesn't matter, I lie. *At least you're alive.*

But he tortured me, till I gave up your secret, I couldn't help it, I'm so sorry . . .

The bony, shrunken mouse in my hand dissolves into sobs. I want to hug her so tight, only I fear she might break.

I put the mouse down on to the hard floor of the ARC laboratory as gently as I can. For a moment she hunches up, a quivering ball of fur. Polly and I glance at each other. Then the mouse shakes herself back into life.

'Is she doing another dance?' asks Polly.

I suspect the time for dances is over.

Mouse, I say softly, *we need to find the man who hurt you. Can you show us where he is.*

I can try, my dear.

She gives her ears one last twitch and then guides us between worktops and tables, dashing under stools or hugging the smooth skirting and walls. She is not as fast as she once was, now and then stopping and wincing in pain.

Not long to go now, my lovely, she mutters, and I'm not sure if she's talking to herself or me.

As we follow her, a voice calls out to me: *And where do you think you're going?*

A voice I recognize.

I motion to the others to stop, and we look around.

The lab is bigger than it appeared on the ultrascreen or sounded in the rat's description. The low room stretches far underground, a puzzling array of glass tanks, flickering screens and cabinets. Again I try not to stare.

Over here, you blithering idiot!

I follow the sound of his voice to some trays of straggling plants under heat lamps – *Keep going!* – and behind them, heavy plastic curtains so fogged with condensation we can only glimpse the drooping outlines of foliage behind. Pushing them apart I find myself in a freezing room of ice-lagged compartments glaring with ultraviolet light, in which nothing appears to be growing at all. Perhaps there was once.

General?

Up here!

His orange shell looks bruised and dark. A glass box barely big enough for him, laced with frost, wedged in an ice compartment. I put my hands in and scoop him out.

You're so cold.

The wretch has been trying to test my endurance. But he has met his match in this General, my boy!

The cockroach, who once barked and buzzed, scuttling over scarves, nipping cullers or spiders, is frozen in my hand. His weak voice is the only sign of life about him. I rub the worst of the ice off and place him in my pocket with care. He grumbles, but he'll be safe in there for now.

Polly summons us back into the lab. 'Kidnapper! I've got something to show you.'

The walls are covered in maps of the planet Stone showed us on the screen. Nova. Polly unfurls a bundle of tracing paper rolls sticking out from a drawer, and finds plans and designs that are hard to make sense of in the low light.

'They look like they're for some kind of machine,' says Polly, turning the drawings this way and that. 'Perhaps for the new planet. A massive one, whatever it is.'

Never mind that. I've got something to show her too.

When Polly sees the frozen cockroach in my hand, a hand flies to her mouth. 'The poor General! Is he alive?'

I shrug. Just.

'Do you think we can do it?' she says quietly. 'Can we really change the world back to how it was?'

There's no way I can answer that question. I put the insect back in my pocket, as the mouse snaps at us from the floor.

Please, my dears! There isn't time to dawdle!

We leave the plans where they are and let her guide us to some concrete steps leading up to a door. It's black with no obvious handle, lock or any means of opening. Not even a swipe strip for a keycard.

The mouse trembles, refusing to go any closer than the bottom of the stairs. *Behind there, my dears. That is where you will find them.*

We gaze at the black door. It doesn't throb or glow; there's no smoke oozing underneath. Only a dull rectangle, that sucks what light there is from the room. The more we stare at it, the more the very ordinary door seems like a black hole, drawing us in. Somehow I know that what lies behind this door is what we have been looking for all along.

Polly lays a hand on my arm. 'Do you think going through there will explain everything?'

There is only one way to find out.

It's a miracle either of you ever makes a decision, mutters the General from my pocket.

Ignoring him, I start up the steps.

The door is ahead of me, silent and dark. It is just a door.

As I get closer, a distant churning noise sounds from behind it.

Then there's someone else on the steps next to me, someone holding a toad. Polly takes my hand. 'Come on, Kidnapper,' she says. 'Together forever.'

Together forever.

We each place our free hand on the door. And it swings open.

'It's not what I was expecting,' says Polly.

I don't know what she imagined. Maybe, like me, the ultimate scientific torture chamber, with my wild wired up to a series of cruel experiments. Or perhaps switches and levers, with Stone's hand hovering over a large red button.

What we definitely weren't anticipating was this.

Complete darkness.

'Where are we?' whispers Polly, clutching at my hand. Her voice echoes, like we're in an aircraft hangar, but I couldn't have told you if the room we were in was any bigger than a lift.

It's as if we really have been sucked into a black hole. The darkness surrounds us in an inky soup. Looking down towards the floor, I spy the faintest gleam from the mouse's eyes. That means there is light coming from somewhere, so we can't be in a real black hole.

There is also something moving in here – something big, heavy and very fast.

'What's this?' says Polly, stepping away from me, and without thinking, following instinct – I yank her back.

Just in time, as the big, heavy and fast thing speeds past, creating a warm rush of air. Churning and spinning, grinding against metal.

But what?

The mouse quails. *I do not fancy this place, my dear. Shall we return to that nice cosy other room?*

Wherever we are makes a torture lab seems cosy. It's that kind of space.

It's also boiling. A wall of heat coming from the speeding, spinning thing. Polly's grip around my hand is damp with sweat, and my skin prickles. The toad moans. He won't last long in here without water.

Well, this is a bit more like it, says the General, warming up in my pocket.

The end of all things is the beginning of all things, mutters the mouse.

Before I can ask her what she means, Polly gasps. 'Kidnapper . . . what's that?'

I have no idea what she's looking at. I'm mute, and right now I'm blind too. I only know Polly is still there because of her hand slipping in mine and her soft breath on my neck.

Sensing why I haven't responded, she raises my hand up, till we must be both pointing in the air.

At a rim of light.

A burning, molten circle, that spins, round and round at tremendous speed. The spinning machine that screams as it grinds past us is on fire at the top.

'I don't know what it is exactly,' says Polly, 'but the drawings we saw in the lab – they were of a revolving machine. It looked like some kind of giant cauldron. Perhaps that fire is coming out of the top.'

A giant cauldron that makes me feel smaller than I ever have. This is a room of machinery, noise, blackness, fire and smoke. There isn't one thing that is soft, human or animal, or even recognizable. The racket made by the cauldron, the screaming of its metal parts as it grinds past, makes me want to press my hands tight to my ears.

I clutch Polly's hand tighter instead, watching the circle of fiery light revolving above our heads. Step by step, trying not to get trapped in the cauldron's orbit, using the air whooshing past as our guide, we feel our way around it in the dark – looking for a way out. Gradually, our eyes adjust.

This way, my lovelies, says the mouse. *I can't see any better than you, I'm afraid, but I can hear something.*

I follow the sound of her voice, taking Polly and the sweltering toad with me.

Her words rise away from us as my foot hits an iron step.

She's leading us up some stairs.

I reach out, and find a handrail. On the other side, the industrial cauldron continues to accelerate around at a terrifying speed. The light from the glowing circle grows stronger and brighter as we wind our way up the side, and so does the heat.

We don't speak as we climb higher and higher, gasping for breath in the boiling air. The tunnel and the lab must be further below the surface than I ever imagined. Perhaps this is what the centre of the earth is like.

I don't know what the centre of earth is actually like, and doubt I ever will – although molten seems to be a word that gets used a lot.

But I do know one thing as we finally reach the top.

This is the centre of the ARC.

We are at the bottom of a deep shaft which soars high above our heads, lined with pods – the ones we saw on the ultrascreen, presumably now packed with passengers. They reach right up into the domed roof of the spaceship, each one glowing with light, the very top levels too far away to see clearly.

What I can see all too clearly, though, is our family – huddled together on a small viewing platform that overlooks the ARC cauldron. They look frightened and pale, even in the scalding temperatures. Littleman is here too, keeping Dad and the Goodacres pressed against the shaft wall with an electric prod. And at the edge of the platform, peering over a slender metal railing at the spiralling vortex of golden heat below, is the man we are looking for.

He doesn't look up as we approach, transfixed by the swirling and spinning beneath him, the glow radiating off his glasses. 'You took your time, I must say,' he mutters.

Selwyn Stone stands up to face us. He is wearing a short grey coat, the sort a factory worker might wear, over his normal suit. Sweat shines on his head.

Dad sees my face. 'It's all right, son, don't worry. Your wild are safe. They didn't let them on-board.'

I nod my appreciation, but I'm not sure where is less safe for them – on here with a maniac, or waiting for flaming rain out on the streets of Premium.

Littleman shoves a prod in his face. 'Did I say you could speak, Beardy?'

Polly doesn't hold back for a second. 'You sent Skuldiss to kill your own brother! Well, they're both dead now, and your stupid cullers too. I hope you're happy.'

Eck's brother smiles and raises his hand as if to shush her, but she won't.

'You tried to stop us finding the omnium fruit, but you couldn't and we've brought it back. It's the secret of the whale's song, and it's going to save the world, so we don't need your stupid planet in the first place!'

She stops, red-faced and out of breath. Her mother is wringing her hands. 'Do be careful, my dear. You'll only make things worse.'

Stone nods, considering his reply. Then, his face as hard as his name, he retorts, 'How?'

'How what?'

'How will this plant of yours save the world from the fire sweeping across the skies towards us?' He turns to the assembled audience. 'A fire, incidentally, that these children started.'

'That's a lie!' snarls Polly, but her parents exchange worried glances.

It's a lie, I repeat to Dad, my voice dead and quiet inside my head. In the shadows, his large head nods in reply.

'Lie or not, it still doesn't answer my question,' says Stone. 'How will some plant from a distant island, however lush, however fast growing, protect a whole planet from skies of fire?' He steps towards us. 'Will it, perhaps, sprout a giant fireproof canopy to cover the city?'

Eck showed us how the palm was fire resistant, and I saw that shoot survive even an exploding plane, but I don't think even the omnium could grow that quick. So instead I am thinking as fast as I can.

Polly looks lost, turning to me for an answer.

'Or maybe,' Stone continues, 'it is a magic plant, which will just spirit away the burning gases in our atmosphere? And they are coming, believe you me. You saw them for yourselves. Our satellites are tracking them.' He glances at his watch. 'They will be here very shortly, and their flames will incinerate this entire city to a crisp. So, I ask you again, you two children who would presume to save this world – how will your plant save our people in a way a whole new planet cannot?'

There is silence, apart from the churning noise fluctuating and swelling beneath us in the cauldron and the distant echo of Coby Cott, calling out the countdown.

I sense everyone's eyes on me. I can feel the General bristling with impatience in my pocket. Polly, taking a step away from me so she can read the reaction in my face. Littleman, grinning childishly. And Dad, waiting.

'Well? The burning clouds come nearer every second,' snaps Stone.

My head is feverish – whether from the heat or my confused thoughts I cannot tell. The omnium will save us from the fire in the sky, because . . . because . . . Because.

And I get it. Because the omnium is everything this metal, robotic, fiery ARC is not. I don't know how, yet, but I know. The whale was right. Eck's omnium, the miracle plant which I last saw curling and stretching out of a hole in the ice, will keep us alive because it is life itself.

The omnium is the secret of life.

I say it to myself, quietly. That must be the answer. Then loudly, to Dad, *The omnium is the secret of life. It will keep us alive because it is life.*

Dad nods and turns to Stone. 'My son says this plant they have discovered will keep us safe because it is the secret of life.'

Stone cocks his head, and a broad smile spreads across his face, cracking it from ear to ear. He rubs his hands with glee.

'But that is just where you are so very wrong.' He returns to the metal railing, and peers over once more. His glasses are lit up in a thousand different yellows and reds as the seas of fire beneath surge and pulse. 'What do you think all this has been for? Why do you think I would go to such effort to achieve my aims, such levels of slaughter and waste? You must have thought I was mad.'

Stone's voice drops, barely audible above the churning and spitting, as he points to the contents of the ginormous cauldron.

'You will wish I was. Because *this* is the secret of life.'

I stare over the railings at the spinning colours and lights below, wondering how they can explain the secret of life. The cauldron does not contain a sea of steaming molten lava. Instead it's a mixture of elements; layers of fire, water, gas and light, interweaving and circling around one another, speeding faster and faster. They're certainly beautiful enough to be such a special secret.

Then Polly steams straight in, almost knocking Selwyn over and into the pit with the force of her words. 'We know all about the secret of *your* life, thank you! Your brother told us everything. How you accidentally killed your younger brother Lucien as part of a game of Dares, and how now all you want is to control life itself. He told the whole story, so don't waste your breath on us, you, you . . . murderer!'

357

'Oh, Polly,' mutters her mother, with a gasp. 'That is very, very rude. Apologize to the poor man at once. We may disagree on many things, Mr Stone, but I do apologize for my daughter. She appears to have left her mind behind as well as her manners.'

But Mr Stone isn't listening to Mrs Goodacre. Polly might as well have stabbed him with a knife. He has gone as pale as the snow outside, clutching at his stomach.

'He said that, did he?' says Stone, his voice still and flat.

'Yes, he did. The wasp and you burning the bush. Everything.'

Stone shakes his head. 'Eck was a very troubled man, I'm afraid. He never forgave himself after the accident with Lucien. Which was his fault just as much as mine.'

I have to hold Polly back before she hits him. 'Liar! You're a liar!' she screams.

Selwyn carries on, unperturbed. 'It drove him quite mad, I'm afraid. Chasing across the world after some miracle fruit, attacking me when I didn't fall for his story of an ever-renewing palm tree that would grow anywhere, refusing to listen to science or reason. He lost his sanity, as well as his job and all his friends – it still makes me very sad to this day.'

Selwyn Stone is the only person I have ever met who smiles like a hyena when they say how sad they are. But the more he talks, the more I do wonder about Eck. He was strange, living all on his own out there, with his tattoos and ragged tie, obsessive over decontaminating every single last leaf, paranoid about rustles in the jungle and convinced we would destroy everything he had fought to protect. Maybe he was a bit crazy.

Then again, he was right to be.

Because that's exactly what we did.

'No,' I say.

'No,' says Polly. 'He wasn't mad. Weird, definitely, but not mad. He believed in something. And you destroyed it.'

Stone smiles again, rubbing his hands. 'And what did he believe in? An island burnt to a cinder, a plant that no longer exists.' He isn't just speaking to us now, but to everyone watching. Even, perhaps, the mouse cowering behind my ankles and the toad sweltering in Polly's arms. 'Shall I show you what I believe in? The hard science right in front of our eyes. Do you know what this machine is called?'

I shake my head. I'm guessing Super-Cauldron isn't it.

'This is a centrifuge. The world's biggest. A machine that spins matter – solids and liquids – at high speeds, to separate them. In this case, the fastest one in the world. It has taken me years to build.'

The strange machinery noises I heard in the Four Towers before.

'To separate them from what?' asks Polly.

'Not from anything else, but to separate their different parts from one another. To isolate cream from milk, sugar from syrup and coconut oil from coconut paste.' I wonder what it could extract from the omnium, but I'm also guessing that isn't top of Selwyn's priorities. 'I first learnt of the centrifuge's extraordinary potential through my experiences in food production. Many of you no doubt wonder how Formul-A itself is made? Well, you're looking at it.'

Our parents and their guards gawp over the railing at the swirling lights and gases, but Stone shakes his head. 'I don't mean this *is* formula, you fools. I mean the process. We created the artificial food from the most unlikely materials – minerals, inedible vegetable matter and reconstituted animal remains stored from before the red-eye. We even tried producing it from quarried stone.' I recall the abandoned Valley of Rock, the cabin door creaking in the wind. Glancing at Polly, I see she is as queasy as me, as we remember how much of his rubbish we have eaten. 'Spinning them together at high speeds until we extracted the vital nutrients and vitamins we needed from them, discarding the waste left behind.'

I don't even want to know what happened to that. Dumped on the Waste Town Mountain, no doubt, or made into pink, the fake formula that burned away Dagger's teeth and tongue.

'What would happen if a person fell in there?' says Polly.

'Oh, very good!' he says, laughing, although he does

step away from the edge. 'As it happens, young lady, Health and Safety are our watchwords at Facto. The centrifuge detects living matter and ejects it. So don't get any funny ideas either – they won't work. Although, speaking of living matter, you might be interested in this.'

He pulls a vial out of his jacket pocket. At first my heart leaps. It looks like a vial of Laura II, the cure for the red-eye Dad developed with our help. But they were different. Not as big, a different colour cap. This larger glass tube glimmers in the ripples of light from the centrifuge as Selwyn studies the contents.

'I had a thought, you see. If we could extract food from rocks and trees, why not go one step further? Perhaps extract the secret of life itself? Tell me, Professor Jaynes,' he says, 'you're a fellow scientist. What powers life?'

Dad looks as stunned as the rest of us, but his brain is still in gear. 'The sun,' he replies after a moment. 'Plants absorb the powerful rays. We eat the plants, and the animals that eat the plants, and process that energy to help us grow, move, talk, reproduce . . . everything.'

Everything on a planet that will now burn to nothing in approximately minus thirty minutes and sixteen seconds, a distant robotic voice helpfully reminds us.

'Precisely, Professor!' says Selwyn. 'Life is energy. You can't make it, you can't destroy it. It circulates, through light, movement, heat – constantly transferring. The energy that makes a newborn baby open its eyes and cry, that helps a tree stretch its leaves towards the sun, that pulls the tides of the ocean, that keeps this planet spinning. That, my friends, is the secret of life.'

An image flashes into my mind of the omnium, a frazzled palm shoot writhing out of the water and smoke in the ice hole on the Ams, clamping itself to the frosted rim.

'And what part of the body stores and transforms this energy, Professor?'

'At the smallest level, our cells. A tiny, nanoscopic element in them that powers everything a body does. They evolved billions of years ago, reacting with oxygen in our blood to turn the food we eat into the energy that keeps us moving, growing and alive. Each one as powerful as a battery, and we all have millions of them inside of us right now. Including the animals, of course.'

'Ten out of ten. You have done your homework. But of course, that's not all we need, is it? How about the energy that keeps the lights on, the cars moving and the houses warm? The energy we get from fossil fuels, stored deep in the ground for billions of years.'

'I believe it was burning those that made this planet so hot in the first place,' mutters Dad. I nod in agreement, distracted by the General, wriggling into life in the warmth of my pocket.

Stone continues. 'What would we do if we all had to flee to a planet where there was no known energy supply? How would we create it?' He holds the vial up high, so it sparkles. 'If only we had a simple solution. Tell me, Professor, those nanoscopic cellular powerhouses you described, in humans and animals – where do you find their secret? The code to produce so much power – where's that kept?'

Dad looks at his feet. 'In our DNA,' he mutters.

'I'm sorry, I didn't catch that,' says Stone, hopping around.

'In DNA.'

'Exactly. Thank you. All that incredible energy-converting ability, stored in something so small as to be invisible to the naked eye. Imagine the number of powerhouses in all the billions of animals in the world. How much energy could that produce? It took this planet millions of years to degrade dead matter into carbon fuels. But what if we could create that much energy in, say, minutes?'

And no matter how hot this room is, every last drop of colour drains from my face. I know, before he says it, what that vial contains. Stone sees the recognition in my eyes.

'Not as dumb as you look, are you? Yes, that's why I was so keen to get your beloved Iris, which I did, thanks to that rodent. A store of thousands of past lives, millions of powerhouses, just waiting to be extracted by my centrifuge. It's taken me a lot of experiments to get it right. I've tried everything from the DNA of stuffed animals to some of your friends here in my lab downstairs, but you handed me the raw ingredients I need on a plate.'

The Iris. What we've been searching for all this time.

The data to rebuild and repopulate this planet – or maybe even a new one – with the animals and plants we've lost. In our eyes the most precious glass vial ever to have existed.

We have been listening to his lecture for long enough, and now an unseen force passes between us, as the Goodacres start forward, only to be buzzed back by Littleman's electric prod, Polly lunging for the vial at the same time as I do.

Stone ducks out of our clutches, holding the Iris over the centrifuge. 'Millions of past lives. An unparalleled store of power. Enough to fuel a new planet. You must admit, it's rather brilliant. The dead of the old planet will fuel the life of the new one.'

And with that –

He drops the Iris capsule into the spinning vortex of light and gas. It disappears without trace . . . at first. No one speaks, hands clutching the guard rail, our faces lit up with the artificial glow.

Then – there is a small, distant explosion at the bottom of the centrifuge, as if a firework has gone off. It spreads and ripples throughout the swirling energy fields. Not just spinning now, they rise and fall, vapours shot through with jagged lines of bright white heat, that when they collide shine like exploding stars.

The chamber echoes with crackles and explosions, each firework seeming to set off another. And then my brain begins to fizz too. It fizzes with a different noise, not the one bouncing off these metal walls from the kaleidoscope of elements beneath our feet, but sounds I have been hearing ever since a cockroach first crawled into my bowl of formula at Spectrum Hall.

The noise of something not human trying to speak to me.

The sounds remind me of the shining-leaf swamp, where I heard the voices of microscopic cells yet to evolve into being radiating through my mind.

So many lives, says the General, who has hauled himself out on to the railing of the centrifuge to watch, his antennae limp with despair.

But they're dead, aren't they? How can they speak?

However you preserved them, you stored their animal voice too. Polly's microdots of DNA. *This vile enemy's spinning magic has released them for a moment in time.*

Now Dad can hear them as well. He clutches his hands to his ears, and the mouse squeals, whisking her tail as if to get rid of the noise.

Millions of living things, crying out.

Voices from things that no longer exist, only the energy they once contained spread before us in a dazzling array of gases and colours, their words hovering invisibly above, each one calling the same thing.

Do not forget.

Then, as fast as their call came, the sound has vanished and the energy field has subsided.

Animals I thought we would bring back. But we can't now. They are gone forever. Everyday cows and sheep and dogs and cats as extinct as dinosaurs and woolly mammoths. All so we can keep on living exactly as we were before on a new planet.

You will only destroy it, said Eck.

I don't want to be part of his story. Or his brother's.

We can change the ending.

I start to run at Stone.

Which is when he produces a second vial from his jacket pocket.

I stop dead in my tracks.

Selwyn Stone grins, as his words echo against the walls of the mighty industrial cavern. 'You didn't think that little tube was the *whole* Iris, did you? There's more where that came from.' He dangles the capsule full of past lives over the swirling iridescent mists. 'Take one step further, and in she goes!'

The vial hangs from his bony fingers, twisting in the light. Thousands more living creatures in a bottle. So much energy, so much life. Perhaps half the history of creation on this planet, not rescued in an ARC, but used to fuel it.

I could save them. These animals are dead already, thanks to us. Do we need to burn them now as well? We could bring them back. We don't need another planet. There is a perfectly good one that can be saved. I believe with all my heart that the shoot of omnium clamped to a hole in the frozen river is a sign.

'Now why don't we sit down and talk about this sensibly over a nice cup of tea,' says Mrs Goodacre, but I reckon the moment for cups of tea has passed.

Think wisely, says Dad in my head. *Be very, very careful.*

Which is when Polly, halfway between me and Stone on the platform, asks him the other question in our heads. 'What will you do with our animals? Take them with you?'

He shrugs. 'No. Let's leave them here to burn. I suspect a new planet deserves new ones, don't you? I fancy designing them myself. Tastier animals, more useful creatures, more beautiful beasts, and none that bite or sting us. And besides, yours might still be incubating the red-eye.' He sounds almost apologetic. 'It wasn't the most perfect virus. Don't know why it didn't attack cockroaches or pigeons. That was clearly an oversight. Because the one thing we will not need on Nova is a cockroach.'

Selwyn looks with disgust at the insect buzzing with rage at him on the railing. The General is making strange sounds I don't recognize, singing a call I can't decipher. He spins round and round, his orange shell catching the light. The voices from the Iris have sent him into meltdown.

'And of course,' continues Selwyn, looking back to me, 'there was the test version. That did attack humans by mistake. I'm so sorry. It didn't even give people red eyes. Just an everyday, lethal, mystery virus. Awful bad luck.'

I look at him, not yet understanding. He isn't smiling any more. His eyes well up, but it's not for the person I'm beginning to think of.

'Kester, I share your pain. I know what it is to lose someone you love.'

It's as if he's thrown me a shot in a game I don't know how to return. And the wheels click into place. The mystery virus. Mum in her hospital bed. Dad not letting me see her just before she died.

Dad's obsession with finding a cure. It was never for the animals alone. The medicine he suggested we give her name, Laura.

Then I can't do anything. Because she's there before me. The floating, fuzzy changing picture of Mum again. She's there between me and Stone, and the Iris. In the same shifting clothes as before, now a cardigan, now a T-shirt.

Everything and everyone else stops, frozen in time.

She's all I can see, shimmering in the air.

369

I'm ready to explode with rage. 'You knew, didn't you? The whole time. Why didn't you tell me?'

Mum shrugs. 'I didn't want to upset you, did I?'

'Bit late for that now.'

'Well, we got there in the end. It's better this way.'

How? Nothing is better this way. She's gone weird in her afterlife.

'Don't you hate him, Mum? Do you want me to kill him?'

She doesn't reply. Just one of those Mum looks that roughly translates as, 'We shall not speak of this again.'

'What do I do?'

'Kes! Like you even need to ask. Do what you can. Be the best human being you can. Don't be like him. That's all I've ever wanted for you.'

'I don't even know what that means.'

'This is no time for sulking, young man. And besides –' she looks up at me, her face shining, her hair wavy as it always was – 'you know this is the last time, don't you?'

I can't speak – not in my head, not anywhere. I nod.

'Be the best human being you can,' she repeats, and then she's gone. Gone forever. Thanks to the man dangling the Iris over a centrifuge. Dad, his cheeks flushed with rage, bristling like a bull ready to charge, if only he could get past Littleman and his prod. Polly looking at me, waiting for the word.

I don't move. I'm staring at the spot where Mum was.

Just another accidental life lost to the red-eye.

Except she was different to all the others as far as I'm concerned.

She was my mum.

A voice from the metallic heavens above breaks my thoughts.

'This planet will self-destruct in T-minus twenty minutes and sixteen seconds, and counting. Prepare for launch.'

The General continues to flutter and spin. It doesn't matter what he's doing. My shoulders sink as I head back to the others. See if I care. We've lost. We're going to Nova. I'll just have to be the Best Human Being I Can on a new planet.

'So is our little drama over?' says Mr Stone. He puts the vial back in his pocket. 'We'll save this treat for later. Mr Littleman, why don't you escort our guests to their quarters for take-off. And as for you –' he says, leaning over the railing – 'this is a pest-free zone, I'm afraid.'

With a bony finger, he flicks the General off into the centrifuge.

He turns in the air, the flickering light of the burning dead catching his shell –

The first of my wild, gyrating, his just thawed wings struggling to beat.

And I'm sorry, Mum, but I can't. If being the best human I can is letting Selwyn Stone get away with that . . .

Then I'm running at him, and Polly is too –

'Not so fast, my dears!' Littleman lunges at us, shooting

crackles of blue electricity from his prod, searing pain up my back and legs, but I don't care.

Our General has disappeared from view.

Stone steps away from the edge, laughing.

We fall in a heap at his feet, writhing with the electric charge, shuddering, muscles clenching in agony, skin burning.

And as I stare at his polished shoes, something runs over them.

It looks like the General. But the General has gone. Cast into the fiery revolving pit. No, another cockroach, the size of the General, definitely ran over Stone's foot.

He recoils.

Then another appears. And another.

We lift our heads as we hear the noise rising above the industrial churn of the centrifuge, a crisking, clacking and scratching. A scratching I have heard once before in a school far away from here. Scuttling up the stairs, swarming up from the depths, streaming up the walls, filling the cavern of the ARC.

Thousands of cockroaches. An army of cockroaches.

They came back.

Shell backs fill the platform, pouring up from the earth below us, the cracks, holes and vents, all the places a cockroach can go. The General was calling them. They swarm, a surging insect tide, rising up and swallowing Selwyn Stone.

The tide washes at the heels and up the legs of

372

Littleman, making him writhe and drop his prod with a clatter. Then he is running and screaming down the stairs, trailing cockroaches behind him as he disappears into the darkness. The mouse does a brief Dance of Won't Be Seeing Him Again Anytime Soon.

Polly looks frightened on her own. I hold my hand out to her, telling her not to worry. But it's not the cockroaches she's frightened of. The girl with the gun isn't scared of bugs. She's frightened of the man emerging from the invading flood. More like a thing than a man.

It tries to walk towards us, as well as someone can who has hundreds of cockroaches covering their body, up his trouser legs, up his sleeves, in his hair, crawling over his glasses and his nose, spilling out of his mouth and ears. Every movement is stiff and jerky, his skin as grey as his name.

'Of all the animals I hate, I hate insects the most,' he says, through half a mouthful of cockroach.

Then I realize he's not walking towards us.

He's staggering towards the centrifuge, with the last of the Iris. The weight of insects on his back overwhelms him and he stumbles, now crawling, an arm outstretched, trying to throw the vial into the energy fields.

What once was Selwyn Stone is hunched on the edge of the platform, covered by a mass of writhing, shiny shells and antennae. He stands up shakily to face us, his body black and pulsing, hands braced against the railings.

There is a strange look in his eyes.

'All I have ever wanted to do is make a profit,' he manages to say.

'Yes,' I say, and then they come.

Finally.

The words come, bubbling up through my throat as before, but now into my mouth, whistling through my tongue and teeth, and out, actually out into the world.

'Yes,' I say. 'That's *all* you've ever wanted to do.'

Polly and I reach out, to help him back. But at the same time, winging out of the fumes, one last cockroach buzzes on to the mass covering his head.

A blackened but still orange cockroach. With white stripes.

A voice hoarse and croaking. *Blasted flames defrosted my wings, didn't they!*

His extra weight is the final straw, making the mound of insects and person topple on the edge, before collapsing backwards.

'Kidnapper! The Iris!' yells Polly behind me.

Without replying, without thinking –

I leap after Selwyn –

And we both fall into the centrifuge.

We fall, wrapped up in one another, cockroaches flying, a black suit of armour fragmenting, swallowed up by the swirling energy field. I twist my head back to see faces peering down at us.

Polly, Dad, the mouse and toad. As if we are below the water, but somehow different. A mist that holds and spins and burns at the same time.

'Kester,' says Polly sounding distant, like she is in another room, 'where are you going? Why do you always leave me behind?'

Mr and Mrs Goodacre, putting their arms around her shoulder, Dad calling in the animal tongue, his voice cracking.

Don't let go.

Don't let go of what? The orange cockroach still

buzzing around our heads? There's no way he's letting go of us.

Then I realize.

The glass vial clutched in Stone's hand. Still there as we're flung around at breakneck speed in a fizzing sea of light and gas. I'm reaching for the Iris, while Stone yanks it away from me, trying to get the top off, and it's hard because we're spinning faster . . . and faster.

And faster.

Now I can no longer make out the faces watching us, as we wheel round and round, Polly, Dad and my mouse morphing into blurred blobs, their cries confused.

And faster and faster.

Feeling sick, something's punching me in the stomach. It's Stone's foot, and I punch back, but it's more than that, it's the G-forces, squashing my insides. The General clinging to my neck for dear life.

And faster and faster and FASTER.

Stone is spitting words at me but I can't hear what they are. The roar of the centrifuge drowns everything out. My hand grips the glass tube and he's biting my wrist, biting so hard I want to let go, but I know I mustn't.

And FASTER and FASTER and FASTER and FASTER.

It's getting harder to breathe, my vision is turning black, but I mustn't let go. I mustn't. For the animals we lost, the ones we could have saved. There is still hope.

A distant voice calls from above, repeating the words through a soup of noise.

Don't let go. I love you, Kester. Don't let go.

The body of my enemy and me are entwined around one another, curled up tight, suspended in a world of flashing red and gold, buffeted by pulses of raw power. Thoughts fade. The mind blanks. My muscles slacken. The only real life left seems to be in the glass vial I now clutch in my hand, which grows warm and trembles as if it might burst.

Then, anounced by a scream that rips right through me, from the man with his arms clasped tight around my back, the centrifuge he designed does exactly what he predicted.

A hole appears in the fiery vapours, a chute sliding open.

Pressure from outside sucking us, pulling us through and propelling us at an unimaginable speed –

Both of us roaring now, the hairs near ripped from our heads, tears and sweat and blood streaming over our faces, our skin ripped by the speed. We fire out, launched by the centrifuge from the centre of the ARC, out above the tall black chimney stacks of Facto, into the night sky.

A haze of escaped energy vapour and snow swirls around us. For a second, I see Selwyn Stone's smooth grey face, lips parting, like he is trying to speak. But Facto's founder will never talk again. He falls away from me,

377

mouth bubbling, hands flailing, swallowed up forever by one of his own chimneys.

The General and I don't fall though.

We rise and rise.

There are hooks in the rags of my T-shirt, hoisting me high. Not little pigeon claws, but large, strong talons.

Eagle.

That'll be me.

Here we go again! says the General cheerily.

I lurch and swing, still clutching the vial in my hand. I can't see, blood is in my eyes, the icy wind is burning my skin, everything cries with pain, but I am here. Ready to vomit, gulping, barely able to breathe, all these things, but most of all I am crying and whooping.

With happiness.

We did it. I have the Iris. Stone is no more.

'We did it!' I yell into the sky, trying to punch my fist in the air and only hitting the eagle.

Wouldn't try that again, if I were you, is all he says.

We jolt through the air, until he lowers me on to a patch of wasteground the other side of the Four Towers. Cold, dirty snow has never felt so good. I lie with my arms outstretched, not caring how freezing or wet I am, not bothered by the pain zigzagging through my entire body. My breath comes out in big puffs and the General retreats to safety in my pocket.

There is a distant robotic voice still booming in the background, but I can't concentrate on what it's saying.

Because there are sloppy tongues licking my face, and I am pushing off both Dagger and my wolf, who are trying to clamber all over me.

You escaped the cullers! I want to hug the wolf for eternity, my head pressed into his fur, the doggy stink of him. He is sticky with blood, I can feel scratches, but he is here.

No human with a dart gun is a match for me, he says in a low voice, tinged with a hunger I have not sensed before.

I pull away to look at him. His eyes are deadly serious. This time I think he means it. He is full grown now in every sense, and I hug him again.

He fought bravely, admits Dagger, also dripping with sweat and blood. *For a wolf.*

Even the white dog who once hated us is laughing, scrapping with the wolf in the snow, the pigeons landing all around us and giving us congratulatory pecks.

I hope you didn't save the Iris? says the white pigeon.

I did save it, White Pigeon, I did!

Half of it, at least. *Oh dear,* he says.

We all laugh because I think he's being silly again. But he doesn't cock his head or narrow his eyes or any of the things he normally does. He shrinks away.

Oh dear, he says again. *Oh no, oh no.* He's jumping around, as if the ground is hot. And it is. So warm the snow is melting, receding away from us like a tide. It's not just the ground, but the surrounding air too. Everything is boiling and noisy. Rumbles booming out from behind us, making the ground shake and our ears bleed. A noise that sounds like a rocket engine.

I twist around, my eyes blinded by the heat and light.

The noise that *is* a rocket engine. Several of them.

The ARC is preparing to launch.

No. *No.*

I run, ignoring the cries of the pigeons and my wolf. Not caring about cutting or bruising myself as I stumble over rocks, hauling myself over fences.

But I can't get near.

A wall of heat has erupted between me and it. Exhaust fumes, chalky and shaggy, ripple out of the Four Towers, tumbling over the walls, obscuring them and the ARC from view. Billowing puffballs that surge along the ground towards us, filling the air too, making us choke and splutter.

I blunder my way back to the birds. They are disorientated and confused. I have never been less confused. I know exactly what needs to happen.

No can do, says the eagle. *That last ride wiped me out. Besides, we'd never even get close.*

Kester, the sky is too hot, and that man-made bird makes too much light and noise. We'll never catch it, say the grey pigeons.

I am too hot, says the white pigeon. *You'll never catch me.*

There isn't time for jokes, or excuses.

Take me.

The birds dither at my feet, the eagle drawing himself in and looking away.

I am your Wildness. I command you. Take me.

There is more cooing and flustered looks between them.

A final robotic announcement is followed by a sharp crack, and a deep-throated growl that feels like it comes from the centre of the earth. The ground shudders, and with a fizzing roar the ARC climbs vertically into the night sky, great jets of flame spurting from below.

TAKE ME!

And they do. The pigeons do. Just as when they first caught me from the cliff, with their beaks and feet, they flock around and we jerk into the air.

The spaceship powers ahead of us into the sky.

The heat is unimaginable, and to even look at the light scorches my eyeballs. I can smell singeing feathers, blistering skin, but I urge the birds closer. We climb higher and higher, until we are, for a moment, level with the silver domed rocket.

Through the haze, I can open my eyes a crack to see one of the windows. There is no longer light pouring out from them, illuminating the city.

But two faces instead. Dad and Polly, looking blank and frightened. A mouse on a shoulder, a toad in their arms.

381

I see them. They see me and raise a hand to wave. They're trying to say something, but I can't hear what. We can't get any closer. There's too much waffling air, the stench of fuel, waves of scalding hotness that want to melt my eyes and peel off my skin.

For a second, I hear Dad in my head. *We'll be all right, Kes. Look after the others.*

Polly whispers into his ear and he speaks for her. *Polly says goodbye. But she also says it will be all right. She said you'd understand.*

How can I understand? She's leaving. Jetting into an unknown world. Forever.

We can't hold you much longer, Wildness, cry the pigeons.

Then Polly – my best ever friend, my first ever true friend – touches the plastic strap hanging around her neck. She raises it up to the glass and points. In return, I touch the watch face hanging around mine.

And I know, as she and Dad begin to frazzle away in a wall of heat and sound –

Disappearing from view, leaving oily clouds behind that choke and blind us –

That it really will be all right.

That as long as I have the watch, we'll be together. She'll be on Nova, and I'll be here. But whenever I miss her, or Dad or Mum, I can remember them.

As the ARC powers away from us, the huge rocket now looking no bigger than a tiny bullet, spiralling into layers of atmosphere and space unknown, I say the first and last actual words I will ever say to her.

'Together Forever.'

Then the birds are sinking, and we drop on to the ground, feathers folding over me. Nobody says a word. They don't need to. My father has gone. My best friend has gone. Along with the mouse, toad and most of the human race.

They are up there now. Gone, and never coming back.

All that remains are the trails of smoke floating along the ground, the black smoke drifting out of the Four Towers. An empty city and the collection of animals gathering around us in the night. A stag. Some wolves. A rat and a white dog.

This is earth. This is who is left.

Underneath gathering clouds of fire in the sky. Not the kind produced by a rocket, but the ones which have followed us across the oceans of this planet. Terrible fires burning in the sky, which we have failed to stop.

The stag does not say a word as I heave myself on his back, caked in soot and blood. He does not need to. The animal dream has come true. Now we must flee, like wild creatures always do.

There is only one place we can go.

There is only one place we could possibly survive a sky filled with fire. A place I never, ever, not in my worst nightmares (animal or not) imagined I would return to – deep underground, in the cool dark.

The Underearth.

The dog is agitating, spit flecking his muzzle. He is scratched and grazed with blood, where he has fought the cullers. *There is little time, boy. Do you not yet trust me?* Above our heads, the sky crackles and spits. *Nature is almighty. We cannot defeat her, or outrun her. But we might survive her.*

The stillness is shattered by an almighty explosion. There is a white-hot flare of explosive light. Way, way up in the atmosphere, above the plumes and billows of smoke from the ARC, it sounds like someone has fired a cannon straight into a hillside. A deafening boom. Then another, another and another. Thunderclaps that rumble above the whole panoply of the sky, rolling out in ripples of noise above Premium's roofs and towers.

Now the flares of light spread through the air. They disintegrate into a shower of sparks, natural fireworks, but these do not fall to the ground. The clouds catch them, and as they do the sparks connect, producing more, setting off jagged electrical lines, which spread through the skies like cracks through ice. Exactly as we saw over Faraway.

In seconds, the whole sky is cracked with fire from side to side, back to front, and all around, as if it might burst. We ride hard through the city. There is no one left to stop us now.

Raining balls of fire strike buildings and ultra-screens

alike, masonry crumbling and falling all around us.

I turn to see the Four Towers collapse in on themselves. The Maydoor Estate ablaze. Across the water, slick with flames, the Glass Towers begin to crack and melt.

Our world is burning and there is nothing we can do to stop it.

The poor, the very young, the weak and the old of Premium, denied entry to the ARC, stream after us, a long caravan trailing behind and across the bridge. We run as the wolf-cub and I once ran before, in pursuit of Polly and a silent dog, past railway tracks and formula trains, under the white road to Waste Town.

But we are too late.

Aida's home is already bright with fire, as the largest rubbish heap takes light, floating upward in mushroom clouds of black smoke.

'Don't look so sad, mate,' says 123, sitting astride his bike. 'We should have torched that dump years ago.'

Not just 123, but the rest of his gang, smudge-faced and wide-eyed on their electric cycles. Behind them, those who remained in Waste Town, bundles of rags and belongings cluttered around them. A few cartons of formula. And sprawled across 123's saddle . . . Aida.

She is unconscious but bandaged and alive.

A fire cloud cracks above our head – a warning.

Yelling at them to follow, I urge the stag on, away from the smoking Waste Mountain, along embankments and cuttings, clopping down the abandoned railway track, following Dagger. The rat curled up on my knees stirs with excitement as we approach his old lair.

Back home together! Will it really be forever this time, old friend?

This time, all bets are off.

Then the white dog is leading us down hidden tunnels, past different ages of man, and we come once again into the great deserted cave temple of the Underearth. The light shining through the dome is now the fierce light of a burning city, rather than dawn, but otherwise not much has changed. Tremors run through the ancient walls, grit tumbling down the old cave paintings, cracks widening.

If we can survive a virus down here . . . starts the dog, but he doesn't finish. Because we are, all of us, humans and animals alike, entering the unknown.

Our planet is on fire.

We are in the dark below.

Where we hold each other, as the world beyond burns.

MY STORY BEGINS

I make my way over the mossy rocks, trying not to slip, and crouch at the water's edge. With my hands cupped, I scoop up a mouthful of water and drink. It tastes as fresh and as clean as it ever did. Glancing around the lake, not much has changed.

There are the same sun spots glittering on the water, the same silvery trees lining the edge, the same ferns and reeds. The white boulder is still here, as are the rotten logs, the shingle on the shore. The one addition is a couple of new trees. Blue rubbery palms with melon-shaped fruit bowing from their branches. We'll need to keep an eye on them.

No, the only thing that has properly changed is sitting at the water's edge, staring at his own shimmering reflection.

Me.

'Hey, you going to sit there admiring yourself all day or what?' calls a voice from behind me.

Aida stands under the yellowing leaves of a birch, arms folded, foot up on a rock. The first human to be allowed into the Ring of Trees since me. Not that there are many other humans still left on earth . . . for now.

'I'm coming,' I reply, and pick my way back over the stones.

The firestorms were twelve months ago. They were as bad as we feared; as terrible as the whale predicted. But they didn't touch us in the Underearth, and they burned themselves out before they reached this far north. So unlike everywhere else, the Ring of Trees got off lightly. The moorland as you approach is scorched, but it will grow back.

Everything will grow back. One day.

I can't tell how long the fires raged high above our heads in Premium. When we stopped smelling smoke and seeing sparks shower through the dome of the cave, we ventured out through the railway tunnel entrance once more.

There wasn't much left of anything. Councillor Clancy-Clay's glass skyscrapers had melted into ragged stumps, like Dagger's teeth. The Waste Mountain was flattened, but good riddance to bad rubbish. No one wants to live on a pile of trash. A combination of the ARC taking off and the fiery skies reduced the Four Towers to smoking mounds.

As I reach Aida under the tree, I glance up at the sky, as I did so much in the early days. It happens less now, perhaps, but still a lot. I'm looking into the blue in the day, at the distant stars at night – and thinking of very special people, on the most amazing journey mankind has ever made. I wonder how far they've got, how they're doing, and whether the ship has reached Nova yet.

I've spent hours and nights and days wondering, as you might imagine.

It's not ideal.

But what can I do to bring a speeding rocket back to earth? I couldn't stop it then, and I can't stop it now. It made me so sad in the Underearth. More sad than I can remember being. A black despair, bubbling up from inside me, obliterating all other thoughts. Some days I found it hard to even wake up.

Aida was patient. The animals were too. They waited for me.

Don't get me wrong – I'm not over it yet.

I'm at last grasping the possibility though, that if enough people actually want to start a new colony on a distant planet – who better to be leading it than my dad and Polly?

A hand touches mine. 'Come. Stop space-staring. We know where that ends.'

I smile. We don't know though. Which is what's so

great about space. It's infinite and could contain any number of possibilities – perhaps a return trip or even the chance that one day we build our own ARC and visit them.

'Hey,' says Aida, not smiling now. 'I serious. Eyes on the ground. We gonna do this or what?'

'Yes.' I mean no. 'Give me a moment.'

The Culdee Sack was razed to the ground, the garden blackened and twisted. That was hard. That was super-hard. I realized when we left home before, on the night the dark wild rose, that we might not return for a while. But I never, ever imagined that one day I would come back to find nothing there.

No trace of my old room, the soft toys and comics. Our shiny kitchen, gone. Dad's lab, a charred ruin. We did find a few things that might come in handy though. Flattened under rubble, a pile of smoke-stained handwritten notes looked interesting. (How-to-activate-the-Iris interesting, in case you're wondering.) Not for today, or tomorrow, or even next year. We don't yet have the raw materials, equipment or skills. But one day . . .

Then we went upstairs to what was left of Mum's bedroom, the one Polly slept in, with the photos and letters and Mum's clothes . . .

I must be careful. Extra careful.

These things, they are deep wounds, so deep I don't know if they will ever heal. I must try not to touch them too much. Instead I touch the battered piece of plastic and glass around my neck. Aida touches the strap around hers.

We look at each other. We don't say the words any more; we don't need to. Because we really are together forever. I don't know what the future holds for sure, except that for me it involves the girl who once broke into my house looking for a flower.

I did find something in the scarred crater our garden had become though. Something that wasn't there before.

Curling out of the coal-black earth, a twisting blue palm.

A palm which grew and spread even during a brief visit.

The kind that can survive even a sky of flames.

Eck called it the omnium. I hope he wouldn't mind, but Aida and I renamed it. (In fact, we've re-titled anything sounding like Premium or Spectrum or . . . Factorium.) We've decided to call it the Tree of Life. Not very original perhaps, but accurate.

I said the city was more or less gone, burned and blistered, blown out of existence by waves of exploding fireballs.

Let me tell you what was in its place.

Forests of palm, snaking over ruins, poking their leaves out of windows and through holes in roofs, searching for the sun. The city of glass and steel, of snow and lately of burnt brick, is now a city of blue and green. One we have called Faraway.

Because we will build a new paradise in our own Island, over the debris. In memory of the whale, Eck and all those who believed in the power of nature.

Fruit swelling on each vine, fresh tendrils twisting around every melted ultrascreen, bringing down what remained of Facto's wire fences with their weight.

Green pollen dust everywhere.

So food hasn't been a problem. Not for us, or the handful of other survivors we found, who hid in basements or underground like us. Outsiders who didn't travel to the city, some of whom we met on our way here, who cowered in farm cellars. No more scraping out formula cartons or eating the chewy fragments of seaweed Aida had held on to from our journey in the *Glass Bottom*.

Real, proper food that tastes of everything, with enough for everyone.

The tree of life isn't without its problems, of course. A growing-super-quick-thing is useful if you're trying to rebuild a world, but it can get out of hand. We need to keep hacking them back, like Eck did on Faraway.

And just as the trees did on the whale's island, they foster life. Where the palm grows, so will other plants around them. Leaf by leaf, the tree is turning our brown wastes vibrant and alive again. The fires purged the world of what remained of the red-eye – as far as we can tell. So it's not just flora that likes the miracle fruit, but fauna too.

The insects crawling along their boughs, the butterflies dancing over the flowers, the deer scraping the trunks.

'Speaking of deer,' I say aloud.

'Yes,' says Aida. 'Come. Get on with it.'

I turn away from the sun flitting on the water to the group of animals standing on the edge of the forest.

This is where I first met them, my wild.

The stag is much older now, gaunt, his rich eyes sunk deeper into his head, grey around his muzzle. But he has a few more runs in him yet.

How very kind, he says. He steps stiffly towards me and for a moment I think he is going to lower his dry horns, but he doesn't. He nuzzles me on the shoulder. *I never thought I would see these woods again. Perhaps I shall look on the hills one last time after all. Thank you.*

Not for the first time, I'm stuck for what to say to him.

So I stroke his face. Already he feels rougher, stranger to the touch.

The other deer gather behind him, rabbits hopping between their feet. A pack of wolves loiter, separate from the others, biding their time. The truce that held such different creatures together is ending, as the ancient laws of nature return.

There are just a few moments left though when I can stroke their leader, and still call him my wolf. His lips pull back in a snarl and then soften.

Will we see you again, Wildness?

I don't want to answer. *Maybe in your dreams.*

*Of course you will be. We must tell ourselves a new

dream now the old one has ended. It will be the best dream ever, because I am going to tell it.*

His white-nosed mother nips his ears. *Foolish boy. No more of that talk. You are the leader of this pack now.*

I know if I reply to him I won't be able to speak, so I do the one thing my wolf – or rather, *this* wolf – has never let me do before, and stroke him between his ears.

An angry voice chirrups in my ear. *Is this sentimental nonsense going to go on for much longer? My army are calling to me.*

With that, the General whisks off my shoulder as abruptly as he arrived in my life, burrowing under a rock. He's right. Time to go.

I stand back and say goodbye to my wild.

All the grey pigeons are massed in the branches above, facing me, the white one on the ground looking in the opposite direction.

Goodbye, Kester Jaynes, thank you for answering our call.

Goodbye, Kester Jaynes, I'll give you a call.

Unlikely. Then they soar off into the air, following the eagle's shrieking cry. The rest of my animals and I, we look into each other's eyes for one last moment, and then, as a breeze moves through the trees, they are gone.

The wild are just that once more. Bounding, crawling and fluttering into the shadows of the old wood. A channel in my brain closes, no longer receiving a signal. The earth is renewed, the gift has run its course.

They must begin again in their way and so must we in ours.

I should be sad. But I understand, wherever I am – whether watching from the undergrowth, or soaring in the skies – they will never be far away.

'Are we done?' says Aida.

Not quite, says the white dog at her side.

(You didn't think I'd actually stop talking to all animals, did you?)

'Race?' I say. Then we are off, chasing after one another over the old paths till we reach the hole in the wire fence that borders the Ring of Trees. We stop to catch our breath and drink in the view.

A long time ago, I said my story began sitting on a bed, looking out of a window.

Maybe that story did.

I had a nightmare that story would end with the planet burning, leaving me alone. That was one ending. But nightmares don't last forever, even animal ones.

Today, I'm standing on the edge of a forest, at the furthest reach of the known world. I'm looking out at the moors, the mountains, the valleys, the rivers and the sky rolling on above. We have lost so much, a loss that only sharpens what remains.

Land, water, rain, sun and air are in ample supply.

Aida takes my hand. We are few, we are young. We will be the best human beings we can be. It will take time.

But now I know, my story really begins here.

ACKNOWLEDGEMENTS

This story started as something else, a long time ago, and I will always be grateful to Rich Mewis for asking the question 'Why don't the animals talk?'

I began the first book at the Arvon Lumb Bank centre; thanks to Jean McNeill and Bill Broady for their encouragement. Much was written at Alexander Duma's home in France: his hospitality has been boundless.

There were only three chapters when Teresa Watkins suggested Jo Unwin take a look. She believed in The Last Wild from the start and I remain indebted to her for her faith, patience, and insight. Carrie Plitt, Rob Dinsdale and Philippa Donovan all suggested vital changes.

My tireless agent Clare Conville has steered the second and third books into being and beyond alongside the incredible Jake Bosanquet-Smith, Alexander Cochran and Alexandra McNicoll at Conville & Walsh.

Any book is only as good as its editor. I am so lucky to work with Sarah Lambert (and Niamh Mulvey) at Quercus Children's, and Sharyn November at Viking Children's in the US. Their passion for seeing these stories told in the best possible way has made them better than I could have imagined.

If the books make any sense, that is due to the forensic copy-editing of Talya Baker and proofreading of Gill Clack.

I do judge books by their covers, so am very fortunate to have designer Nicola Theobald, illustrator Thomas Flintham and typesetter Nigel Hazle making these ones look so fine inside and out.

There's no point in writing books if nobody knows about them. Plenty do, thanks to Alice Hill, Bethan Ferguson, Lauren Woosey and Ella Pocock, not to mention Ron Beard and Therese Keating, who made sure they really were available in all good bookshops.

Numerous friends read early drafts, and everything they said helped: in particular Milo Bates, Jack Bootle, Sonya Walger and Orlando Wells. Eoin Colfer, Eva Ibbotson and Francesca Simon all said lovely things and let me quote them.

Books on the vanishing natural kingdom around us by Melanie Challenger, Caspar Henderson, Philip Hoare, Elizabeth Kolbert and Callum Roberts played a big part in my reading and I apologize if I have inadvertently misrepresented any of their real observations in creating a fantasy world.

When you're trying to finish a book it's your family who matter the most; I'm so grateful for the love and support of my husband Will, my brother Nick, my mother Jane and my late father Paul.

Finally, I want to 'thank' the animal species whose desires and fears I have taken in vain to draw awareness to the plight of non-human life forms on this planet. We can't save them all, but we can save some. No one has all the answers, but I hope these books have perhaps prompted some questions. We could begin by respecting all other species as the biological miracles they are (even the cockroaches) and we should always listen out for them, because you never know . . .

If you would like to do something practical to help conserve wildlife in this country,
a very good place to start is the Wildlife Trusts:
http://www.wildlifetrusts.org/

WWW.THELASTWILD.COM